P9-BYB-997

Praise for Sabrina Jeffries's previous novels

"Best-selling Jeffries brilliantly launches her new Duke Dynasty series with another exemplary Regency-set historical brilliantly sourced from her seemingly endless authorial supply of fascinating characters and compelling storylines."

—*Booklist* on *Project Duchess*

"Anyone who loves romance must read Sabrina Jeffries!"

—Lisa Kleypas, *New York Times* bestselling author

"Quick pacing, witty dialogue, and charmingly original characters set Jeffries's books apart."

—*Publishers Weekly* (Starred Review)

"Master storyteller Jeffries is at the top of her game."

—*RT Book Reviews* on *The Secret of Flirting*

"Quick wit, lively repartee, and delicious sensuality drive the elaborate plot of this sinfully delightful addition to Jeffries's latest series."

—*Library Journal* (Starred Review) on *The Pleasures of Passion*

"With its irresistible combination of witty banter, well defined characters, and a wonderful surfeit of breathtaking sensuality, the latest in Jeffries's Sinful Suitors series is a straight flush."

—*Booklist* (Starred Review) on *The Danger of Desire*

"Lovely, poignant, and powerful."

—*Kirkus Reviews* on *The Study of Seduction*

Books by Sabrina Jeffries:

Project Duchess

Seduction on a Snowy Night
(anthology)

The Bachelor

Who Wants to Marry a Duke

Published by Kensington Publishing Corp.

Who Wants To Marry A DUKE

SABRINA JEFFRIES

ZEBRA BOOKS
KENSINGTON PUBLISHING CORP.
www.kensingtonbooks.com

ZEBRA BOOKS are published by

Kensington Publishing Corp.
119 West 40th Street
New York, NY 10018

All Kensington titles, imprints, and distributed lines are available at special quantity discounts for bulk purchases for sales promotion, premiums, fund-raising, educational, or institutional use.

Special book excerpts or customized printings can also be created to fit specific needs. For details, write or phone the office of the Kensington Sales Manager: Attn.: Sales Department. Kensington Publishing Corp., 119 West 40th Street, New York, NY 10018. Phone: 1-800-221-2647.

Zebra and the Z logo Reg. U.S. Pat. & TM Off.

First Printing: September 2020
ISBN-13: 978-1-4201-4857-2
ISBN-10: 1-4201-4857-5

ISBN-13: 978-1-4201-4861-9 (eBook)
ISBN-10: 1-4201-4861-3 (eBook)

10 9 8 7 6 5 4 3 2 1

Printed in the United States of America

To my daddy, who always has a big smile
for his "firstborn," quirky daughter.

And to my mom, who tirelessly takes care
of my daddy these days.

Thanks to both of you for all the love you give.

Lydia's Husbands

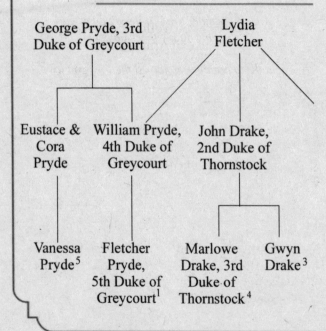

George Pryde, 3rd Duke of Greycourt

Lydia Fletcher

Eustace & Cora Pryde

William Pryde, 4th Duke of Greycourt

John Drake, 2nd Duke of Thornstock

Vanessa Pryde [5]

Fletcher Pryde, 5th Duke of Greycourt [1]

Marlowe Drake, 3rd Duke of Thornstock [4]

Gwyn Drake [3]

1 *Project Duchess*
2 *Seduction on a Snowy Night*
3 *The Bachelor*
4 *Who Wants to Marry a Duke*
5 *Undercover Duke*

and Children

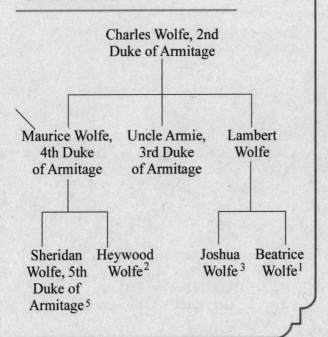

Charles Wolfe, 2nd
Duke of Armitage

Maurice Wolfe,
4th Duke
of Armitage

Uncle Armie,
3rd Duke
of Armitage

Lambert
Wolfe

Sheridan
Wolfe, 5th
Duke of
Armitage [5]

Heywood
Wolfe [2]

Joshua
Wolfe [3]

Beatrice
Wolfe [1]

Prologue

London
April 1800

Having finally come into his title as the Duke of Thornstock, Marlowe "Thorn" Drake leaned against a pillar to survey the crowd at the Devonshire House ball. Why hadn't his twin sister returned to England with him when he'd asked? If Gwyn were here, she'd be mocking the fops with their excessive cravats and taking bets with him on which gentleman would make a drunken fool of himself first.

She'd be keeping him well entertained.

God, how he missed her. Until now, they'd never been apart, and it still chafed him that she'd blithely watched him sail away without her. He'd never counted on feeling so alone in the land of his birth. He was English, damn it, and this was his rightful home. Since he'd never felt as if he belonged in Berlin, despite having lived there almost since birth, he'd expected matters to be different in his native country.

Instead, everything smelled and tasted odd, from the

weak coffee his servants gave him in the morning to the strange liquid he was drinking now, which bore a faint— *very* faint—resemblance to the *Glühwein* he'd drunk in Prussia, although not nearly as good.

"So what do you think of your first marriage mart?" asked his half brother Grey, who'd come up beside him.

Fletcher "Grey" Pryde, the Duke of Greycourt, had returned to England at the age of ten to be educated for his future role as duke. That probably explained why he seemed comfortable with English life. He'd had fifteen years here. Thorn had only had six months.

Not that he would let his older brother see his discomfort. "*This* is a marriage mart?" Thorn snorted. "I'd imagined something a bit more . . . mercenary, with mothers sniffing the crowd in search of eligible gentlemen for their pretty vixens."

Grey laughed. "That's not far off the mark, at least for ladies who have only their looks to commend them. With heiresses, it's more like the fathers sniffing about—trying to ferret out the fortune hunters."

"Then I suppose I should be glad Gwyn did *not* come with me." Thorn pushed away from the pillar. "Father and I had enough trouble keeping the fortune hunters at bay in Berlin."

"I would have helped you with that." Grey gazed up. "Gwyn would have loved that ceiling. She would have tried to sketch it for her book of architectural wonders. That's why I can't figure out why she refused to come back with you." He fixed his gaze on Thorn. "Do you know why she chose to stay in Berlin?"

"She said Mother needed her," Thorn replied.

"Nonsense. Mother is perfectly capable of fending for herself. Besides which, Mother has Maurice, who dotes on her. There's got to be another reason."

Thorn had a pretty good idea of what it was, but Gwyn had never admitted it, and he wasn't about to speculate to Grey. "What are you doing at a marriage mart, anyway?"

Grey turned grim. "I lost a bet."

"Ah. What are the terms?"

"I have to stay until midnight . . . or until Lady Georgiana is introduced to me, whichever comes first."

"Devonshire's daughter? The one coming out this Season?"

"Precisely."

"Then you'll be able to leave soon enough," Thorn said. "They'll introduce her to you first of anyone."

"And you. Or have you forgotten your exalted station?"

"No." How could he? Every time he entered a room, people bowed and curtsied for all they were worth.

"Never lose sight of who you are," Grey said. "You're not accustomed to how devious matchmaking mamas and their scheming daughters can be. Look at it this way: They're the hunters, who want to hang your ducal coronet on their trophy wall. So keep an eye out."

"I plan to. As soon as I see the Devonshires coming, I'll flee."

"I didn't mean keep an eye out for the *Devonshires*, for God's sake," Grey said. "They take precedence over us both. Fleeing would be like giving them the cut direct. Even I am not so reckless as all that. I may need one of them someday."

Thorn would rather risk that than take one step awry in conversation with them. Although earlier he'd had someone point them out to him, this would be his first time to actually meet the powerful Duke and Duchess of Devonshire, and he was a bit shaky on the protocol. In Prussia, Thorn had been the only English duke around since Grey had left for England.

"First of all," Thorn said, "I don't have your ambition to own half of London. Second, I can escape a ballroom without being noticed if I have to."

"You think so, do you? Look around, little brother. Half the young ladies in here have their eyes on you."

"Or you. When the exalted duke and duchess introduce you to their daughter, everyone will be so fixed upon that august event that no one will even notice I've vanished." Thorn grinned at him. "Besides, I've no need to marry as well as you. I can be content with one of the pretty vixens, as long as she's also clever and amusing."

He heard a snort behind him, but when he looked back, he saw nothing. He must have imagined it.

Grey frowned. "From what I've heard, Lady Georgiana is neither. Supposedly, her mother eclipses her in that respect as well as in looks."

"That's a damned shame. For you, anyway. Would you marry her for her connections in spite of it all?"

"Only if the gossip is wrong about her and she proves to be, as you put it, clever and amusing. And pretty." He smiled at Thorn. "I want everything in a wife."

And he'd probably get it, too, once he decided to settle down. Grey had the sort of wavy black hair that always looked as if he'd just left some woman's bed, and his blue-green eyes and chiseled features ensured that he could get back there anytime he pleased. Unfortunately for the ladies, he was very particular.

"That's probably why you haven't yet married. You set the bar ridiculously high." Thorn sipped some of the mysterious liquor in his glass and grimaced.

"How can you stand to drink that?" Grey said.

"I keep trying to figure out what it is. It tastes like port, but it's too thin for that and far sweeter. Nor would I expect port to be served at a ball for ladies making their debuts."

"And yet it is. What you're drinking is negus, a punch the English have concocted out of watered-down port and whatever spices are lying about. Or so I've surmised through years of trying to drink it without making a face."

"It's vile." Thorn looked around for one of those footmen who took the glasses away. Instead, he spotted the Devonshires heading in their direction. "And I believe it's time to make myself scarce. Our hosts are approaching."

Grey nodded. "I see them. I know Devonshire himself well enough to speak to, but I've never met the duchess or her daughter. The duchess is rumored to be a fascinating woman. Are you sure you don't wish to stay around?"

"Another time, perhaps," Thorn muttered.

At twenty-one, he was hardly ready for marriage. Right now he could barely make his way through the myriad rules in London society and manage the properties of his dukedom, much less drag a woman along with him. Nor was he yet comfortable enough with the brother he hadn't seen in years to admit that.

The Devonshires now paused to speak to another acquaintance, so he circled the pillar in search of a balcony where he could hide out. Then he collided with another guest and spilled negus on the front of his waistcoat.

He stared down at the prominent red spots. "Damn! Why don't you watch where you're going?"

"Why don't *you*? I was just standing here minding my own business."

His head snapped up to find a fetching female with fire in her eyes staring him down. Like many of the young ladies, she wore white silk, but the curious embroidery of gold thread along her bodice drew his gaze to her full breasts. And he did like a buxom woman.

Instantly he changed his manner. "Forgive me. I didn't

mean to offend. I simply wasn't paying attention to where I was going."

"Clearly, Your Grace. You were too busy trying to escape poor Lady Georgiana, who is the nicest person one could ever meet."

He grimaced. "I take it you overheard my conversation with my brother." That explained why his effusive apology hadn't softened her. And he refused to apologize for not wishing to meet Lady Georgiana. Why should he? This chit shouldn't have been eavesdropping on a private conversation.

Drawing out his handkerchief, he began to dab at the spots on his waistcoat.

She shook her head, sending the fringe of blond curls around her face bouncing. "You'll make it worse trying to get it out like that. If you come with me, I can clean it."

"Really? How in God's name do you mean to do *that*?"

"With champagne and bicarbonate of soda," she said, as if that made all the sense in the world.

It piqued his curiosity. "What is bicarbonate of soda, and where the devil do you intend to get some?"

"I carry it in my reticule, of course."

Of course? "Because that's what all young ladies carry in their reticules, I suppose."

"Do they? I thought I was the only one." Before he could even respond, she added, "But if we don't act quickly, those spots will stain your waistcoat for good."

He could afford to replace his waistcoat ten times over, but he hadn't even had a chance to dance, so her offer to wipe away the spots had merit. Besides, he wanted to see what magic she meant to conjure up with her odd ingredients—and if she really did have bicarbonate of soda in her reticule. "Then by all means, lead the way."

With a nod, she took his glass of negus and replaced it

with a glass of champagne sitting abandoned on a nearby tray. Then she guided him out onto a balcony. "The hall to the Devonshire library isn't too far. We can do it there."

Do what *there?* Thorn nearly asked. Did the pretty wench really intend to whisk away his spots? Or did she have some other, more lascivious purpose in mind?

Now *that* would be a result he'd embrace. The woman's bodice was intriguingly low cut. He'd assumed from her gown's color that she was a debutante, but he might have been lucky enough to have stumbled over some fast-living married woman.

One would think that if the young lady was *that*, she'd be curtsying and flirting like all the other females he'd encountered in society. Then again, London society was wilder than Berlin's. He was still trying to figure out the rules.

As the stepson of the British ambassador to Prussia, Thorn had been expected to behave appropriately, which had generally meant not having any fun. But in the six months since he'd left home for England, he'd begun to loosen his strictures, encouraged by other young bucks he'd met. Still, this was the first time a young *lady* had tempted him to misbehave.

They're the hunters, who want to hang your ducal coronet on their trophy wall. So keep an eye out.

He would. But he'd enjoy this intriguing encounter, too. There had been few enough of them since his return.

They traversed the balcony, then passed through a pair of French doors into a hallway not frequented by the rest of the guests. That roused his curiosity even further.

"Since you mean to save my hapless waistcoat, perhaps we should introduce ourselves," he said. "I am—"

"I know who you are, sir," she said curtly. "*Everyone*

does. My good friend Lady Georgiana pointed you out to me from the moment we entered the ballroom."

"Is that why you were eavesdropping on my conversation with my brother?"

"Hardly." She shot him a mutinous glance. "I was there first, you know, trying to hide from my stepmother."

"Why?"

She blew out a frustrated breath. "She keeps trying to match me up with gentlemen I don't care for. I do not need or want a husband, but she refuses to believe me."

He figured he'd better not say what he was thinking: that perhaps her stepmother was right. As sulky as his unnamed companion was, she also seemed an odd blend of innocent and seductive, the sort that could easily get into trouble with a gentleman. He didn't yet know what to make of her.

"I see," he said, for lack of anything better to say. "But I still don't know your name."

"Oh! Right." She shot him a faint smile. "I tend to forget such niceties."

"I noticed."

Her smile vanished. "Well, you don't have to rub it in."

He burst into laughter. "I swear, you are the most bewildering female I have ever met. Aside from my twin sister, that is." He bent close to whisper, "I'll give you her name if that helps you to offer me yours. Hers is Gwyn. And yours is . . ."

"Miss Olivia Norley."

She said it primly, which he found delightful, though he was a bit disappointed she wasn't a lustful married woman.

Then she stopped outside an open door. "Anyway, here we are. Shall we go in?"

"If you wish, Miss Norley. This is your endeavor, after all."

"Right." She marched inside without a single swish in her step.

He followed, suppressing the urge to laugh at her purposeful manner. At least she had the good sense to situate them at the far end of the room, where they wouldn't readily be seen by anyone passing by.

She set the glass of champagne on a table that also held a lit candelabra, then opened her reticule and pulled out a small box. It proved to contain quite a few vials.

"Good God, what is all that?" he asked.

"Smelling salts and cosmetics for Mama, since she has no room in her own reticule for them." She opened a vial and tapped it until a white powder filled her palm. "This is bicarbonate of soda. It's good for indigestion."

"And removing wine stains, apparently."

"Exactly."

She smiled up at him, and he caught his breath. Her smile transformed her from a pretty woman to a breathtaking goddess. As she moved the candelabra closer, he could see that her eyes were the warm green of jade. She had a sumptuous mouth, peach-tinged cheeks, and a nose that tipped up ever so slightly. He found all of it charming.

"Forgive me," she said, seeming oblivious to his staring, "but I must put my hand beneath your waistcoat in order to clean the stain properly."

"Would you rather I removed my waistcoat entirely?" he asked, knowing that the request was inappropriate and wondering how she would respond.

She brightened. "Oh, yes! That would make it much easier."

Clearly she wasn't put off at all by his lack of propriety, which he found amusing. He shucked off his coat, then unbuttoned and removed his waistcoat before handing it to her. After placing her handkerchief beneath the waistcoat, she went right to work on the spots, first dousing them with the champagne and then covering the diluted stains with the white powder she called bicarbonate of soda. The spots foamed up, taking him by surprise.

She held out her hand. "Give me your handkerchief, if you please." After he did so, she used the clean parts to blot up the foam.

To his amazement, he could hardly see the stain anymore. It looked as if he'd merely spilled some water on his waistcoat. "Where did you learn to do that?" Thorn asked.

She took his waistcoat over to the fireplace and waved it back and forth in the heat from the fire, ensuring that even the water would evaporate. "From my uncle. He's a chemist."

What an odd family. No doubt she'd amassed all sorts of cleaning formulas from her relation. According to Gwyn, women were expected to know such domestic things even if they didn't perform the cleaning tasks themselves.

Miss Norley came toward him with his waistcoat. "There. That should get you through the evening at least. Although you should have your servants give it a proper cleaning as soon as you get home."

"I will keep that in mind," he said, attempting to match her serious tone. Taking the waistcoat from her, he put it on. "How can I repay you? Perhaps with some eye of newt and toe of frog to fill out your vials?"

"Why would I want those? They would be of no use to me whatsoever."

Clearly she'd never read *Macbeth*. Or if she had, she'd forgotten the toil and trouble scene with the witches.

Chuckling, he buttoned up his waistcoat. "Then perhaps I'll ask you for a dance."

A look of sheer horror crossed her face. "Don't you

dare! I'm the worst dancer in Christendom. And since young ladies aren't allowed to turn gentlemen down—"

"What? I don't know that rule. Though it does explain why everyone always accepts my invitations to dance." He winked at her. "And here I thought it was because of my irresistible charm and dashing good looks."

"Everyone accepts because you're a duke, sir. So please don't ask *me* to dance, or I'll end up making a fool of us both. You wouldn't like it, I assure you."

He shook his head. "You're an unusual woman, Miss Norley. I'll give you that."

When he pulled a bit of his cravat out at the top, she frowned. "Oh, dear. You have spots there, too. I should—"

"No need. If you will just rearrange the folds of the cravat to hide the spots, no one will be the wiser. I'd do it myself, but there's no mirror in here."

"Right." She began to tug here and tuck there, reminding him of his initial suspicion of why she'd brought him in here in the first place.

"You do that very well," he said. "You must have practiced at it."

"My uncle has no valet, so I sometimes have to do the honors if he's expecting a guest."

"Admit it, Miss Norley. You did not lead me in here solely to clean my waistcoat and reorder the folds of my cravat."

Her gaze shot to his. "I don't know what you mean. Why else would I do it?"

Smiling down at her, he cupped her face in his hands. "So we could indulge ourselves. Like this."

He kissed her gently, and she drew back, her eyes going wide. "Oh, *my*."

A chuckle escaped him. "Oh, my, indeed," he murmured, then kissed her again.

This time her hands caught his waist, and she leaned up to meet his lips more fully. Ah yes. Sweet as cherries, those lips. But bold, too, as if she'd done this before.

Not that he cared if she had. It had probably made her into the delicious armful of woman she was, one he could happily kiss all night. Her wonderfully warm mouth tasted of champagne, which he discovered when he ventured to deepen the kiss, and she opened it to his tongue. After a moment she tangled hers with his, and his blood rose.

Oh, hell. She made him want to throw caution to the winds and do more than kiss her, but he dared not. So he settled for exploring every inch of her mouth, finding all the lovely secret places of it. With a moan, she wrapped her arms about his waist, firing his need even more.

God, she smelled delicious, like tropical hothouse flowers. He wanted to sink into her scent as one sank into a hot bath.

He ran a hand down one shoulder to beneath her arm and along her ribs. Why not? He had just begun to wonder if he *did* dare to cover one of those ample breasts with his hand when another voice thundered in the room.

"Olivia Jane Norley! What the devil do you think you're doing?"

Olivia jerked free of him, looking a bit disoriented, not to mention disheveled. His stomach roiled. He'd been well and truly caught. He feared he knew exactly what that meant.

He turned to face an elegantly dressed matron whom he could only assume was Olivia's stepmother. How had she found them if Olivia had truly been hiding from her as she'd said? And the woman was accompanied by a few friends, too. Witnesses. That was bad. Very, *very* bad.

In a flash he remembered where he'd heard the name Norley. Baron Norley was supposedly a member of Grey's club, which Thorn had visited a few times while trying to decide if he wished to join. That meant Miss Norley was the *Honorable* Miss Norley, probably in search of a husband and simply more clever at it than the other young ladies at this affair.

"This is not how it looks, Mama," Miss Norley began. "His Grace spilled negus on his waistcoat, and I was cleaning it up."

Lady Norley's friends laughed at the very idea.

Lady Norley did not. "Olivia, please step into the hall. I need a private word with the duke."

"But—"

"*Now*, young lady."

Miss Norley's shoulders drooped as she left the room. With a word, Lady Norley banished her friends to the hall as well. Then he and the woman were alone.

"Lady Norley—" he began.

"I expect to see you at our town house first thing in the morning, with an offer of marriage in hand."

Marriage! God help him.

He attempted to climb out of the hole he'd so unwisely fallen into. "There's no need for such precipitate behavior. I only just met your stepdaughter tonight, and although she is a nice girl—"

"Yes, she *is* a nice girl and barely eighteen. I will not allow her reputation to be damaged one jot because of your . . . animal desires."

Striving to look the part of a duke, he drew himself up and put ice in his voice. "It was just a friendly kiss."

"That you removed your coat to engage in."

Bloody hell. He'd forgotten he was standing here in his shirtsleeves. That *was* damning, and he'd done it to himself.

Remembering Grey's warnings, he scowled. More

likely, Miss Norley had done it to catch him, and her stepmother had been lying in wait to finish the deal. That possibility infuriated him.

His anger must have shone in his face, for Lady Norley neared him and lowered her voice. "In case you're considering *not* showing up to offer marriage in the morning, you'll force me to make publicly known a certain secret about your family I've kept to myself all these years."

A chill swept over him. "You don't even know my family. What secrets could you possibly have heard about them?"

"Actually, I knew your parents quite well years ago. Your mother and I came out together, and your father was a friend of my family's. That's why I happen to know exactly where he was headed when he had his fatal carriage accident."

That caught him off guard. "He was going to London," Thorn said warily. "That's no great secret."

"Yes. But he was going there to see his mistress."

For one horrible moment, the bottom dropped out of his world. "*What?*"

"He had a mistress before he met your mother, and he never gave her up."

Thorn wouldn't have been surprised to hear that *Grey's* father had possessed a mistress, but his own? It wasn't possible.

He tried to remember if his mother had ever said what had provoked his father's sudden trip to London from Berkshire, but nothing came to mind. What Mother *had* said was that she and Father had been mad for each other. According to her, their marriage had been the only love match from among her three husbands. Either his father had never had a mistress . . . or he'd hidden the fact so well that his mother had never suspected it.

There was a third possibility—that Mother had known and all this time had been lying to him and Gwyn about the state of her marriage to their father. God, he couldn't even bear to consider that. Because it meant that the great romantic love Mother had always spoken of so passionately to him and Gwyn was a sham.

That was assuming Lady Norley spoke the truth. As the woman must know, there was no way to confirm or disprove the "secret" she was using as blackmail, not with his mother abroad. As it was, it took months for his correspondence to reach Berlin.

But even if it were a lie, the baroness could still spread the tale. She might even know enough to give it the trappings of truth. And he refused to let this she-devil hurt his mother by doing so. Having such gossip bandied about in the papers would wound Mother deeply, once it *did* make it to the embassy. Nor would it help the career of his stepfather, the British ambassador to Prussia.

"Do we understand each other, Your Grace?" Lady Norley asked, not an ounce of indecision or fear in her voice. She had him in a corner, and she knew it.

He said, with all the nonchalance he could muster, "I'll be there in the morning."

Olivia sat stiffly on the drawing room settee the next day while her stepmother fussed with her curls. "Once you marry His Grace, I shall have to instruct your new maid about the proper way to arrange your hair."

"*If* I marry His Grace," Olivia said woodenly.

"Not that again." Her stepmother pinched Olivia's cheeks. "Of course you'll marry him. He's handsome *and* wealthy. You can't go wrong. You must have thought so, too, given the clever way you got him off to yourself."

"I wasn't . . . I didn't expect that we would be . . ."

Her stepmother raised an eyebrow.

Olivia sighed. She probably shouldn't admit that she hadn't expected to be caught alone with him. "What does Papa say?" She hadn't seen him last night, since he'd already headed off to his club.

Her stepmother waved her hand. "You know your father—too busy with his own affairs to care about ours. But he did promise that once you accept the duke's offer, he would entertain that selfsame offer himself. To that end, he is staying in his study until the duke has finished with you."

After Olivia's mother had died when Olivia was eight, Papa had withdrawn from her life, leaving the care of her to nursemaids and governesses while he indulged in gentlemanly pursuits . . . like drinking, gambling, and going to his club. Sometimes she suspected he'd only married her stepmother so he wouldn't have to deal with his daughter.

His awkward, chemistry-loving, no-nonsense oddity of a daughter.

"Are you both that eager to get rid of me?" Olivia asked, hoping she hid her hurt well.

To her gratification, her stepmother looked truly shocked by the question. "Get rid of you? Don't be silly, my dear. We just want to see you marry well. And once you do, you and I can have so much fun shopping and riding out on Rotten Row and paying calls to all the best people."

Leave it to Mama to choose entertainments that Olivia didn't remotely find "fun." "You're assuming that the duke will actually make an offer."

"Oh, don't you worry about that." Her stepmother's tone had turned steely. "He *will* offer for you."

She seemed oddly sure of it. Not for the first time since last night, Olivia wondered how Mama had persuaded him to agree. Or was he simply that much of a gentleman?

Somehow she doubted that, having seen his face as he'd stormed from the library last night. He hadn't even stopped to bid her good-bye. That had wounded her, but she couldn't think about it right now. She had to figure out what she would say if he *did* offer.

It was a hard choice. After all, he was the first man ever to kiss her on the mouth. It had been shocking. Delicious. Utterly unexpected. She'd always thought kissing on the lips sounded unpleasant, but she'd enjoyed it. A lot. It still gave her swirly sensations in her stomach. Who could have guessed?

And when he'd slipped his tongue inside her mouth . . . Oh, Lord, she'd felt entirely out of her depth. He'd slid his tongue in and out, so slyly and pleasurably that it had enticed her to do the same with hers.

That had seemed to startle him, but not for long. With a groan, he'd caught her about the waist and pulled her up against him. It had been wildly exciting. She supposed most ladies would call it romantic, but she didn't know about that. She wasn't sure what "romantic" was, exactly, having never really experienced it for herself.

The clock sounded the hour, and she jumped. Now was the time when everyone paid calls. Not that anyone ever called on *her*. Olivia wasn't good at offering pleasantries or making small talk about the weather, so she didn't draw scores of admirers like some of the other ladies. It had never bothered her. Indeed, the daily ritual of waiting for callers was just something she had to get through so she could go to her uncle's and help him with his experiments.

Part of her hoped the duke didn't show up at all. Then she wouldn't have to decide what her answer should be. She'd been weighing both sides all night, and still hadn't made up her mind.

On the one hand, he was very handsome and apparently

found her attractive enough to kiss. He was good at the kissing, too, though she had nothing to compare it to. And there was another point in his favor—if she married him, she need never make small talk again. He didn't strike her as a small talk sort of person. That was certainly an advantage.

On the other hand, she doubted that His Grace would allow her to run her own chemistry experiments or to help with her uncle's. A man of his consequence would expect an obedient, domestic sort of wife, and she wasn't that. Why, she wasn't even sure how she felt about bearing children.

And a small, foolish part of her—the part that had read fairy tales as a girl—wanted affection, even love, in her marriage. But that seemed a bit much to hope for from Thornstock.

The knocker sounded on the door downstairs, and she tensed. Several minutes later, the Duke of Thornstock was announced.

As he entered, she and her stepmother rose and curtsied. His Grace looked positively grim, which reinforced her fear that Mama had somehow forced him into offering.

That impression was only confirmed when he stood staring at her as if seeing right through her. "Good morning, Miss Norley. You look well."

"As do you, Your Grace." Heavens, but he did. His straight, dark brown hair had a reddish sheen, and his eyes were so light a blue they were nearly translucent.

He glanced at her stepmother, then back at her. "Miss Norley, I hope you will do me the honor of becoming my wife."

She froze. He couldn't have been more abrupt. For the first time in her life, she wished there had been a wee bit more small talk. "Why?"

That seemed to catch him off guard. Then he narrowed

that ice-blue gaze of his on her. "Because last night I damaged your reputation irrevocably. And marriage is the usual recourse for that."

Of course it was. Yet something wasn't right here. Surely a duke could wriggle his way out of marriage to a virtual nobody, yet he stood there looking like a thief being dragged to the gallows.

She had no desire to be his executioner. If she must marry, it wouldn't be to save her reputation. And it certainly wouldn't be to a man who obviously now despised her. "Thank you, Your Grace, for your kind and generous offer. But I regret that I must decline it."

"Olivia!" Mama said.

Olivia scarcely heard her, too intent on watching his reaction. She'd expected relief, but the only emotion replacing his cold arrogance was hot anger.

What right did *he* have to be angry? She'd saved him from being forced to marry her. He could at least be grateful.

Her stepmother tried to smooth things over. "What my stepdaughter meant to say was—"

"—exactly what I said," Olivia put in. "I have no desire to marry His Grace. And I suspect he has no desire to marry me either." She headed for the door to the drawing room. "Now if you both will please excuse me . . ."

She had to escape. She couldn't bear to see his triumphant expression once he realized he was truly free. But she only got as far as the hallway before her legs failed her, and she sank onto the nearest hall chair to try and settle her nerves.

From inside the room, she heard her stepmother say, "Your Grace, you must give her a chance. Like any young woman, my stepdaughter wants to be courted and petted. Surely in time she—"

"I do not like being toyed with, madam," he cut in. "As far as I'm concerned, I have met the terms of our bargain."

Bargain! Oh, this day only got worse and worse. What could her stepmother possibly have offered him to gain his compliance? Was Olivia really so dreadful that a young man wouldn't even consider her for a wife without some inducement? Granted, she had a middling fortune, but that wouldn't tempt *him*. Everyone knew he was rich as sin.

He went on in a voice devoid of the playfulness he'd shown Olivia last night. "I offered; she refused. So we are finished. And if you ever make good on your threat from last night, I will make your life—and that of your stepdaughter—a misery. Good day, Lady Norley."

Those words galvanized her into action. He was about to leave the room! And she couldn't bear to be caught listening at doors. She jumped up and headed for the stairs, praying he took his time about walking out on her stepmother.

When she glanced back, she noticed he hadn't even seen her on the stairs. He was too intent on making his own escape. No doubt he'd finally had the good sense to realize he'd narrowly missed marrying a near stranger.

For the merest moment, she wished she had accepted him. Their kiss had tempted and entranced her. She knew she'd never have another like it.

But kissing wasn't enough. She could easily guess what marriage to a man of his consequence would be like. He would dictate her days—and her nights. Like Papa, he would have no use for her or for what she wanted. Her desire to be a chemist would fade away just as every woman's ambition seemed to do once she had to subjugate her dreams to a man's needs.

It sounded awful. And in such a case, who wanted to marry a duke? Certainly not her.

Chapter One

Thorn broke into a smile as he saw Gwyn heading across her modest ballroom toward him. Leave it to his sister to celebrate her and her husband taking ownership of their new town house by throwing a ball. He didn't regret one bit selling the house to them. She'd turned the place into a home, and it showed, especially in here. The new floor had the perfect gloss for dancing, and the new chandeliers lit the room much better than the old ones.

It meant she was sure to stay nearby for a while, thank God. And now that she'd married Major Wolfe, who could well protect her, Thorn could relax and stop worrying that some scoundrel might run off with her for her inheritance.

He could focus on his writing for a change, although it was getting harder to hide it, especially from Gwyn. She thought him nothing but a rakehell. His whole family did. In truth, Thorn the rakehell was a character every bit as much as Thorn the playwright and Thorn the duke. None of the roles felt real. Except Thorn the brother, of course. At least that role was genuine.

"You're wearing a suspiciously secretive smile." Gwyn kissed him on the cheek. "What mischief do you have up your sleeve tonight?"

"Nothing that would concern you, *Liebchen*."

She laughed. "How disappointing. I love being part of your schemes. Or I used to at home, at any rate."

Home. Prussia was still home for *him*, too. "Do you miss Berlin?" he asked, genuinely curious.

"Sometimes." A faraway look crossed her face. "I'd sell my soul for some *Eisbein mit Sauerkraut*."

"You should have said so before. My new cook makes it."

She gaped at him. "And it's good? As good as in Berlin?"

"Since my new cook is German, it's every bit as good."

"How on earth did you find a German cook?"

"There *are* Germans in London, if you look for them, sis." He grinned. "I'll send some *Eisbein mit Sauerkraut* over tomorrow."

"You are a dear man." She grabbed his head and kissed both his cheeks. "I shall hold you to that."

He chuckled. "I'd expect nothing less of you."

"Anyway, I'm glad I caught you before you fled." She adjusted her gloves. "You're always terribly elusive at affairs like this."

"What sort of affairs do you mean?"

"Marriage marts. You know."

"It's October. Too late in the year for marriage marts. Besides, I thought this was just to celebrate your move into your new home. I see plenty of guests who would never be invited to a marriage mart. Like William Bonham."

"Stop that," Gwyn said with a nudge of her arm. "I know you don't approve of his interest in Mama, but he's been a perfect gentleman to her."

"He's a man of affairs."

"He's *Papa's* man of affairs. I swear, you've become dreadfully high-in-the-instep now that you've been in England nearly a decade. And Mama says she's not interested in him romantically, anyway."

"She said the same thing about our stepfather, but that didn't stop her from marrying him."

"Surely you aren't complaining about that. Without Papa, we wouldn't have Sheridan and Heywood as brothers. And we would never have had the experience of traveling across Europe and growing up in Prussia."

"True." Without their stepfather, he wouldn't have had to choose between his twin and his dukedom either.

No, that wasn't fair. He'd mucked that up himself by not being more honest with Gwyn before he'd left Prussia. He should have told her from the start that he'd paid off her favorite suitor, that the arse had taken the money and run. He and Gwyn were slowly growing close again, though he feared there would always be a bit of a rift between them. They had once been of the same mind always, but years apart had made him more cautious and her more . . . self-sufficient.

Nothing showed that like the fact that he'd never told her of his playwriting. Of the painful secret about their father. Of the one woman Thorn had offered marriage to.

What the hell? What had made him think of *her*?

Remembering Father's secret, no doubt, the one Thorn had continued to keep through the years because he'd begun to fear it might be true.

After the Devonshire ball, Thorn had written his mother to see what she'd answer if he mentioned running into her supposed "friend," Lady Norley. To his surprise, Mother had told him, "give my good friend Lady Norley my regards." Apparently the baroness hadn't lied about their friendship, which was enough to make him cautious about mentioning anything else to Mother.

"So if Mama likes Mr. Bonham and he's good to her," Gwyn was saying, "what's the problem? It's not as if they'll have more children."

"Thank God."

"And speaking of marriage and children—"

"You're enceinte."

"How did you know? I thought my gowns hid it fairly well." She sighed. "Joshua told you, didn't he?"

Thorn smirked at her. "What do you expect? He's the proud papa."

"I can see I won't get to give the news to anyone," she said petulantly. "Anyway, that's not what I was hinting at. I was trying to point out that there are plenty of unmarried ladies here."

He stiffened. Now that *she* was happily married, she wanted to see everyone in that exalted state. Judging from his mother's marriages, his father's possible infidelity, and the many women who'd tried to snag Thorn through the years for his title and wealth, love in marriage was a falsehood. So Gwyn's matchmaking efforts were wasted on him.

He was about to tell her so, when she added, "More than one of those ladies is just begging for a partner."

Ah. He'd misunderstood. She was chiding him for not doing his duty as a bachelor at a ball. That was different. He knew the rules. "I tell you what. Before I leave, I promise to dance one set with the lady of your choice. Will that exonerate me?"

"Perhaps." She narrowed her gaze on him. "And after that?"

"Are you demanding to choose *more* than one dance partner for me?"

"I know better. Although I'd rather you stayed later, of course, what I meant was, where are you off to when you leave here?"

"No idea. Covent Garden, I imagine. Or my club." He tapped his finger on his chin. "Is Vauxhall still open? I wonder if those fellows who bought it might let me have a go at the tightrope. I've only had one glass of wine—I might manage it."

She rolled her eyes. "You should be the one writing those plays, you know."

He tensed. "What plays?"

"The ones by your German friend, Mr. Jahnke. The first, I think, was *The Adventures of a German Gentleman Loose in London*."

"First of all, it's Juncker, not Jahnke," he said irritably. "And second, there's no mention in the title of his character Felix being German. It's *A Foreign Gentleman*, not *A German Gentleman*."

She eyed him closely. "I hardly think it matters whether Felix is German or foreign. All I'm saying is you'd make the adventures more exciting."

Thorn couldn't decide if she was baiting him. Had she guessed that his poet friend, Konrad Juncker, was standing in for Thorn himself? "According to Juncker, the adventures please the audience well enough to make him wealthy. The original work has run off and on for years, and the subsequent plays have . . ." When Gwyn started to smile, he caught himself. "I merely think them fine as they are."

"Well, of course you do. You're loyal to your friend. Personally, I only enjoy those scenes with Lady Grasping and her hapless daughter, Lady Slyboots." She grinned. "I do like their shenanigans. They always make me laugh."

"Me too."

He hadn't intended to keep the comic characters once his anger at Miss Norley's refusal had waned. But now the two had become an integral part of the works. Vickerman, the manager at the Parthenon Theater, which had produced all of Juncker's plays, had insisted that Grasping and Slyboots appear in every new one.

Gwyn was still watching him. "I sometimes forget you're the only member of the family—other than Mama, of course—who actually enjoys the theater. Now that she's out of mourning, have you taken *her* to see the Juncker plays? I daresay she'd like them a great deal."

"Not yet. I've been busy." And he didn't want to risk Mother noticing the turns of phrase that might show his hand. She was often more clever than his siblings gave her credit for. If anyone could find him out, it would be her. Or Gwyn.

"Yes, I can guess what you've been busy doing." Gwyn scanned the ballroom. "Speaking of busy, I should return to my guests. You may be my favorite, but you're not my only." She wagged her finger at him. "Don't forget—you must dance with the lady of my choice. I'll be back soon to introduce you."

He stifled a groan. Gwyn would pair him with a wallflower for certain. She had no idea about his preferences in women. He lost sight of her as she marched across the room, but within moments another woman caught his attention.

It couldn't be. But it was. He would recognize that face anywhere.

It was *her*.

After all these years without so much as a moment's encounter between them, Miss Olivia Norley—or whatever her name was these days—had the audacity to show up here at his twin's home, where she had no right to be. Well,

Thorn meant to inform the chit of that fact. Right before he had her removed from the ballroom.

He motioned to a footman, but got no further before he spotted her companion, a woman equally attractive but not nearly as devious: his new sister-in-law, Grey's wife Beatrice, the Duchess of Greycourt.

Miss Norley and Beatrice were in league together? What the devil was going on?

He watched as they drifted across the room, coming closer to him by the moment. Fortunately, Beatrice was stopped every few feet by some acquaintance, and that gave him a chance to assess the changes time had wrought on Miss Norley.

There weren't many. She'd be about twenty-seven now, yet she still had the youthful appearance of a woman who'd borne no children. She wore her blond hair almost exactly as she had years ago, but her gown in a brilliant Pomona green skimmed her form more lovingly than a husband, a testament to how fashions had changed.

So had he. After his encounter with her, he hadn't looked at women in quite the same way. Now he always hunted for their hidden purpose before he indulged. And he'd indulged a great deal, thanks to the gossip Lady Norley had spread, about how her daughter had refused him because of his wild ways.

The gossip had actually enhanced his appeal. People who'd considered him odd because of his German habits now saw him as a typical English duke. And once Lady Norley had given him a scoundrel's reputation, he'd figured he might as well live the part.

But these days he used his sojourns into the stews mostly as fodder for his plays. He was getting a bit too old for whoring.

A fellow came by with glasses of ratafia, and he took

one. Tonight he found himself in need of strong drink, and the juice-flavored brandy would be just the thing.

He'd only taken his first sip when Beatrice approached him with Miss Norley, whose eyes glittered in the candle-light. Clearly she didn't want this meeting any more than he did. That was something of a surprise, given her propensity for trapping men.

"Gwyn told me to remind you of your promise, Thorn," Beatrice said. "In keeping with that, I'd like to present my new friend, Miss Olivia Norley. Miss Norley, this is the Duke of Thornstock, my brother-in-law."

He fancied he saw her pale at that last bit, but he couldn't be sure. In any case, one mystery was solved. After all this time, she was still unmarried. Then again, so was he.

"We've met," he said tersely, giving her the slightest of bows. If not for having made Gwyn that idiotic promise, he would have given Miss Norley the cut direct.

As it was, Beatrice blinked at him, obviously surprised to see him be so insolent to a woman. She must be unaware that Miss Norley wasn't a woman—she was a she-devil like her stepmother.

But Miss Norley clearly understood his behavior be-cause she tipped up her chin and said saucily, "You're drinking ratafia, Your Grace? Don't you think that's unwise, given your tendency to spill beverages at balls?"

He narrowed his gaze on her. "And how is Lady Norley these days? I assume she's in hiding somewhere around here." He scanned the ballroom. "Is she still trying to throw titled gentlemen into your lap?"

Miss Norley didn't so much as blush. "Fortunately, no. Now that I'm considered a spinster, my stepmother gener-ally leaves me be at balls."

"How lucky for you," he snapped. "And quite a kind-ness to the chaps she would try to corral on your behalf.

Although I'd hardly call you a spinster. You're younger than my sister, and she still managed to snag Major Wolfe."

"Thorn!" Beatrice said sharply. "What has come over you? You're being very rude to Miss Norley. Not only is she a guest, she's a particularly important one to me and Grey."

That brought him up short. "How so?"

"He didn't tell you? He has engaged Miss Norley to test his father's remains for arsenic using her new chemical method. The three of us leave for Carymont in the morning."

Carymont in Suffolk was the family seat of the dukes of Greycourt, where Grey's father had been entombed in the grand family mausoleum.

So Beatrice's pronouncement set Thorn back on his heels. Yes, Grey had recently begun to suspect that his father, presumed to have died of an ague in Grey's infancy, might actually have been poisoned all those years ago. But to go so far as to exhume the man's body? That seemed extreme. And why in hell would Grey choose *Miss Norley* to test the remains?

This was madness.

Thorn downed his ratafia, then scanned the ballroom. "Where's Grey?"

"Why?" Beatrice asked. "You're supposed to be dancing with Miss Norley."

Miss Norley stuck her chin out. "There's no reason His Grace should—"

"Oh, I fully intend to dance with you, Miss Norley," Thorn said icily. "But first I must speak to my brother."

"What do you want to know?" asked a sonorous voice behind him.

Thorn whirled to find Grey standing there. Seizing him by the arm, Thorn muttered, "Come with me. I wish to talk to you privately." Then Thorn headed for Wolfe's study . . . and its convenient store of liquor.

As soon as they entered and Thorn closed the door, Grey said, "You're being as theatrical as Mother usually is. What's got you so agitated?"

"I hear you're having your father's remains tested for arsenic."

Grey headed for the decanter. "I'm hoping to, yes."

"Are you even sure it can be done?"

"I am, actually. A short time ago, I came across a Prussian newspaper from 1803 in some of our stepfather's things. It contained an article about Sophie Ursinus, a Berlin poisoner. A German chemist named Valentin Rose developed a test to check for arsenic in the body of one of Ursinus's victims, and the results were used in her trial." Grey poured himself a glass of the amber liquid and took a generous swallow, then spit it back into the glass. "God, that's rum!"

"The major prefers rum. Something to do with his having been at sea for so long, I believe." Thorn poured his own glass. He could tolerate rum in the absence of brandy. "And don't change the subject. Is that why you're looking for a chemist?"

"Precisely."

"And you hit upon Miss Norley, of all people?"

"Yes." Turning stone-faced, Grey set down his glass. "Why do you care, anyway? It's *my* late father who's involved, and I can ask whomever I please to do the testing."

"But I'm assuming you want someone minimally competent in the field. Miss Norley surely has only a dilettante's interest. So why use her instead of a legitimate chemist?"

Grey scowled. "I tried to find 'a legitimate chemist,' as you put it. But every one I spoke to refused."

"For what reason?"

"Many were unfamiliar with the test Rose had developed. Some said they couldn't get results on a body so long deceased. Others said they didn't have the time. I suspect that's a polite way of saying they want nothing to do with the possible murder of a duke."

"You can hardly blame them. Dead men of great rank have live friends of great rank who don't want to risk being dragged into a trial and might go to extraordinary lengths not to be. Which would leave the chemist who proved the poisoning in an awkward position."

"Exactly. I even approached Mrs. Elizabeth Fulhame, a published chemist whose work is admired by others, but she has her own experiments that take up much of her time. She did, however, suggest a friend of hers—"

"Miss Norley."

"Yes. And when I learned of Miss Norley's experience as a chemist, I thought engaging her was my best recourse."

Thorn sipped some rum. "The chit actually has experience?"

"You must have little faith in me indeed if you think I'd entrust this task to just anybody. Miss Norley comes highly recommended by her uncle, a well-known chemist himself, as well as by Mrs. Fulhame."

Thorn had forgotten about her uncle, whom she'd mentioned on their first encounter. "So, a relation and another female. I hope you're not paying Miss Norley too much for her dubious experience."

Grey's eyes turned the dark blue that showed he was reaching the end of his patience. "Not that it's any of your concern, but I'm not paying her at all."

That took Thorn by surprise. "Then why is she doing it?"

"Why do you care?" Grey leaned against the nearby

desk. "For that matter, how do you even know Miss Norley?"

Thorn sighed. "Do you remember the Devonshire House ball, and how I was caught in a compromising situation with a young lady? I vaguely remember telling you that she turned me down when I proposed marriage."

He'd been in such a temper when he'd left the Norley town house that he'd ranted to Grey about it. All these years later, he still regretted that. He didn't like having people, even his half brother, know his secrets.

Grey's jaw dropped. "Miss *Norley*?"

"The very one. Her stepmother set me up to be caught, and her daughter was the one who baited the trap." With her knowledge of chemistry, actually. But being able to get a stain out of a waistcoat hardly meant she could do testing that would hold up in court. It was little more than a parlor trick. "Now you see why I'm concerned about your fixing upon her to do this."

"Actually, no, I don't see."

"Trust me, Miss Norley's reasons for her actions are generally suspect. For all you know, she wants to seduce you and ruin your marriage for her own shady purpose."

Grey laughed. "Dear God, the woman certainly put *your* back up. You forget that I've met her. She hardly seems the consummate liar you make her out to be. Or, for that matter, the consummate seducer."

"Appearances can be deceiving," Thorn muttered, unnerved by his brother's logical arguments.

Grey cocked his head. "I should point out that if Miss Norley 'baited the trap' for you, why did she then refuse your offer of marriage?"

That question had plagued his nights. Through the years, Thorn could come up with only one reason. "She thought refusing me would entice me to court her and possibly rouse jealousy in some fellow she really wanted."

Better that than her rejecting him because she'd found him wanting during the short span of time between when she'd lured him into the library and when her stepmother had shown up on cue to "catch" them.

"You think she would prefer some other fellow over a wealthy duke?" Grey asked. "So why didn't this other fellow offer for her? Since she has never married, she is obviously bad at baiting traps for men."

Now fully in a temper, Thorn marched up to his half brother. "Whose side are you on?"

Grey crossed his arms over his chest. "We're taking sides now, are we? Over my choice of chemist?"

"She is not a true—" Thorn stifled a sigh. "Look here, just because she carries a box of chemicals in her reticule doesn't mean anything."

"How do you know what's in her reticule? For a man who is barely her acquaintance, you seem oddly aware of her habits and surprisingly sure of her character." Grey looked smug. "Admit it, you're being irrational. You don't like her merely because she once had the audacity to turn you down."

"So did Bea," Thorn shot back, "the first time you proposed to *her*."

As Thorn had known it would, that sally wiped the humor right off Grey's face. "Who told you that?"

"Her brother." Thorn smirked at Grey. "Who is now my brother-in-law. Trust me, I've heard all your dirty secrets."

"From Wolfe? I doubt that. He's more tight-lipped than I am." Grey crossed his arms over his chest. "And obviously, Beatrice accepted me the second time, so perhaps you should offer for Miss Norley again."

"Not on your life." Thorn fought a grimace. Why was Miss Norley's refusal still such a sore subject? It had happened years ago.

"Then offer for another woman. You're getting a bit long in the tooth to be a bachelor."

"Don't be absurd," Thorn said, though he'd thought nearly the same thing earlier. "I'm only thirty. Just because you fell into Bea's arms like a trout into a fisherman's net doesn't mean I should give up my carefree bachelor life too young. Besides, there are plenty of women to be had without a man needing to marry one."

"Ah, now I understand," Grey said lazily. "You haven't offered for any other woman because Miss Norley saw right through your easy charm and rattled you."

"She was impressed enough by my 'easy charm' to let me kiss her years ago."

"Oho!" Grey grinned at him. "You never told me that part, you devil, you. She must have found something wanting in your kisses, indeed."

Thorn gritted his teeth. "She seemed rather enthusiastic at the time."

"Are you saying she's a trollop?"

"Of course not. But once you pair her with her stepmother, who forced my hand to make sure I offered for Miss Norley, you'll realize that the two of them—"

"Who said anything about her stepmother?" Grey lifted an eyebrow. "Miss Norley made it quite clear she did *not* want Lady Norley to come along. The baroness doesn't approve of her stepdaughter's experiments."

"So why did Lady Norley agree to let her go with you?"

"Because she doesn't know why we invited Miss Norley. We told her that the young woman is coming to the estate to serve as Beatrice's female companion during her confinement. I think Lady Norley was more than happy to allow her stepdaughter a chance to mingle with a duke and duchess. None of us saw any point in mentioning Miss Norley's real purpose."

"You don't know what her real purpose is," Thorn growled.

"Neither do you." Grey straightened his shoulders. "Don't take this the wrong way, but if anything, Miss Norley's rejection of you makes me trust her even more. She has a spine, something sorely lacking in most society women, and she's unimpressed by your title and wealth. So consider me forewarned, but I remain firm in my decision to have her do these tests."

Grey's refusal to see what seemed obvious to Thorn pricked his pride. "Very well. Then I'll go with all of you to Carymont."

"I haven't invited you."

"I daresay I can get your wife to do so."

"You probably could, you silver-tongued arse. She won't want to cause trouble in the family." Grey mused a moment. "All right then. Join us. I suppose that could be useful. Once we have the results of the test, you and I can think through the next part of our strategy—finding out who administered the arsenic."

Thorn drained his glass. "Assuming she finds any. And that her results are reliable."

Grey headed for the door, then paused to look back at Thorn. "I warn you. If you so much as attempt to ruin my plans with unfounded accusations against Miss Norley, I will send you packing so fast you won't know which way is up. Do you understand?"

"Perfectly."

At least he could be around to make sure Miss Norley

didn't cause any trouble. Or her stepmother, for that matter, who was liable to go marching off to Suffolk to "rescue" Miss Norley from the licentious duke half brothers.

After all, Grey had gained a reputation for wild living himself before he'd married. And in Thorn's mind, Miss Norley and Lady Norley went hand in hand no matter what the young woman had told Grey.

Lady Norley's "secret" concerning Father had even more potential to hurt Mother than it had when she'd been abroad. So far the baroness hadn't said a word about it publicly, so it was probably best not to upset the family by telling them. Indeed, all these years he'd considered it well in the past . . . until Miss Norley had shown up here.

Protecting Mother was paramount now that they were digging into who might have killed their fathers. If he and his half brothers proved that their fathers had been murdered, then she'd have more than enough secrets to deal with.

Unless she'd known about it all along. Unless *Mother* had murdered Father because she'd found out about his mistress.

Thorn shook his head. The very idea was absurd. How would she have managed damaging a carriage to cause the accident? Assuming there had been any damage to the carriage—they couldn't even be sure of that.

But it *was* possible that his father's mistress—if he'd had one—might have had an irate husband. It was something they should all consider . . . *after* Thorn had investigated the accident. He'd put that off long enough. If Grey was taking steps to find out who was killing off the dukes in their family, then it was high time Thorn do the same.

Until he could get home to do it, however, he must keep an eye on Miss Norley. Even if he hadn't entirely averted the crisis over Grey's choice of chemist, he'd at least put himself in a position to mitigate it. Now he must take her on. Time to let her know he'd be watching her every move. And he hated to admit it, but he was looking forward to that.

Chapter Two

Olivia got more nervous the longer she made small talk with the duchess. While waiting for a dance with the Duke of Thornstock. Who'd once been the sole subject of her fantasies.

Drat him. Why had he shown up again just as she'd finally erased him from her memory?

Supposedly he'd spent the intervening years in unsavory pursuits. That didn't surprise her. Clearly, Mama had been right—he was a scoundrel who'd only been dallying with her that night and who'd only offered for her because Mama had pushed him into it.

But Olivia had never learned what he'd meant when he'd spoken of Mama's threats and their bargain. She'd asked, but her stepmother had never given any specifics—just that she'd threatened to ruin him in society.

Obviously Mama hadn't realized whom she was dealing with. Dukes were immune to such gossip, although through the years Mama had done her best to blacken his reputation. Why he hadn't fought back as he'd threatened years ago was anyone's guess. Was it perhaps because after his temper had cooled he'd recognized that he'd done plenty to blacken his own reputation?

Mama had said Olivia was better off without him, duke or no, so Olivia had struggled to put him out of her head. But at night after leaving the laboratory, when Mama had insisted she embroider fire screens and cushions, Olivia's mind had wandered to when he'd kissed her. The only time anyone had *ever* kissed her.

Like the embroidery she'd worked on, she'd embellished their brief moments together—a stitch here and a loop there—until she'd no longer been sure exactly what was memory and what was fantasy.

But nine years was a long time, and eventually she'd been able to put the duke from her mind for days and then weeks at a time. Now he was here, threatening to overturn all her hard efforts. A pox on him. She wouldn't fall prey to his charm again, especially now that she knew how little it meant.

"I can't imagine where those two have gone off to," the duchess said kindly. "I assure you, Thorn is generally much more polite."

Not to me. Although she felt as if she'd given as good as she'd got during their exchange, it had been exhausting. "Honestly, it's fine, Your Grace."

"Please call me Beatrice. We'll be spending quite a bit of time together, I imagine."

Olivia certainly hoped so. She liked the duchess. Beatrice never seemed to put on airs. "Then you must call me Olivia," she countered.

"I will, thank you. And I'll ask you this before my mother-in-law does: were you named after the character in *Twelfth Night*?"

"Papa says I wasn't. My mother never said, or if she

did, I don't remember. She died of consumption when I was eight, and Papa remarried very quickly. Lady Norley has been my mother in all respects for the past nineteen years."

Beatrice stared across the room. "My mother died bearing me, so I never knew her at all. I'm named after Dante's true love, but my mother-in-law prefers to think I was named after the Beatrice in *Much Ado about Nothing*. I don't mind. It means I fit right in with the family. The dowager duchess gave all but Gwyn playwrights' surnames for their Christian names. And even Gwyn is named after an actress."

"That's unusual, isn't it?"

Beatrice nodded. "They're an unusual family. Why, my husband and Thorn are so close one would never guess they're only half brothers. They were raised together for a time, and it appears to have strengthened their filial bond."

Olivia wondered if Beatrice was warning her not to get between the two brothers. Then again, Olivia had never been good at reading such subtleties of behavior, and the duchess seemed genuine and open, not the sort to hint at things.

"It's lovely that they get along," Olivia said. "I have no siblings, I'm afraid. I often wonder if I would have liked some. Or if they would merely have proved a nuisance."

"I have only the one brother, Joshua—now Gwyn's husband—and he can be both a nuisance and a pleasure, sometimes all at once." Beatrice laughed lightly. "But I wouldn't trade him for anything."

Olivia was a bit jealous. With Papa absent most of the time, her stepmother always trying to push her in one direction or another, and her uncle only speaking of chemistry, Olivia wished she had someone nearer her age with whom to commiserate.

Beatrice scanned the ballroom yet again. "I may have to go fetch Grey and Thorn myself. We've already monopolized too much of your time this evening as it is, so I know you're probably looking forward to a dance."

With Thornstock? Hardly. Thank goodness she wore gloves, because the very thought of being in his arms again made her hands grow clammy. Especially given that he was so unreasonably angry at her. "Actually, I tend to prefer *not* dancing. I enjoy watching people far more than I do participating."

The duchess smiled. "I understand. Grey is very patient with me on the dance floor, but I just learned some of the newer steps in the past year, and I'm not quite as steady on my feet as he is."

"I used to be awful at it, but my stepmother hired a dancing master for me, and after far too many lessons I feel a bit more comfortable." Olivia cast Beatrice a rueful smile. "A tiny bit."

"Thankfully, Thorn is light on his feet. Follow his lead, and you shall have no issues, I assure you."

"Unless he carries me about," Olivia said grimly, "I fear I most certainly will have issues."

The duchess chuckled. "You're among friends here, so don't worry. The dancing is all in good fun. We can overlook a misstep or two."

Was she among friends? She rather liked the thought of that, but she dared not pin her hopes to it. She'd been without friends her age for so long that she'd taught herself to enjoy the solitude. Sometimes she even believed she truly did.

A sly look crossed Beatrice's face. "And speaking of

friends, I gather that you and Thorn have met before. Dare I ask how?"

Olivia searched for the best way to put it. "We had a brief encounter at the Devonshire House ball during my debut."

"That sounds fairly innocuous. Your conversation did not."

Dear heaven, how could she possibly explain the complicated situation her stepmother had put her in that night? "Well, we . . . er . . . did have a misunderstanding of sorts, which has left your brother-in-law disgruntled with me and my stepmother for all these years."

"Disgruntled. Hmm. No matter. You shall have one dance with him, and then you need not see him again."

Olivia didn't want that either. But what *did* she want?

The impossible. For him to be attracted to her the way she was to him. For him to wish to marry her while also supporting her work as a chemist. Neither of those was likely to happen.

She sighed. Although she'd guessed he was being forced into offering for her, her refusal of his proposal had clearly also stung his pride and fired his temper. It made no sense. She simply did not understand men and their . . . odd reactions.

That was why she preferred chemicals to people. Chemicals behaved in predictable ways. One merely had to figure out what those ways were. Chemicals didn't up and change their properties one day out of the blue, and they certainly didn't lose their tempers for no good reason.

"There they are!" Beatrice said as Greycourt and Thornstock entered the ballroom. "I began to wonder if they'd left entirely."

If only Olivia could be so lucky.

As the two half brothers approached, she studied

Thornstock, looking for signs that he'd changed since they'd first met. Unfortunately, he hadn't. His form was still as pleasingly fit as it had been in his youth, and his dark chestnut hair not only had no gray, but its short-cropped Titus style suited him better than his wild, untamed look from before. If she were a typical female, the very sight of him approaching with that icy look in his eyes would make her swoon.

But she was not, and it did not. By the time Thornstock and Greycourt had reached them, she had braced herself for an argument. She half expected to hear that Thornstock had talked his brother out of engaging her, and that her trip to Carymont was no more. So help her, if he had done so—

"Miss Norley," Thornstock said, "would you do me the honor of standing up with me for this set?"

He really meant to go through with their dance? Very well, she'd do her best not to let the arrogant, nosy fellow cow her.

She stared him down. "Certainly, Your Grace."

He surprised her by smiling. It threw her off guard, since she'd intended to be as cool to him as he'd been angry at her.

Then he offered her his arm, and a new sort of emotion hit her. Fear. She had exaggerated how far her dancing master had gone in improving her ability to dance, and the thought of having Thornstock see her bumbling about terrified her.

"Follow his lead, and you'll be fine," Beatrice whispered in her ear.

Olivia cast the duchess a grateful glance as Thornstock took her off to the floor. Fortunately, the dance was familiar, and the steps were ones she'd practiced often. She could almost enjoy the music.

Almost. Because his smile had vanished. The whole time they were doing the steps, he was staring intently at her. Glowering, really.

He stepped closer in the dance, his presence suddenly oppressive. She fancied she could feel the anger emanating from him, which was absurd. No experiment had ever proven that people could project their feelings into the air. Yet she would swear she felt palpable waves of bad temper coming from him.

She ignored the unsettling sensation. "Why are you so angry?"

"You know why."

"Because I refused your offer of marriage years ago?"

"Certainly not! Damn you, I am not the one at fault here."

They parted once more, and her heart began to clamor. How was *she* at fault? For that matter, what was she at fault for?

When they danced down the center of the two lines of other dancers, she was painfully conscious of his hand in the small of her back steadying her, of his other hand coming across to grip one of hers.

Beatrice had been right about one thing—Thornstock led very well. But this position was rather intimate. How could he hold her hand so tightly, yet still be angry at her? Feeling a need to understand him, she said, "I didn't realize the Duke of Greycourt was your brother, you know, when I agreed to his request."

Thornstock cast her a sidelong look. "Would it have made a difference?"

"Not really. But it seems to have angered you that he has engaged me to . . . er . . . perform these chemical tests."

"I have good reason to be angry. You are not—" He broke off, apparently noticing that people were trying to overhear their conversation. He lowered his voice. "The woman I thought you were at first."

"That's not *my* fault. I was always ever myself. I cannot help it if you perceived that differently."

He pinned her with his crystalline gaze. "I remember you telling me you weren't a good dancer. But clearly *that* was a lie, given how beautifully you're following my lead."

She wasn't sure whether to be pleased he approved of her dancing or annoyed that he thought nine years had passed without a single change in her. "My stepmother made me take more dancing lessons than I wanted. This is the result."

"I gather that you hated them," he drawled. "The lessons, I mean."

She shrugged. "I did them only to please my parents. Chemistry was my primary interest then, and it's my primary interest now."

"Hmph," he muttered, sounding unconvinced. They took their positions next to each other, waiting while the remaining couples danced their way down the middle. "And why are you so interested in this particular chemical endeavor? Surely you aren't doing it out of the kindness of your heart."

"No, indeed. Science and hearts have naught to do with each other."

That seemed to startle him into smiling. "I'm sure there are those who would disagree."

"Are there? How peculiar. All that matters in science are the results of experiments. That's why I prefer it. Facts don't lie. An experiment either proves something or it does not."

He lowered his voice. "And you mean to prove the existence of arsenic in . . . er . . ."

"Yes. It has been used by villains for centuries. I wish

to put an end to that by developing a better test to detect it. If my method proves to work as planned, then others can find out for certain when their loved ones are murdered by poison."

A nearby dancer gasped, and Thornstock glared at the woman. Then he said in a lowered voice, "I'm afraid that murder isn't a suitable topic for the ballroom. We should not speak of your . . . er . . . aims until we are done with the set and can be more private."

She nodded. But she would have preferred to continue talking about her experiments. Or anything, really. Because when he'd spoken of being "private" it had sent electricity through her blood. And when she wasn't talking, she became too aware of His Grace's capable hand in hers or on her waist or turning her toward him in the dance.

It wasn't particularly warm in the room with all the doors open toward the garden, but her cheeks still felt hot. Every step they took together made her stomach do that same somersault as on the night he'd kissed her. She didn't understand it. He knew nothing about science and cared nothing for her personally. So why did he have this effect on her?

His sister-in-law hadn't lied about how adept a dancer he was. Olivia didn't want to admire him for it, but she did. Through her many lessons, she'd learned how much work went into looking so effortless on the floor.

The music finally ended, and he took her hand so they could promenade away. "Shall I show you my sister's new garden? Gwyn is inordinately proud of it."

Olivia could only nod. She knew he wanted to speak to her privately, and she wanted to be done with it. She would explain her reasons for taking on Greycourt's task, and then Thornstock would give his approval.

She wasn't entirely sure if Greycourt *needed* his half

brother's approval, but if laying out her plans put an end to Thornstock's objections, it would help her achieve her goal.

Now if only she could stop her heart from thundering in her chest around him.

Thorn led Miss Norley into the refreshments room, which was mostly empty now that another set had begun. He waited until no one was watching, then swiftly guided her through the door and down the stone steps into the garden.

As soon as they'd found a quiet spot near a fountain, he turned to her. "So tell me, Miss Norley, why are you doing this?"

"Coming out into the garden with you? You gave me little choice."

Was she deliberately being obtuse? "That's not what I mean, and you know it," he said irritably.

"Oh! You're asking why I agreed to test the remains of your half brother's father for arsenic."

"Exactly. I know you're not being paid for it."

"Your brother offered me payment, but I have managed to learn a few of the unspoken rules of society through the years, and one is that a woman of rank may not work for money. So of course I refused to take any for my efforts. My parents wouldn't approve."

He fought a smile. "But they approve of what you're doing?"

"Well, no. If they knew of it, they probably wouldn't. Papa would blame Mama for not looking after me better, and Mama would simply be appalled. She prefers I live the life of a pampered lady of rank." She sighed. "I find that sort of life boring."

He couldn't blame her—the older he got, the duller he

found circulating through polite society himself. Wait, why was he sympathizing with her? "In other words, you don't *always* follow the rules, unspoken or otherwise."

"Now you're baiting me." She looked away, studying the water of the fountain as if to determine what made it shimmer in the moonlight. "You know perfectly well I broke the rules rather spectacularly when we first met. I generally try to follow them. I just don't always succeed."

Her reference to their night at the Devonshires' ball sent him right back to that dimly lit library and the feel of her feminine curves, the taste of her mouth, and the smell of frangipani and jasmine that seemed to follow her everywhere—an exotic fragrance for a decidedly unexotic woman. He wondered if she still tasted as luscious, if her skin was still as silky.

He ached to touch her and find out.

The thought made him stifle an oath. Clearly she *wanted* him to remember their kiss. That was her way of getting him off the subject. But he wouldn't let her distract him.

"So you're not taking money for these experiments," he said coldly. "You're just doing them to enliven your boring life? Or perhaps you have no intention of performing them at all. Doing experiments on a corpse doesn't sound like the sort of pastime a young lady enjoys. So perhaps you merely mean to spend a week or two away from home, having a lovely time at a wealthy duke's expense."

For a moment she gaped at him. Then a scowl marred her smooth brow. "You really are the most annoying fellow I have ever met."

When she turned, as if to march back into the ballroom, he caught her by the arm. "You're not leaving until you explain your real reason for doing this."

"First of all," she said as she snatched her arm free, "not that it's any of your concern, but I will not be experimenting on the corpse. As the local magistrate, your brother will be overseeing the exhumation of his father's remains, and I have given him a list of what parts will be useful for testing."

That took him aback. It implied a certain amount of planning that he wouldn't have guessed she would involve herself in.

"Secondly, I am doing this to gain better credentials. This set of experiments will establish me as a chemist of renown, since none have succeeded in using the existing tests for arsenic on a long-buried body."

That raised a different concern. "So you intend to publish your findings."

"A chemist is only as good as his—or her—publications, and I have only one to my name." She tipped up her chin, sending moonlight flowing over her golden hair. "Of course I intend to publish the results. Why wouldn't I? Other chemists do."

"Other chemists aren't testing the remains of a duke of the realm." He swore under his breath. "Does my brother know of your plans to publish?"

"If he doesn't, he's not very bright. Why else would I take on the task?"

"But you haven't explicitly told him."

Her lips tightened. "No. I assumed there was no need."

"He might feel differently." Catching her by the shoulder, he turned her to face him. "Here's another unspoken rule of society for you. Dukes don't dabble in anything scandalous. And nothing is more scandalous than murder. My brother isn't going to want his private affairs talked about in the press simply because you wish to enhance your standing as a chemist."

She stared at him unblinking. "But his father's murderer

can't be brought to justice without a trial, and nothing is more public than that."

The chit was clever. He'd give her that. "Still, your test can't prove *who* poisoned Grey's father—just that it was done. We don't want to tip our hand to the murderer until we've actually found the villain. That means you might have to keep quiet about your results for some time. Are you willing to do so?"

Looking wary, she searched his face. "If that's what it takes to gain justice for your brother's father, I am perfectly willing . . . for a while, anyway. It benefits me to have my name linked to the case eventually. That is how Valentin Rose's methods became known, after all. So it behooves me to wait until after a trial before I publish."

"No matter how long that takes?"

She cocked her head. "Well, obviously not if it goes on for years. Someone else might discover the same methods I have, and that person's publication will become the most important by virtue of being first. I did take this on to gain credentials; I can't risk having someone else chronicle the experiments before me."

That made sense but was hardly the point. Would Grey really want the world to hear about his father's murder if there was no way of proving who did it? Somehow Thorn doubted that.

And Miss Norley had it in her power to force Grey's hand. Thorn's bargain with Lady Norley might have held, but he hadn't made any such bargain with *Miss* Norley. Assuming that the young woman knew the same gossip as her stepmother, Thorn would have to handle her with kid gloves. While Grey wouldn't care if the reputation of Thorn's father was damaged, he *would* care about protecting their mother from hearing about it. So Miss Norley could end up forcing all of Lydia's children to dance to her tune.

There was another matter to consider, too. "What if you don't find arsenic? What if Grey is wrong, and his father *did* die of an ague?"

Her frown told him she was hoping for a different outcome. "Then I'll have to find another way to prove that my methods could withstand the rigors of a trial."

He shook his head. "I must confess, I'm shocked to meet a woman so interested in chemistry that she's willing to do experiments on the dead to prove her hypotheses. I'm a man, and even I have no interest in such a thing."

She shrugged. "You're not a man of science. Or so I've heard."

That caught him by surprise. Again. "What else have you heard about me?"

Her eyes widened. "I . . . um . . . well . . ."

"Miss Norley," he said, surprised by her unexpectedly feminine response, "there's no need for embarrassment. I am well aware of my reputation."

"Then you don't need me to tell you what it is," she said matter-of-factly.

He couldn't help but laugh. The woman was like no other female he'd ever met. "Indulge my curiosity. I never know how much young, unmarried ladies are told about me." He took a stab in the dark. "Though I'm sure your stepmother didn't mince words on the subject."

"No, she did not," she said dryly. "She rarely does."

Ah, so the young woman *had* learned about his reputation from her stepmother. He stepped closer. Would Miss Norley also admit that her stepmother had told her the gossip about his father? Had Lady Norley even done so? On the chance that she had not, he refused to tell

Miss Norley himself, but that didn't mean he couldn't question her.

"What exactly did your stepmother say about me?" he asked.

"That you were a ne'er-do-well."

"A duke can't be a ne'er-do-well, my dear, especially not one as wealthy as I."

The lady didn't look impressed. "Mama said you spend your evenings with . . . loose women rather than with respectable people."

"I don't deny it. Like you, I sometimes find the life of a person of rank rather dull."

"Yes, but I fill my hours doing something useful."

He chuckled. "So do I. Loose women need entertainment, too. Not to mention, money. I provide them with both. Isn't that useful of me?"

She shook her head, clearly fighting a smile. "You are hopeless, Your Grace."

"So they tell me. And there's no need to keep calling me 'Your Grace.' Everyone calls me Thorn. You might as well, too." He wished it weren't too dark to see if she was blushing. He pushed further. "And I shall call you Olivia."

"That's rather forward of you, isn't it?"

"My sister-in-law is calling you Olivia. Why can't I?"

He waited for her to make the standard argument that a woman could call another woman by her Christian name when a man could not.

Instead, she eyed him askance. "Fine. But not when Mama is around. Or any of your family."

"Very well. It will be our little secret." He tucked one of her errant curls behind her ear, pleased when the intimacy elicited a shaky breath from her. He wasn't sure of her motives with this chemistry business, but clearly she was still attracted to him. "And speaking of your 'Mama,'

I daresay she's frustrated that you won't oblige her by looking for a husband."

Olivia thrust out her chin. "She and Papa insisted upon my having a debut. I did. No one offered for me. So I refused to repeat the process."

"*No one offered for you?* I seem to recall a certain duke offering for you, and being refused."

"That was different." Her eyes gleamed in the moonlight. "You didn't mean it. When you kissed me you were just having your usual sort of fun. Until Mama forced you into making an offer, you had no intention of actually marrying me."

"My 'usual sort of'—Wait, you *knew* your stepmother was forcing me?"

"Of course I knew. You made it painfully obvious."

That didn't mean she knew about the blackmail. And he certainly didn't intend to tell her. The less people knew about it, the better.

Then the rest of her statement registered. "I didn't realize I was obvious."

Her face was hard as stone. "Well, you were. And I didn't want a husband who had to be dragged to the altar."

"I didn't want a wife whom I'd known only an hour."

"That's fair." She folded her hands behind her back. "But that doesn't explain why you got so angry when I refused you. I only did what we both wanted."

When she put it that way, he sounded mean spirited. Or was that how she wanted him to feel? "Are you saying that if I'd spouted some compliments and begged for your hand, you would have accepted me?"

She frowned. "Er . . . probably not."

He advanced on her. "Because our kiss didn't thrill you?"

"I didn't say that." She looked downright nervous now.

Good. He liked her nervous. She let her guard down then. "So our kiss *did* thrill you."

"I—I'm not sure. . . ."

"Not sure?" He took another step forward, and she backed up toward the fountain, nearly falling in before he slipped his arm about her waist to steady her. "Well, *Olivia*? Which is it? Because our kiss certainly thrilled me. And I could have sworn I wasn't alone in that."

Her eyes widened and her fetching mouth fell open.

"But perhaps I should make certain of it," he went on. "For both of us."

Then lowering his head, he sealed his mouth to hers.

Chapter Three

Olivia grabbed his shoulders, but only to keep her balance. Not because she liked his kisses.

Oh, devil take it, she *did* like his kisses, which were as combustible as sweet oil of vitriol and nearly as dangerous. She'd forgotten how delicious his lips tasted, how him holding her close made her heart race and her knees wobble. He conjured up feelings she couldn't comprehend. And as usual, whenever she didn't understand something, she threw herself into it with even more enthusiasm until she did.

So she joined her hands around his neck—probably crushing his shirt collar and cravat—and opened her mouth to him in anticipation of him kissing her as he had before.

Instead, he drew back to search her face. "You never answered my question. Is your stepmother here? Is she hiding out in the garden somewhere?"

"How should I know if she's hiding in the garden? I've been dancing with *you*. But yes, she's at the ball somewhere. She's my chaperone."

He narrowed his gaze on her. "I'm trying to determine if this is another attempt to trick me into offering marriage."

"*Trick* you! Dear heavens, you're full of yourself." When he bristled at that, she added, "*You* were the one who brought me out here, so only *you* would know why you did. For that matter, you were the one to initiate the kiss."

"Ah. Right." A self-deprecating chuckle escaped him. "Excellent point."

She shook her head. She didn't know what to think of him. "If it makes you feel any better, I promise to turn you down again if you *do* offer."

"I have no intention of offering," he said in a brittle tone.

She ignored the quick stab of disappointment in her chest. Even if she *did* like kissing him, she had no desire to marry such a self-important, arrogant fellow. He was too much like Papa in his habits. "Then since I have no intention of accepting, we're in agreement. But as you seem ridiculously concerned about being caught kissing me, we should probably go back inside and—"

He smothered the rest of her words with his mouth.

She considered protesting. He was waxing hot and cold, and it got more confusing by the moment.

But then he did what he'd done before and thrust his tongue inside her mouth, and she melted. Kissing him in that fashion was like heaven. No wonder he was arrogant. He kissed the same way angels surely did.

He nibbled her lower lip, another strange behavior that made her go all hot inside. "You mustn't read too much into this," he whispered.

Ignoring the pang those words gave her, she whispered back, "Neither should you."

"Just because I like kissing you doesn't mean I—"

"More kissing," she muttered. "Less talking."

With a chuckle, he drew her over to a bench where

they'd be hidden from view if anyone came into the garden. That should have alarmed her. It did not.

He pulled her down beside him, then set about feathering delicious little kisses along her cheekbone to her ear. "Are you sure you're a chemist?"

She leaned back to lift an eyebrow at him. "Are you sure you're a rakehell? Because you certainly aren't acting like one."

"Then I'd best begin doing so," he rasped.

This time he kissed her neck. He even licked her pulse at her throat, which should have disgusted her and instead made her wish to do the same to him.

Would he like it? Did she dare?

She tried it, reveling in his scent of rosewood oil and soap. The scrape of his whiskers delighted her, too, and so did the way he groaned and buried his mouth between her breasts. How wicked!

How thrilling. She gripped his head, meaning to pull him from her bosom and instead tugged him closer. Oh, dear. She was rapidly losing her way. He must be a rakehell after all.

"Your skin is like satin," he murmured into her breasts. "And you smell so good. I can only imagine how you would taste if I—"

"Olivia?" a voice called from somewhere behind them. "Are you out here? Gwyn wanted me to find you so we could all chat."

It was Beatrice. Thorn put a finger to his lips, but Olivia didn't plan to wait until the woman came down here and discovered them together.

She rose from the bench. "I'm here. I was sitting and admiring the fountain." She hurried up the stone steps to where Beatrice stood near the door. "The Wolfes truly have a lovely garden, don't they?"

"They do," Beatrice said as she peered beyond Olivia into the darkness.

Olivia wasn't good at deception, but if she let Thorn get caught with her again, he would *never* believe she hadn't done it on purpose somehow. He was so absurdly suspicious.

She looped her arm in Beatrice's. "I'm quite eager to talk to Lady Gwyn. When Mama and I were introduced to her as we entered this evening, she and I barely got to say two words. There is such a crush here tonight, don't you think? It's precisely why I came out to get some air."

Lord, she was babbling. She'd never babbled in her life. Because she'd never before practiced to deceive.

Apparently, tonight was to be full of firsts for her.

"Have you seen Thorn?" Beatrice asked, looking suspicious. "I could have sworn he was with you when you came out here."

"Oh. He . . . um . . . merely showed me the garden and hurried back inside. I believe he was headed in search of more ratafia."

Beatrice's face cleared. "That does sound like my brother-in-law." She patted Olivia's hand and headed for the door. "I'm sure we'll run into him again."

Olivia hoped not. Her body couldn't take much more of a practiced rakehell's attentions.

Thank goodness she wouldn't have to see him after this. She and the Greycourts were leaving for their estate tomorrow, and she could bury herself once more in her work.

Now if only she didn't have fresh fuel for her fantasies, her nights would be calm. But she suspected it would be a long while before that happened.

* * *

Thorn sat on the bench, waiting until he was certain that Beatrice and Olivia were gone, then waiting a while longer for his arousal to subside. Damn it all to hell. He'd handled matters badly. He'd intended to inform Olivia he'd be keeping an eye on her at Grey's estate.

Instead, he'd fallen right back into doing things with her that were most unwise. It didn't bode well for his ability to keep her at bay at Grey's.

Perhaps he shouldn't go.

Like hell he shouldn't. He still wasn't convinced of her motives for doing this. And even if she proved as transparent as she seemed, she could very well be incompetent as a chemist. What did *he* know about chemistry? What did *Grey*, for that matter?

He rose. The ladies were gone. And he had a long night ahead of him. Presently Vickerman was awaiting his latest play, so Thorn—or rather, Konrad Juncker—would have to put the theater manager off again if Thorn meant to join Grey and the others for the trip to Carymont tomorrow.

It couldn't be helped. He would make that clear to Juncker. Having grown up in London, Juncker was no more German than Thorn, but the two had become fast friends over the writing of Thorn's plays.

Thorn had been reluctant from the beginning to let it be known he was a working writer. One reason was the freedom that using Juncker afforded him. Thorn could easily move about the stews without anyone realizing he was doing research.

The other reason was to protect his family. Before the death of his stepfather, the only father he'd ever known, he'd been loath to hurt Father's career as ambassador to Prussia. And now that all his family was here, Thorn was even more wary of exposing himself and them.

Juncker was happy to oblige. The adventures had made

him famous, and that in turn helped him get his poems published. Once in a while, Juncker even wrote a bit or two for the plays. Poets didn't make much, after all, and Thorn was happy to pay his friend for the use of his name and any writing he wished to do for Thorn's works.

Thorn walked into the ballroom, only to find himself surrounded by half his family. His mother was standing with Bonham, which grated on Thorn, and Olivia stood beside her, which did not. He glanced around for Lady Norley, but she was across the room chatting with Mother's closest friend, Lady Hornsby. Judging from their animated gestures, they had known each other long enough to be comfortable together. Hmm.

"Oh, look who's come in from the garden *now*," Gwyn said with a twinkle in her eye. "How odd that you and Miss Norley chose to get a breath of fresh air at nearly the same time."

"Leave them alone, my dear," Mother said. "Thorn isn't so foolish as to take a young, respectable woman he's just met out into the garden. I'm sure they didn't even cross paths."

Thorn could tell a subtle warning when he heard one. It was her way of slapping his wrist. "Mother's right. Miss Norley is perfectly safe from me. And anyway, I was actually out in the mews, looking at that new gelding Major Wolfe keeps bragging about."

"He's a prime goer, isn't he?" his brother-in-law put in.

"Indeed, he is," Thorn lied.

Gwyn and Beatrice exchanged glances. They didn't believe him for a minute. Even Grey narrowed his gaze on Thorn, while Olivia merely stared serenely at the company as if butter wouldn't melt in her mouth.

That only proved, once again, that she couldn't be trusted. Most ladies would have *some* reaction to being teased about being caught with a man. Yet not even a blush stained her cheeks.

Come to think of it, he wasn't sure he'd *ever* seen her blush. Unfortunately, that only made him wonder what it would take to gain one.

Damn it to hell.

"Mother, I'll be away from town for a while. I'm planning on traveling with Grey, Beatrice, and Miss Norley to Carymont tomorrow."

Olivia's gaze shot to him and color stained her cheeks. Ah, so he *could* make her blush, though her embarrassment quickly turned to anger, judging by the daggered glance she shot him. She was clearly none too happy, which was precisely what he'd intended. To put her on her guard. To let her know that she'd best behave herself around his relations.

But a quick survey of his family's reaction showed that throwing his cannonball into the cozy group had roused more than Olivia to anger.

"Grey!" Beatrice exclaimed, with hurt in her voice. "You knew about this and didn't tell me?"

Grey shot Thorn a foul look. "It was just decided tonight, sweetheart. A short while ago, as a matter of fact. I was about to tell you when Thorn interrupted."

Beatrice looked unconvinced.

"I'm hoping to purchase some property in Suffolk," Thorn lied blithely, "so I thought I might as well travel there with family to observe the place and then hire a post chaise to return."

Out of the corner of his eye, he caught Gwyn and Mother smirking at him. Let them smirk. They saw love matches everywhere, and if they thought he was sweet on Olivia, they wouldn't give him much grief about his comings and goings.

Major Wolfe, on the other hand, was hard to read. Thorn's brother-in-law was *always* enigmatic, but tonight he was positively inscrutable. What was the man thinking? Wolfe already knew quite a bit about Grey's suspicions concerning his father's death, so he might be drawing his own conclusions about the trip to Carymont. For that matter, Beatrice might have mentioned to him the real reason for it. She and her brother were very close.

Well, at least the major was in *their* corner. Bad leg or not, Wolfe would make a formidable foe for anyone.

"Forgive me, Lady Gwyn," Olivia said, without so much as a glance his way, "but if I'm to be traveling tomorrow, I had best get plenty of sleep tonight. So I believe I'll fetch Mama and have your footman call for our carriage."

"Of course, my dear," Gwyn said, shooting him a knowing look. "Given the circumstances, we're pleased you even managed to attend. I'll walk you out."

Damn. He shouldn't have told everyone about going to Suffolk. Now he would have to endure questions from Gwyn and Beatrice and Mother for the rest of the night.

The hell he would. As soon as Olivia and Gwyn had walked away, he went over to kiss his mother's cheek. "I'd best be off, too, Mother, for the same reason as Miss Norley. I don't want to be the one to hold up Grey's leaving in the morning. You know how he hates getting a late start."

"I mean to leave at eight a.m.," Grey said with a taunting smile. "Or earlier, if you can manage it."

Thorn stifled a groan. "In other words, your usual crack of dawn departure. I'll do my best."

"But Carymont isn't far, is it?" Bonham interjected. "So you should have an easy journey even if you *do* get a late start."

Thorn stared the fellow down. Bonham had no right even to enter the conversation, much less stand there making calf's eyes at Mother. What she could see in the man escaped Thorn entirely. He was handsome for a gentleman in his sixties—with a full head of graying hair, a robust body, and no sagging jowls—but Thorn still resented his presence.

"We'll have an easy journey regardless," Thorn said. "Traveling with *family* is always pleasant."

Bonham flashed him a ghost of a smile. "With family and Miss Norley, you mean."

Damn him. "Of course."

Then, as Mother chuckled, Thorn walked off. He tried not to fume as he left, knowing that he'd been rude, but also not caring. His encounter with Miss Norley had put him in a foul mood, and his talk with Juncker about the play wasn't likely to improve it. Olivia might get some sleep tonight, but he doubted *he'd* get any.

Fortunately, he found Juncker at his lodgings in the Albany Hotel and didn't have to go hunting through taverns half the night to run the chap down. Juncker's rooms were nicer than any bachelor could want, which he could ill have afforded without Thorn's money.

Thorn wasn't surprised when the fellow met him at the door clearly dressed to go out. "Thorn!" Juncker cried. "You're just in time to join me. I'm going to that new tavern on Piccadilly where the barmaids have nice arses and even nicer—"

"I can't." Pushing past Juncker, he dropped onto the aging sofa. "I'm leaving for Suffolk in the morning."

Juncker's mood changed at once. With a scowl, he shut the door. "What about the play? You said you'd have it finished this week."

"I know, but something came up. I'll work on the ending while I'm traveling."

"You always say that," Juncker grumbled, "yet you

never do. Once you leave London, I have no hope of seeing any writing from you."

Juncker began to pace, his beetled brow appearing fearsome indeed. His height alone would intimidate, but his dark blue eyes and wildly disordered blond hair—what was called the "frightened owl" style—made him look like a madman. Gentlemen usually steered clear of him.

Ladies did not. Juncker was the very figure of the tortured writer, and women always swooned over that.

Juncker glared at him. "I don't understand why you don't just tell Vickerman you write the plays. Then every time you leave town, he'll be more than happy to allow you a reprieve. Hell, he'd be ecstatic to have a duke in his arsenal."

"That's the problem. I don't want people knowing I wrote them, and Vickerman would only succeed in keeping it secret for the space of a day. If that."

"I suppose."

"Besides, if you don't write for me, how will you live so well?"

Juncker's shoulders slumped. "True."

"So stop fretting, for God's sake," Thorn said irritably. "Vickerman will understand. Just tell him your muse is on holiday."

"He doesn't believe in muses. He believes in cold, hard cash, as you well know. And he gets damned disagreeable when I can't produce the work for him because you're off doing as you please." Juncker stalked up to pin Thorn with an accusing look. "He's not the only one. If you aren't careful, I'll write the damn plays myself, and to hell with you."

Thorn laughed. "All the characters will speak in iambic pentameter, I suppose." When Juncker didn't rise to the bait, Thorn added, "If it's money you're worried about, I can advance you some until Vickerman pays for the play."

Juncker snorted. "It's not money. Not yet, anyway. I just . . . It's been a while since we had a play in the theater. People seem to be losing interest."

"If they are, *c'est la vie*. All good things must come to an end eventually."

"That's easy for you to say. You don't have to worry about the money. I'm the one who'll be out in the cold."

Seeing his friend's doleful look, he rose to place a hand on his shoulder. "You know I was merely joking about the iambic pentameter, don't you?"

Juncker's terse nod struck Thorn to the heart.

Thorn sighed. "You're a fine poet. And a fine writer in general. What happened to that novel you were working on? What I read of it was damned good, and now that you're famous in London circles, you would probably have no trouble getting published."

"If I finished it." His friend pulled away. "Unlike yours, *my* muse went on holiday, fell off the ship, and drowned. I haven't gone beyond chapter five." Juncker tapped his head. "I'm dry as dust up here, cobwebs everywhere."

"I know the feeling well," Thorn said. "Just keep writing. It will come."

"Sounds like you need to take your own advice," Juncker muttered. "You've been working on that ending for months now."

"True." He'd been in the doldrums. Until tonight, that is. Something about sparring with Olivia had roused more than just his desire. It made him itch to have a pen in hand, if only to skewer a character or two with his barbs. "I tell you what. How about I walk you out, and you can visit that tavern? It will cheer you up. Perhaps it will even sweep out those cobwebs."

"Perhaps," Juncker said. "You're not joining me, I suppose."

"Not tonight."

Thorn had a few hours yet before he must show up at Grey's. And he meant to spend them productively. He might actually finish the play while he was traveling, after all.

Chapter Four

It had taken Olivia half the night, but she'd finally managed to get her panic under control in time for their departure the next morning. So what if His Grace, the dratted Duke of Thornstock, was riding with them? It sounded as if the coach trip was the only time she'd have to endure his . . . his pompous smiles and knowing smirks.

And his flirting. His clever, annoying flirting that made her stomach flip over, and her blood heat. The man should bottle that charm of his and sell it. She would buy a bottle just to analyze the ingredients.

But apparently she wouldn't have to worry about him today. The moment he entered the carriage and settled into the seat next to his brother, he laid his head back against the squabs and promptly fell asleep.

Olivia tried not to watch him obsessively, but that was difficult. She'd never seen a man who looked more blissful—or attractive—in repose.

Particularly the differing parts of his facial hair. Unlike her father, who always looked overgroomed, and her uncle, who always looked undergroomed, Thorn looked perfect. His side whiskers weren't bushy, his eyebrows were clipped but not overly so, and his hair lacked pomade. She hated pomade—it just seemed . . . greasy.

And heavens, but he had long lashes, like little, dark brown half-moons against his lightly tanned skin. Clearly he spent time outdoors, although not as much as his elder brother, who had more deeply tanned skin. She would have to ask Beatrice about it later.

Would that be rude? She wasn't sure. She could never keep the rules of society straight. Especially the ones that didn't make sense.

When after a short while, Thorn started to snore, Greycourt chuckled. "It never ceases to amaze me how Thorn can sleep anywhere at any time. I once saw him dozing in the midst of a heated debate in the House of Lords. The rest of us were riveted; Thorn would have fallen off the bench if I hadn't poked him awake."

Without even opening his eyes, Thorn muttered, "That's a despicable lie. I have never in my life fallen off a bench, poking or no poking."

Beatrice and Olivia burst into laughter.

"Go back to sleep," Beatrice said soothingly. "We promise to be quiet."

"I promise no such thing," Grey said. "It's not *my* fault he decided to come along at the last minute. He probably spent last night in the stews."

Thorn opened one eye. "I spent last night settling some financial affairs, I'll have you know. And if you hadn't insisted on leaving at dawn, I'd be far more chipper." He opened the other eye, straightened on the seat, and finger-combed his hair, which now miraculously looked as if he'd just left his barber.

His clothing wasn't even rumpled! His white cravat was still crisply tied, his blue morning coat lay properly, and his tight pantaloons accentuated his muscular thighs. No doubt whoever coined the term "sartorial splendor" had done so after meeting the Duke of Thornstock.

"And if you lot are planning to talk about me while I doze," Thorn went on, "I believe I'll stay awake." He flashed her a most devastating smile. "I can't have you telling Miss Norley lies about me."

She fought the silly burst of pleasure that his smile gave her. She knew better than to trust that talent of his. "I already know about your reputation, Your Grace. So it's not as if they could tell me anything that would surprise me."

Greycourt slapped his brother's knee. "Clearly, you've met your match in Miss Norley, old chap. She doesn't fall for your sly attentions and droll wit."

How she wished that were true. Thorn's smile had faded, but his eyes still danced as he stared at her, and she desperately wished he would go back to sleep.

No such luck. He had fixed on her now, and like an entomologist with a beetle, he was determined to pin her to his board.

"I'm curious about these experiments of yours, Miss Norley," he said in a too-casual voice that put her on her guard. "What makes you think you can succeed in finding arsenic in the remains of Grey's father when other chemists think it impossible?"

"From what the duke has told me about his dealings with other chemists, they aren't even willing to try."

"Not even this Valentin Rose fellow?" Thorn asked.

Surprised that he knew of Rose, she said, "Alas, Mr. Rose is dead."

"Ah," Thorn said.

"There have been others who developed tests for arsenic. In preparation for your brother's task, I studied and tested all the known ones by chemists Scheele, Metzger, Rose, and Hahnemann. Sadly, all but Hahnemann are dead, and Hahnemann lives in Saxony, so bringing him here would not be feasible."

Thorn looked surprised that she even knew of the men who had tried the task. It irritated her.

"Each of their tests have flaws," she went on. "I have, through stringent experimentation, found a better one that uses the best of their methods. Mine would be useful in the courts. That's why your brother has engaged me for this task—because my uncle and Mrs. Fulhame felt that my test could be successful in this instance."

Thorn was looking at her as if she'd sprouted wings.

"What?" she said. "Do you have an opinion of your own about the proper method? I welcome any suggestions, if they will better my results."

"Er . . . no suggestions. I wouldn't even know where to begin, honestly." He stretched out one leg, brushing her skirt.

She swallowed hard, though she doubted that Thorn had done it intentionally. She was just reacting to his general nearness. She'd never shared a carriage with two such handsome gentlemen, and certainly not with a man who'd kissed her more than once.

As usual, her nervousness brought out her tendency to babble. "My method isn't that complicated. Once the exhumation is complete, I mean to see what is left of the previous Duke of Greycourt's remains to test. His Grace tells me his father was embalmed, and if so, that may be a problem because arsenic is sometimes used for embalming. But assuming I can find relevant samples that aren't contaminated, I will first subject them to nitric acid and then combine that with zinc. The formula for that would be $As_2O_3 + 6\,Zn$—"

"I beg you, Miss Norley, no formulas!" Greycourt said. "They're meaningless to me and my brother, I assure you. And if Thorn tells you otherwise, he's lying."

"Grey is absolutely right," Thorn said. "I only like chemistry to the extent that it improves the liquor and wine I drink. But that leads me to my next question. Why are you even sure that the poison used would be arsenic?"

"I'm going by the duke's description of his father's symptoms," Olivia said. "They are that of an ague or cholera, which are also the symptoms of arsenic poisoning, and arsenic *is* one of the most common poisons. There's a reason, after all, that the chemical is called '*poudre de succession*.'"

Beatrice glanced at her husband, who said, "Inheritance powder. That's the French nickname for arsenic."

"But to be precise," Olivia said, "when we speak of the white arsenic used as a poison, we really mean arsenic trioxide."

"Oh, by all means, let's be precise," Thorn said. "And speaking of precision, how will you do all these tests without a laboratory?"

"Your brother has been generous enough to create one for me," Olivia said.

Beatrice patted Olivia's hand. "We asked her for a list of what she would need to do her work. Then Grey bought all the necessary items and had them brought to the estate."

"I'll still have to formulate some items from their components," Olivia added. "And I did bring a few items that would be hard to find anywhere."

"Of course," Greycourt said, "we had no idea how to set all the chemicals up to Miss Norley's satisfaction, so at the moment they're sitting in boxes in our old dairy. But the building should serve well enough for a laboratory."

"Why not put it in the house?" Thorn said, his expression veiled. "God knows you have the room for it."

"Miss Norley was concerned about having dangerous chemicals in our residence, where they might harm us or the furnishings."

Olivia could tell Thorn found that suspicious, although she couldn't imagine why. "Some of my chemicals are combustible. If they somehow ignited and spewed toxic fumes that hurt Beatrice's baby, I would be quite upset."

"You and I both," Greycourt said. "I would hope that wouldn't happen anyway, but you're wise not to take any chances. It's much appreciated. And I do think the dairy will suit your purposes."

"You were able to fit enough shelves on the walls, weren't you?" Olivia asked. "And a few tables?"

Greycourt smiled. "I made sure everything was done to your specifications. The rest is up to you."

"Thank you, Your Grace."

It took all of Olivia's strength not to show how excited she was at the thought of having her very own laboratory, with the latest equipment and plenty of chemicals. She couldn't wait to get there and set everything up.

"So," Thorn said, leaning forward to rest his elbows on his knees, "I'm unfamiliar with the chemists you mentioned, but I assume they are well-known in scientific circles."

"They are, indeed," she said. "I brought their journal articles along so I could review them in the evenings. You're welcome to do so yourself if you wish."

Greycourt chuckled. "Doesn't that sound like riveting reading, Thorn? It should keep you far more entertained than your usual diet of Shakespeare, Fletcher, and the oldest playwrights you can find."

Thorn's only answer was to shoot his brother a foul glance.

"Thorn's favorite pastime," Greycourt explained, "is either attending the theater or reading plays. You should see his collection of dramatic literature. It's quite extensive."

"I do read journal articles sometimes," Thorn said sullenly.

"About chemistry?" Beatrice asked.

Now *Beatrice* was the recipient of a foul glance, which only made the duchess grin.

"Actually, I quite like the theater myself," Olivia said, though she wasn't sure why she felt the need to defend Thorn, of all people. "I attend with Papa and Mama as often as I can. I don't read many plays—they only come alive for me when I see them acted. But once I do, I can then go back and read the play with enjoyment."

Thorn sat up. "Most people don't understand that you have to *see* a play to get the full effect."

"Exactly!" Olivia said, pleased to find someone else who understood that. "The first Shakespeare play I read was *Much Ado about Nothing*, and I missed at least half of the funny bits. I didn't understand why Shakespeare was considered such a great writer. Then I saw it performed—"

"The one at the Theatre Royal in Covent Garden with Charles Kemble as Benedick?" Thorn asked, his eyes alight.

"Yes!" Olivia said. "It was spectacular. He's every bit as good as his more famous brothers."

"His wife was great in the role of Beatrice, too," Greycourt put in. When Olivia and Thorn gaped at him, he added, "I go to the theater from time to time. What do you think I am—a know-nothing?"

Thorn arched one brow. "I can count on one hand the

number of times you've gone with me to the theater. And even then, I had to drag you there."

"I don't like all the shouting," Greycourt said defensively. "If the audience would behave themselves, I would enjoy myself better."

"Oh, I quite agree with you there," Olivia chimed in. "I don't like the shouting and throwing of oranges and the like, either. But Mama tells me it's far better now than in her time. She said that back then, whenever Malvolio used to take the stage, the jeering and catcalls grew so loud that no one could even hear his lines."

"Ah, yes, *Twelfth Night*, another of my favorites." Thorn cocked his head. "Were you perhaps named after—"

"No!" she and Beatrice said in unison. Then they laughed together.

"I already asked her that," Beatrice said.

"*Everyone* asks me that," Olivia added. "Everyone who likes Shakespeare, anyway."

"Oh, I understand, believe me," Beatrice said. "The irony of everyone assuming I was named after the character in *Much Ado about Nothing* is that I've never even seen or read the play."

"You'd like it, I assure you," Olivia said. "And Beatrice is a wonderful, sharp-tongued heroine."

"That does fit our Beatrice, to be sure," Thorn said. When Beatrice swatted him with her reticule, he laughed, then returned to questioning Olivia. "So I take it you prefer Shakespeare's comedies to his tragedies?"

"I prefer anything that makes me laugh. As your brother so deftly demonstrated, chemistry can be a very dry subject. I love it . . . but sometimes I also need something to take me out of it for a time. Lately, my favorite playwright is a fellow named Konrad Juncker. I think he's German, although the name could be Danish or Swedish."

She met Thorn's gaze, surprised to see that his smile had abruptly faded. "Anyway," she went on, "his stories about a foreigner named Felix living the life of a rakish buck in London always make me laugh myself silly. Have you seen them?"

"I doubt it," Thorn said. "Although recently I went to a wonderful new play at Covent Garden that—"

"You did see at least one of the Juncker plays," Greycourt broke in. "I remember because you were the one who dragged me to it." He mused aloud. "It wasn't *The Adventures of a Foreign Gentleman Loose in London*—that one I've never seen—but a later one. Perhaps *More Adventures of a Foreign Gentleman Loose in London*?"

With a long-suffering look, Thorn crossed his arms over his chest. "Whatever it was, it must not have made much of an impression on me. I don't recall it."

Olivia turned her attention to Greycourt. "Might it have been *The Wildest Adventures,* et cetera, et cetera? That one packed the theater. I would never have been able to see it if Papa hadn't had a box."

Greycourt tapped his chin. "That might have been it. Was that the one with Lady Grasping and Lady Slyboots?"

"Actually," Olivia said, "they've been in all the plays so far. I know, because the pair are my favorite comedic characters bar none."

"Even over Shakespeare's?" Thorn asked, with a skeptical arching of one brow, though he also seemed terribly interested in her answer. Which was flattering, she supposed.

"Well . . ." She had to think about that one. "Yes, I believe so. Because they're so much more real to me than Shakespeare's, even though written by a foreigner."

"I don't think Juncker is a foreigner, actually," Greycourt said. "Just his name is German."

"That would explain his extraordinary knowledge of English society," Olivia said. "You can meet matchmaking mamas and scheming young ladies like Grasping and Slyboots in any London ballroom. He describes them masterfully and mocks them so well that I laugh until my sides hurt."

"In the play I saw, whatever it was titled," Greycourt said, "Lady Grasping gets the idea to have Lady Slyboots, her daughter, demonstrate her skill at needlepoint to impress an aging marquess who's seeking a wife. But Lady Slyboots gets so distracted by the handsome Felix who's flirting with her that she sews the marquess's breeches leg to her embroidery. Then, of course, the marquess is trying to leave but he can't, and he pulls hard enough to rip the fabric over his backside, exposing his drawers, and her mother faints. . . ."

"Ooh, ooh, I love that scene!" Olivia said. "It's in *The Wild Adventures of a Foreign Gentleman Loose in London*."

"I think that's it, yes," Greycourt said with a satisfied smile.

"*My* favorite part," Olivia said, "is when Lady Grasping takes Lady Slyboots to Bath for the first time. They go to the Grand Pump Room to see and be seen, and Lady Grasping tells Lady Slyboots to fetch her a glass of champagne. Lady Slyboots gets what she thinks is champagne from a footman offering glasses of the mineral water, and she gives it to her mama. Of course, Lady Grasping drinks it, then spews it all over an eligible earl she's been trying to snag for Lady Slyboots, and he walks off in a huff, with Lady Slyboots running after him offering him what she still thinks is champagne."

Olivia sat back. "Anyway, it's very funny when performed in the theater with good comic actresses."

"Grey, you must take me to see one of these Juncker plays," Beatrice said. When Olivia looked at her, astonished that the duchess hadn't already been to one, Beatrice added, "I came to London for the first time not quite a year ago. Until then, I'd never seen a play of any kind anywhere."

"Oh, you poor thing!" Olivia uttered a sigh. "You might have lost your chance with the Juncker ones, though. Rumor has it he isn't planning on writing any more of them."

"Where did you hear that?" Thorn asked.

"From one of the gossip rags, I think. Or perhaps in the theater? I don't recall."

"How many of these plays have there been, anyway?" Beatrice asked.

"Five, I believe," Greycourt said.

"Six," Thorn said. When their gazes all shot to him, he said, "What? I go to the theater often. I know the schedules for plays I've never even seen."

Greycourt frowned at his brother. "Wait a minute, isn't Juncker a friend of yours? I forgot that."

Thorn stiffened noticeably. "A mere acquaintance, really," he said with a dismissive wave of his hand.

"Next time you see him," Olivia said, "do ask if he plans to write any more."

"Now I understand why you're so annoyed by this conversation, Thorn," Greycourt said. "You're jealous."

"What?" Thorn said. "Why the hell would I be jealous of Juncker?"

"Excellent point," Olivia told Greycourt. "Your brother is a duke. I don't see how he could be jealous of a mere playwright."

"*I'm* a duke," Greycourt said. "Trust me, we have the

same human emotions as the next person. And what you don't know about my brother is that in his salad days, Thorn dabbled in writing himself. Never could finish anything. So he's jealous of this fellow's success at having five whole plays in the theater—"

"Six," Thorn said wearily.

"Right. Six," Greycourt said. "Hmm." He looked at Olivia. "So the gossip is that he's not writing anymore?"

She bobbed her head.

"I can see why. Six is a damned lot of plays to write on what is essentially the same subject. I mean, how many ways *can* a man get into trouble in London?"

"You'd be surprised," Thorn muttered under his breath.

"Don't enlighten us," Greycourt said. "You'll scandalize the ladies."

"Or have us clamoring to join you on your next adventure," Beatrice said, with a wink for Olivia.

The wink startled Olivia into a laugh. She hadn't expected to enjoy this coach ride quite so much. Apparently small talk could be delightful with the right people to share it.

"I know what we should do," Beatrice said, a mysterious twinkle in her eyes. "We should see if we can guess which of Juncker's adventures Thorn has also experienced."

Thorn's icy gaze would have frozen stone. "First of all, the adventures aren't Juncker's. They're his character Felix's. Secondly, guessing at how my adventures line up with Felix's would be rather difficult, since the only one of us who's seen all of Juncker's plays is Miss Norley."

"Fine, then Miss Norley should pick the adventure," Beatrice said, as if that had been her aim all along. "Then we'll guess if you ever took part in a similar one, and you can tell us who guessed right. It sounds like quite a fun game."

"Or an absurd one," Thorn muttered.

Greycourt lounged against the squabs. "I don't know, old chap. I think it could be quite entertaining. And we do have a long ride ahead of us."

Despite Thorn's objections, Olivia was already mentally thumbing through the adventures in the plays. "How about this one? Felix gets drunk—"

"So far I can safely say that Thorn has done that, and more than once," Greycourt said, earning him a glare from Thorn.

"Let her finish," Beatrice chided her husband.

"He gets drunk and mistakes a countess for a courtesan," Olivia said, "then tries to engage the lady's services for the night."

"Half the bucks in London have probably done that," Greycourt said.

"*I* haven't," Thorn said. "Now can we please stop this nonsense?"

"It sounds rather clichéd, I know," Olivia said, "but it's really clever in the play. Felix mistakes what the countess says, and she mistakes what *he* says, and they go round and round for quite a while."

"Going round and round does sound like my brother when he's flirting with ladies," Greycourt drawled.

"You aren't even making sense now," Thorn grumbled.

"Perhaps I should think of a different adventure," Olivia said. "One that's not so debatable."

Then they felt the carriage slowing. Thorn looked out. "We're at Great Chesterfield, and I'm starving. I had no breakfast. Let's see if the innkeeper can provide us with sandwiches and a jug of ale."

"Oh, yes, sandwiches sound heavenly," Beatrice said. "I'm famished."

"And no wonder," Grey said dryly, "you only ate three eggs and sausages this morning instead of your usual five."

"Nothing but the best for your heir," Beatrice quipped.

Greycourt's expression softened as his gaze dropped to his wife's belly. "Or my pretty daughter, who I'm sure will be as clever as her mother."

The tender moment roused a strange envy in Olivia. Her father and stepmother had never shown any such depth of feeling for each other, and neither had her father and mother, from what she could recall. Olivia had always assumed that was typical of all aristocratic unions. Indeed, the glimpses she'd had of other society marriages had only confirmed her assumption.

But watching Beatrice and Greycourt together made her wonder if she'd been wrong. Perhaps it *was* possible to have a different sort of marriage. Even with a duke.

Just not with Thorn, who was as prickly as his name when it came to enduring the idea of marriage.

"We do still have a few hours to go," Greycourt said, "and we have to stop to change horses anyway. So we can have a bit of food at the inn here." He grinned at his brother. "But don't think you're off the hook with our game. We can continue it once we're back on the road."

"Great," Thorn said sarcastically. "I can't wait."

Olivia perked up considerably. *This* was going to be fun.

Chapter Five

Once they returned to the carriage, Thorn tried to derail his companions' "game." But it soon became evident it was no use. They were determined to plague him, especially Olivia, who really must have read all of his plays, because so far she'd pulled an astonishing number of adventures out of her memory.

The score was presently two correct guesses for Beatrice, four for Grey, and three for Olivia. The little baggage was proving able to guess his past activities nearly as well as his family could.

"Oh!" Olivia said brightly, "I've got one from the third play. Felix and a friend go to Ranelagh Gardens with their mistresses. Once there, Felix starts a rumor that the two demireps are really middle-aged but have partaken of an elixir that makes them look half their real age. When the vainest men and women of the company beg Felix for some of the elixir, he 'reluctantly' gives it to them."

Olivia chuckled. "But it's actually plum schnapps, a strong German liquor, and before long, Felix has them all drunk. He assures them that they're now looking quite youthful. As you might imagine, that leads them into all sorts of amusing situations, with one man even telling his own servant his name, sure that he has become so youthful in appearance that the servant won't recognize him."

Thorn brightened. He knew *this* adventure very well. What's more, Felix's "friend" in the play was based on Grey. Thorn cast a sly look at his brother.

Grey's face was already clouding over. "That seems like a very convoluted tale to be anything Thorn might have done."

"I agree." Thorn tapped his chin. "Although it does sound an awful lot like the time you and I went with Juncker to Ranelagh Gardens, along with our—"

"It does not," Grey interrupted. "Not in the least."

Beatrice smirked at Thorn, who winked at her. "When did the three of you go to Ranelagh Gardens?"

"It would have to have been before the place shut down in 1803," Thorn said. "So it wasn't long after I arrived in England, back when Grey and I used to act like feckless ruffians occasionally."

"*Very* occasionally," Grey said while glaring at Thorn.

"Then that was long before he met *me*." Beatrice was clearly fighting a smile. "So, what was Grey's mistress like, anyway? He won't give me any details, although I know he had at least one."

Grey laid his head back against the squabs to look heavenward. "God help me."

Eyes widening, Olivia glanced first to Grey, then to Thorn. "You really had mistresses? Both of you?"

It was Thorn's turn to be uncomfortable, although he couldn't imagine why. "I did," he said belligerently. "Half of my peers did, too. I was young and new to London and . . ." Trying to prove something to himself after a certain young lady had inexplicably turned down his offer of marriage.

"And what?" Olivia prodded, with the same curiosity she showed for arsenic tests.

"I was sowing my wild oats like any other buck of the first head." He hated that he sounded defensive. "It was a long time ago." His voice hardened. "And this is a highly inappropriate conversation."

Beatrice snorted. "You've never balked at inappropriate conversations before, Thorn."

"Very well," he said coldly. "If you truly want to hear all about our mistresses—"

"Can we *please* talk about something else?" Grey said with a groan.

"Feeling all those little chickens coming home to roost, are you, my love?" Beatrice said lightly.

"You find this amusing, I suppose," Grey muttered.

"Vastly so," Beatrice said with a teasing smile.

Thorn laughed. "That's what you get, Grey, for inventing a stupid game in an attempt to make *me* look bad." And to unwittingly expose his secret.

Although no one seemed to have put that together. Perhaps because Juncker had been with them. Or perhaps because of Grey's ridiculous claim that Thorn was jealous. Thorn was allowing that to stand. It was as good a way as any to protect his secret self.

"Fine, I concede defeat," Grey said, a red flush creeping up his neck. "I give my points to Miss Norley. That makes her the official winner."

"I won!" Olivia said, seemingly oblivious to the undercurrents between Thorn and Grey. "Do I get a prize?"

"Do you *need* a prize?" Thorn countered.

She cocked her head. "There's hardly any point to winning if one doesn't get a prize."

"I can think of a number of prizes I can give you, Miss Norley," Thorn said in a low, husky voice, hoping to rouse a blush again, "though I don't think your parents would approve."

"*Thorn*," Grey warned. "Watch where you're treading."

Thorn stifled a curse. "Here." He handed her the newspaper he'd brought along to read. "Will this do for a prize?"

Olivia shot him a blazing smile. "Oh, yes, thank you! I love this one, because they always include the news about science."

When she smiled like that he wanted to buy her a thousand newspapers.

What was wrong with him? He must be tired. Or ill. Or out of his mind.

She opened the paper and clearly sought out a certain section. Then with a happy sigh, she settled back to read.

Damn her for being even more stimulating than he remembered. She did seem to know a great deal about chemistry, and she certainly enjoyed talking—and reading—about it. That made her more of a bluestocking than the schemer he'd envisioned. Then again, he didn't know any bluestockings, so he wasn't sure if Olivia fit the type.

Actually, she fit no type whatsoever. Take her gown, for example. The bluish green reminded him of her gown last night. Other women never seemed to wear the same color twice, but Olivia did as she pleased.

God, he must have been a heedless arse nine years ago not to have seen her unusual qualities. Now he knew how to appreciate a woman as unique as she, no matter how badly she danced or what lapses she had in following societal rules.

Or what part she'd played in her stepmother's scheme? He wasn't sure if she'd played any part at all. He still couldn't tell, not from what she'd said and not from how she'd behaved.

Last night she'd thrown herself enthusiastically into

their kiss, but she'd gone out of her way to hide their encounter from the others. He didn't know what to make of that. She said she would turn him down again if he asked. Was she trying to impress Grey concerning her scientific ability by not showing herself to be the usual female scheming to marry a duke? Or was she really not interested in marriage despite being interested in kissing?

Not that her motive—or lack of one—mattered. He still had no intention of renewing whatever interest he'd had in her.

Then again, he couldn't believe she enjoyed his plays. It didn't fit with his picture of her as a young woman whose entire focus was on ensnaring a husband. Or even his newer picture of her as a bluestocking.

Either way, he must be on his guard concerning Juncker. When she'd mentioned Lady Grasping and Lady Slyboots, he'd nearly cursed aloud. She must never guess who they were based on. She wouldn't understand. She'd be hurt.

Why he *cared* whether she was hurt was a mystery he didn't want to examine very closely.

Olivia put down the paper with a sigh of pleasure. "That was the best prize you could give me. I feared I would miss getting to read *The Chronicle of the Arts and Sciences* while I was away. Thank you."

"You're welcome. I subscribe." He had to keep up with what was going on in theater, after all.

"So do I," Grey said. "Feel free to read my issue if you wish. Mother always does. I send it to her once I'm done."

"Wait, I do that, too," Thorn said. "Mother is getting two issues every week? Why didn't she say something?"

"Probably didn't want to hurt our feelings," Grey said. "And she may very well be passing one on to her friends. You know how generous she is."

Beatrice shifted on her seat. "Speaking of your mother

and her friends, did either of you know she had her come out at the same time as Grey's Aunt Cora?"

"I certainly didn't," Grey said. "How can that be? Mother is nine years younger than Aunt Cora and married at seventeen, which, if they came out at the same time, would mean that Aunt Cora had her debut at twenty-six. But I suppose it's not terribly unusual to wait that late, is it, my love?"

When Olivia looked confused, Beatrice said, "My husband is alluding to the fact that *I* was presented at court at twenty-six, after I had already married."

"And Gwyn wasn't presented until thirty," Thorn pointed out. "But she'd been living abroad. And Beatrice had an inattentive guardian in her Uncle Armie. He never did his duty by her."

"In my aunt's case," Grey said, "her family wasn't wealthy, and they had four daughters. She was the youngest and had to wait until they could afford a London Season for her, although I've been told she was beautiful in her youth."

Thorn mused on that a moment. "Actually, Lady Norley told me she came out with Mother, too."

"When did she tell you *that*?" Beatrice asked with a particularly devious smile. "I thought you only met her last night, and I didn't see you talking to her at the party."

Grey's eyes twinkled. "Nor I."

Feeling Olivia's gaze on him, he said, "Mother wasn't aware of this, but I had actually met both Lady Norley and Miss Norley years ago." Then to stave off more questions along that line, he added hastily, "And don't forget that Lady Hornsby and Mother also came out together. They've been friends for years. Is it purely coincidence that we know all four women?"

"Of course not," Beatrice said. "Our ages are roughly within a span of ten years, so it follows that our mothers might have known each other or even been close friends. Besides, ladies who have their debuts together have an unbreakable connection, forged of spending so much time in each other's company. They meet the same men, go to many of the same events, and possibly even see the same sights, if they haven't been to London before."

Thorn glanced at Grey. "'Meet the same men.' Are you thinking what I'm thinking?"

"Sorry, old chap, but I haven't yet developed a talent for reading minds."

Huffing out a breath, Thorn said, "If the four women met the same men, then they might also have competed for those men. And, with the obvious exception of Mother, one of the ladies might have been angry that your father didn't pick her to marry."

"Angry enough to *poison* the man?" Beatrice said.

Thorn frowned. Lady Norley had been angry enough to stoop to blackmail, so it was possible she at least would go so far as that. Although it was hard to see what she might gain by murdering the other dukes.

He looked over to find Olivia listening wide-eyed to the conversation. "Perhaps we should leave this discussion for family."

"Why?" Grey said. "Miss Norley knows we asked her to Carymont to find out if my father was poisoned. So she obviously knows that we think he was murdered. No reason to mince words about it now."

Olivia paled. "Wait a minute. Are you saying my *step-mother* might have poisoned the previous Duke of Greycourt? Out of spite that he hadn't picked *her* to marry? By that criteria, it could have been any one of the whole group of women debuting that year. That's bound to have included twenty ladies at least."

"Excellent point," Grey said. "Although they'd also

have to have been guests at Carymont for my christening, because that's when my father took ill. And that's why the most likely candidate would be my aunt Cora. I daresay she married my uncle in hopes that he would one day inherit the dukedom. Getting rid of my father would have taken her one step closer."

That seemed to reassure Olivia, for her face looked less pinched now.

"Actually, Grey," Thorn said, "didn't you tell me there were a number of people at Carymont for the christening? That your father invited several of his and Mother's friends to witness the blessed event?"

"Yes, but I doubt the group included Lady Norley."

"There's no telling." Thorn avoided Olivia's gaze, though he fancied he could feel the force of it anyway. "As Beatrice said, they were all in the same crowd of ladies having their debuts."

"With twenty or more other women," Beatrice reminded him.

"None of whom were particular friends of Mother's or relations of Grey's father the way these three were," Thorn said.

Olivia thrust out her chin. "You don't know that. There could have been others."

"And I still say my aunt is the most likely candidate." Grey frowned at him. "Or even Lady Hornsby, who, as a close friend of Mother's, would almost certainly have been at the house party for the christening."

"We could probably get Mother to tell us who was invited," Thorn said, "although we'd have to give her some reason for our wanting to know."

Grey nodded. "The point is moot until we're certain whether he was poisoned. So speculation will get us nowhere just now. Let's worry about getting the tests done, and if the results show poisoning, we can think about what to do next."

Beatrice was staring out the window. "We're nearly there, anyway. Thank the good Lord. I swear, this trip seems to take longer every time we make it."

Grey smiled at her indulgently. "My wife would stay her entire life at Carymont, Miss Norley, if she had the choice. She's not one for town."

"It was fun at first," Beatrice admitted. "I did like seeing the menagerie at the Tower of London and listening to the music at Vauxhall. Highbury Barn was wonderful entertainment, too, with its bowling green. But in general, I find that London is too dirty, too noisy, and has too few dogs of any breeding."

"Also, she finds the Season, with all its parties and people, very wearing," Grey said.

"As do I." Olivia cast Thorn a pointed glance. "There are so many people who can't be trusted. Or who always see the worst in others." She forced a smile for Grey and Beatrice. "Although I do enjoy the theater and the lectures on science. Oh, and I like that I can find any sort of chemical I need. That isn't the same in the country, trust me."

"Then it's probably a good thing you had us order the chemicals ahead to be brought here," Grey said. "I can promise that our nearest town, Sudbury, wouldn't have had many of them."

"Speaking of that, Your Grace," Olivia said, "as soon as we arrive, I should very much like to start putting my laboratory together, if that's all right."

"You know," Greycourt said, "there's no need to stand on ceremony with me and keep calling me 'Your Grace.' My friends call me Grey, so you must, too."

"Then you must call me Olivia. I have few friends in society, since I'm almost never around it, but as your wife already knows, I would be honored to consider you and her my friends."

"And me?" Thorn drawled.

She flashed him a frosty look. "I think of you as more of an adversary, Your Grace."

That irritated him. She was clearly angry at him for lumping her stepmother in with the others, but what did she expect? Surely she knew of Lady Norley's Machiavellian side.

"Getting back to setting up your laboratory, Olivia," Grey said, "if you wish to do so at once, that's fine by me. Once the exhumation is finished, we'll need to move quickly anyway."

Beatrice laid her hand on Olivia's knee. "But don't you want to rest a bit first or have some refreshments? I'm already parched and quite ready for a cup of tea and a bit of a nap."

"Yes, but you're enceinte," Olivia said with a smile, "and I am not, so I still have the energy to do some work before dinner. Indeed, I'm eager to get started."

For no reason Thorn could fathom, he flashed upon a scene of domestic bliss, with Olivia, not Beatrice, at the center. She'd make a fine wife and mother. Surely she'd also be relieved not to have to worry any longer about her chemistry pursuits.

Chemistry was my primary interest then, and it's my primary interest now.

Then again, he might be wrong about that.

He scowled. It didn't matter how she felt about her unusual pastime or whether she'd make a good wife and mother. She would not be wife to *him*. Once he decided to settle down, he wanted a woman he could trust, a woman without secrets. A woman who was prepared to be a duchess in every way, who put nothing else above that.

The way he put his dukedom above everything else? He groaned. He did his duty by his tenants, and he tried to be a good steward of the land, as his stepfather had taught him before dying unexpectedly. He'd even found taking his seat in Parliament more entertaining than he'd expected, though he didn't crave power the way others in the House of Lords did.

But he took no pleasure in London society and its constant gossip. Granted, at first he'd enjoyed having women fall into curtsies and men eye him with envy every time he entered a ballroom. But he'd soon discovered it was lonely being of such lofty rank. How much lonelier would it be if his wife enjoyed and thrived on her rank when he did not?

At least Olivia had a purpose in life. He had none beyond writing entertaining plays, looking after his properties, and counting the days until death.

God, she was making him maudlin.

"Very well, Olivia," Grey said. "I'll have a footman accompany you to the old dairy, and help you with unpacking and setting out everything."

"If you can spare a footman," Olivia said, "that would be wonderful."

"There's no reason for that," Thorn said. "I'm perfectly happy to show you to the dairy and help you with your unpacking. I need to get my blood moving again, anyway, after sitting so long in this carriage. Besides which, I'm curious to see this laboratory unfold."

If she'd insisted on a separate building for her laboratory to keep suspicious people at bay, she was in for a surprise. He meant to shadow her today and every other day.

"Now I feel positively decadent," Beatrice said. "I'll be lolling about while the rest of you do things."

"Feel free to loll about as much as you wish, sweetheart," Grey said. "You have good reason." He raised an eyebrow at Thorn. "Unlike my brother, who means to blunder in where he doesn't belong."

"Because one of your footmen knows so much more than I about unpacking chemicals and laboratory equipment?"

Grey's lips thinned.

"There's no need for you to trouble yourself, Your Grace," Olivia bit out. "Surely you'd also like to have some tea and settle into your room."

Olivia's wary expression raised his suspicions even more.

"Nonsense," Thorn said. "I'd enjoy keeping you company." He looked at Grey. "As for tea, I'm certain my brother would be happy to send some over to us."

"We'll have it done at once," Beatrice said hastily, clearly bent on continuing her matchmaking. "And I trust you'll be able to tell us if Olivia's laboratory meets all her needs. I fear she's too polite to admit the truth."

Never was there a less likely description of Olivia's character. Even if he'd been convinced she was as innocent of scheming as she pretended, she was too blunt and frank not to give her benefactors a thorough assessment of the laboratory they'd bought for her. He couldn't wait to hear her list all the ways in which it was inadequate. Perhaps then they wouldn't be so hasty to champion her.

Right. Because Grey and Beatrice just hated blunt and frank speech.

Thorn sighed. They'd probably make her an honorary member of the family for it. Well, he refused to let her charm him again until he figured out what she was up to. And whose side she was on.

"We're here!" Beatrice said cheerily.

He looked out to find that they were indeed heading up the long drive to the front of the majestic house, a residence as big and stately as Rosethorn, his own family seat in Berkshire.

"What a beautiful manor house, Your Grace . . . I mean, Grey," Olivia said in ill-disguised awe. "Are those carvings of sandstone?"

"You have a good eye." Grey smiled. "The walls are of red brick, but the cornices and other decorative elements are sandstone. As soon as you finish setting up your laboratory, I'd be happy to give you a tour."

"That would be lovely, thank you."

As they climbed down from the coach, a wide-eyed Olivia continued to scan her surroundings.

But before Thorn could do more than disembark, Grey pulled him aside. "I need a word with you." As Olivia began explaining to the footmen which of her trunks should be taken inside and which taken to the laboratory, Grey lowered his voice. "What are you up to now? You practically accused Olivia's stepmother of killing my father."

"You don't know that she didn't. That might be why her stepdaughter readily agreed to your proposition, because she knows her mother had something to do with his murder, and she wants to hide that fact by having control over the tests."

"Except she didn't even know her mother might have done anything until we proposed it just now."

Thorn gritted his teeth. Grey had a point.

"Nor do we have any evidence whatsoever," Grey said, "that Mother and Lady Norley were close friends back then."

"That's not true, actually. I couldn't say this in front of Miss Norley, but I happen to know for a fact that they were. Lady Norley told me that herself when I offered for Miss Norley."

"Still, it doesn't prove that Lady Norley could have killed my father. Or that she was even interested in him." He crossed his arms over his chest. "And none of this explains why you insist on viewing Olivia's laboratory."

"Has it occurred to you that left to her own devices, Olivia—Miss Norley, I mean—could very well twist the results of her tests in order to get what she wants out of this?"

Grey thrust his hands in his greatcoat pockets. "And what, pray tell, do you assume that is? Her mother exonerated of a crime we don't even know was committed?"

"Don't be an arse. Miss Norley wants to publish her results. To make a name for herself as a chemist. You didn't know that was her goal, did you?"

"No, but it makes sense. That's the goal of every man or woman of science. To be known. To discover new ideas, new tests. I have no issue with it."

"Well, I do," Thorn said. "It makes her methods suspect. How can we be sure she won't doctor the results so she can gain her credentials as a chemist?"

"By that score, you would find every chemist's methods suspect, since all of them wish to publish their results." Grey stared him down. "At some point, Thorn, you simply have to trust a person to do what they promise."

That brought him up short. "I don't have to trust anyone. And I don't plan to, either. Beyond my family, I mean."

His brother shook his head. "So *that's* why you wish to help her with her laboratory. To make sure she isn't up to anything suspicious."

"Exactly. I can fathom a great deal about her knowledge of chemistry from watching how she sets up her laboratory."

Grey laughed outright. "The way you fathomed her

methods after she started reciting formulas you could no more comprehend than I?"

"That's the point. She knows we're ill-educated when it comes to her field, so she can fob anything off on us, and we'll be impressed. But it's hard to hide that one knows little about chemicals when faced with a laboratory full of them."

"True. I'm sure you'll prove your ignorance the moment you step inside."

"I meant *her*." Thorn hadn't forgotten her wary expression when he'd said he'd be helping her.

"I knew what you meant." Grey shook his head. "You're a hopeless case. If I were her, I'd find your constant suspicion wearing, especially when it's borne of a blow to your pride years ago. So I tell you what. I won't insist upon sending a footman with you if you promise this will be your last test of her."

"Fine," Thorn said. "I promise."

With any luck, this would tell him once and for all whether she knew what she was doing, whether her goal was deception, and whether he was right about the sort of person she was.

And if she was? If she proved to be everything she seemed? Then what did he mean to do with her?

He'd cross that bridge when he came to it.

Chapter Six

Olivia wished she had waited until Thorn wasn't around to ask Greycourt if she could get right to work on her laboratory. She wished she'd told Thorn she didn't want him there.

She wished she'd never laid eyes on the man. Why, he actually thought Mama could have murdered Grey's father! The devil! How dared he? When it came to her and her family, he always thought the worst.

The dratted man even meant to intrude in her laboratory! He would *not* ruin this chance for her. She wouldn't let him.

"You're very quiet," Thorn said as they walked along a gravel path that wound through the gardens.

"Is that a problem, Your Grace?"

He cursed under his breath. "You weren't calling me 'Your Grace' last night when we were kissing."

"You weren't accusing my stepmother of murder."

"I wasn't—Damn it, all I'm saying is that she was a member of the group of ladies having their debuts in the same year. I just made the obvious conclusion that one of them might have—"

"Murdered your half brother's father. Yes, I know all

about your conclusions. I'm not sure how obvious they are, but you're certainly free to make them. Just leave me out of it."

They walked a few moments in blessed silence, but he of course couldn't leave it alone. "What other explanation do you have for why someone would poison Grey's father?"

"First of all, as a woman of science, I prefer not to speculate on anything. I amass facts, and then I prove my hypothesis. I have no facts yet concerning the possible poisoning of Grey's father. Until I do, I can only postulate that his cause of death is undetermined."

"All that aside," Thorn snapped, "I'm not saying it was necessarily your stepmother who poisoned him. Just that there are three women who had the means and possibly the motive to murder him."

"*Four* women," Olivia shot back.

"I beg your pardon?"

"Your mother had the means and 'possibly the motive' as well."

His face darkened. "My mother had nothing to do with his poisoning, I assure you."

She halted to face him. "Based on what evidence?"

"She was caring for her infant son, for one thing."

"No matter what men think," Olivia said primly, "a woman can take care of a child and do other things at the same time." Though she truly didn't believe his mother—or any of the other ladies—had killed Grey's father, she was trying to make a point: At present he had no more evidence to prove her stepmother guilty than she did to prove *his* mother guilty.

"It wasn't my damned mother!" he cried. When she lifted her eyebrow, he added, "There's more to our suspicions than you know. Than we can reveal until we have additional information."

"That's precisely what *I'm* saying. Until we prove Grey's father was poisoned, we shouldn't speculate about who fed him the poison."

"Fine. I will ignore my tendency to speculate for the time being. Will that satisfy you?"

"Perfectly." She marched off down the path. Him and his secret suspicions. He was no better than Papa, slipping off into the night to do whatever he pleased.

He matched her stride. They went quite a way without speaking before he said, in a toneless voice, "The dairy is just around the bend ahead at the top of a hill."

She walked on, but he had offered an olive branch, so she felt she should take it, at least for the moment. "I gather that you know your brother's estate well."

"Well enough. Grey and I used to travel up here to get away from town. Carymont is his nearest property to London. Sometimes we'd even invite other bachelors and make a house party of it."

"Without any women present?"

"We-e-ell—"

"That's what I thought." She stifled the urge to torment him about it. "You and Grey are very close, I suppose."

"Yes. Although less so now that he's married." He stared off ahead. "I don't know how it happens, but once a man takes a wife, he seems to replace all his bachelor friends with her. And with other couples."

"That's probably why my uncle has never taken a wife. He prefers the company of his Oxonian friends."

She could feel Thorn's gaze on her. "And you," he said.

"Yes. But not at the same time. A niece is different than a wife. No matter how much I tidy his rooms in town or he champions my work as a chemist, when his friends are there, he wants me nowhere around."

Thorn surprised her by chuckling. "Probably because he doesn't want them eyeing you with lust."

"What? I'm sure they don't even know what lust is."

He snorted. "They're men, aren't they? Trust me, they know. Your uncle is probably just trying to protect you. Especially if visits from his friends involve substantial amounts of ale, wine, and spirits, which visits of that kind generally do."

"For *your* friends perhaps. Not his."

But the observation gave her something to consider. She'd assumed that although her uncle was proud of her among certain circles, he was still too ashamed of her being a female chemist to introduce her to his lofty Oxonian friends. That it might be something more like Thorn described soothed her hurt pride.

They'd reached the dairy now. It wasn't at all what she'd imagined. In keeping with the only other one she'd ever seen, she'd expected a tiny building. That's why she'd asked the duke about the shelves and tables.

But the pretty brick building would provide her with all the room she could want. And when she walked in, she was pleased to see that there were not only plenty of shelves, but a nice amount of floor space for the tables she required.

Grey had explained that his father had built a new dairy of a better design, so this one was no longer used. But it still had sufficient windows to give her light during the day and a fireplace to drive away the cold. She might need that fireplace, but she'd have to be cautious with it. No telling what residue of coal and wood ash might be lingering in the chimney. It wouldn't do to have a dangerous chemical reaction happen because of negligence.

In the meantime, she would place her main worktable near it so that if she *did* have chemicals catch fire, she could at least sweep them into the hearth where the fumes could rise and be dissipated in the air.

Thorn might not realize it but his constant challenges of her ability to do these tests had begun to make her uneasy. What if she *couldn't* manage this? What if she discovered nothing?

She couldn't think about that now. Grey was counting on her. So she would ignore the effect Thorn had on her and get to work.

"Turn the box around so I can see how it's marked," said Olivia, Thorn's pesky taskmaster.

"Perhaps you should have put the markings on all sides," Thorn grumbled as he shifted the box. The very heavy box. Damn, how much did laboratory equipment weigh, anyway?

"Perhaps you should have left the work to a footman as I originally suggested. The one who brought our tea would have been happy to help."

She had a point. Thorn hated that. "Think of it this way—how often will you get to order a duke about? Besides, I wouldn't dream of missing the chance to see a woman of science at work."

"I would consider 'woman of science' a compliment if I didn't know you were being sarcastic." She gestured to a table. "Put the box over there."

Of course she would pick the farthest table from them. He was getting enough exercise to fill a session or two of practice fisticuffs at Gentleman Jackson's. Olivia had already taken half an hour deciding which table should hold which part of her laboratory, a process that had involved him moving boxes more than once. Then she'd required another half an hour to sort the boxes either to tables or underneath the shelving to be put up later.

He paused to pull out his handkerchief and mop his forehead. He'd removed his hat long ago, and she her bonnet. He tried not to notice how fetching she looked without it, tried not to imagine how much hair made up that fat chignon and how desperately he wanted to see that hair tumbling down about her waist.

He glanced around and realized that all the boxes had been sorted. "That was the last one." Thank God. "So what's next?"

Tucking one of her golden curls behind her ear, she broke into a smile. "The best part. Unpacking."

"*That's* the best part?"

"For me it is. The contents of the boxes should mostly be where they belong, but some items will still have to be moved around."

"I take it that I'm going to be the one moving them around."

"It depends on what they are. I'm perfectly capable of moving a jar to another table or onto a shelf. But we can stop for another cup of tea, if you'd like a rest."

At her minxish smile, he gritted his teeth. The woman knew just how to prick his pride. "I'm fine. Besides, the tea is probably cold by now, and we ate all the lemon cakes."

That seemed to startle her. She glanced over to where the footman had earlier set up a small table, two chairs, and a tray of refreshments. "Oh. So we did." She flashed him a rueful smile. "I get quite caught up when I'm working on a project, and I don't realize how late it's getting to be."

"I noticed." He drew out his pocket watch. "Grey and Beatrice generally keep country hours, but not on days they're traveling, so we still have a while before dinner."

For the next hour, he got to unpack boxes and leave her to examine each item to decide where it went. She wore a look of pure bliss as she moved from table to shelf, arranging and organizing and setting up equipment that had been broken down for the journey.

There were names of ingredients he'd never heard of— aqua regia, nitrate of potash, muriatic acid, green vitriol, salt of wormwood, spirit of ether, and a dozen other mysterious compounds.

"What? No eye of newt?" he quipped.

"It's right there," she said, gesturing to a jar.

"That says 'Mustard Seed' on the label."

"I know. The mustard seed shouldn't have been included. I won't need it." When he gaped at her, she added, "Oh, *that's* why you joked all those years ago about paying me with 'eye of newt.' You thought it really was the eyes of lizards. Sorry to disappoint, but 'eye of newt' is mustard seed."

"You're joking."

"Not a bit."

"What about the other ingredients for the witches' brew in *Macbeth*?" he asked. "'Toe of frog, wool of bat, and tongue of dog'?"

"'Toe of frog' is buttercup. 'Wool of bat' is holly leaves."

"Ah, but surely the 'tongue of dog' is exactly what it says."

She laughed gaily. "'Tongue of dog' is hound's-tongue, sometimes also called wild comfrey. The witches' brew comprises a variety of natural ingredients, most of which you can find in any good herb garden."

"That's vastly disappointing."

"Why?"

He hadn't expected that question. "They're witches. They're supposed to be . . . well . . . wicked and frightening."

"I think their wickedness comes from how they use their predictions to tempt Macbeth into murdering the people who stand in his way. But yes, Shakespeare took advantage of the multiple names of herbs to choose ones that sounded particularly gruesome."

Olivia gestured to another jar. "Chemicals also have a variety of names. That nitrate of potash is sometimes called saltpeter, for example. Names of ingredients evolve as we learn more about them."

"You have ruined *Macbeth* for me," he said crossly. "The witches might as well be my French chef mixing up a salad in the kitchen."

"To be honest, I never liked *Macbeth*. Too many people being killed. I prefer the comedies."

"So you said." He found her love of humor endearing. The fact that she enjoyed his plays, too, was gratifying, but rather surprising for a woman of her unique ambition. Then a thought occurred to him. "Why choose chemistry?"

"What?" she said distractedly.

"You could have been a naturalist or an astronomer. There are a few women already who discover comets and the like, so astronomy wouldn't be as difficult an area to explore. Why chemistry?"

"For one thing, I grew up watching my uncle do fascinating experiments, and discovering elements no one had isolated before, like chlorine. For another, I like the purpose of chemistry—to discover the chemical components of our world. That enables us to manipulate those chemicals to the good of mankind. Astronomy can't do that."

Thorn gestured to where a large jar held pride of place on one worktable. "That arsenic isn't good for mankind. And I may not know much about chemistry, but I do know that saltpeter is a key ingredient in gunpowder."

"Saltpeter is also used to salt meat. Even arsenic is useful in producing glass. Chemicals are just bricks. They can be used to create buildings or they can be used as weapons. So don't blame the chemicals. Blame the people who use them."

He watched as she checked items off a list packed in the trunk she'd brought from home. Now she walked over to that same trunk and pulled out some notebooks.

"Are those the journals you were speaking of?" he asked.

"Clippings from them, yes. I'll need to refer to them as I work." She set them out on a table with a couple of jars on it. Then she turned to open the box on the far end that purported to contain several pieces of some contraption, most of it made of glass.

Chemistry laboratories seemed to have a great deal of glassware, as evidenced by his sore muscles.

"I suppose you're going to assemble what's in that box," he said.

"Why? Do you think I can't?"

Her belligerent expression told him it was probably time he admitted something. "I know you can. Any remaining doubt I had concerning your abilities as a chemist vanished somewhere around the time you set up that other complicated piece of laboratory equipment." He flashed her a faint smile. "And without so much as a list of directions, I might add. *I* would need directions, at the very least. At home, my servants usually do all the assembling of laboratory equipment."

He'd expected her to laugh or make some pert remark. Instead, she continued to stand there with her back to him, staring down into the box.

"Don't misunderstand me, Thorn," she said. "I greatly appreciate your help this afternoon. But there's nothing left for you to do now, so you should probably return to the house and dress for dinner."

He stepped toward her. "Why? Is my presence bothering you?"

"Of course not." The way she turned her attention to arranging the notebooks she'd already arranged told him differently. "I just don't want to keep you from your family."

Walking up behind her, he murmured, "I spend time with my family often enough. But in all these years, you and I have not once encountered each other in society since our initial meeting. And I like encountering you. Talking to you." He laid a hand on her waist, giving her plenty of time to move away. "Touching you."

She dragged in a heavy breath but remained where she was. Taking that as an invitation, he slid his other arm about her waist to pull her closer so he could kiss her temple. When her pulse quickened beneath his lips, he was emboldened to kiss her ear. Then the nape of her neck.

"God, you always smell so good. How do you manage it?"

"With perfume," she said lightly. "How else?"

He bit back a laugh. Most women pretended they didn't use anything—that their scent was utterly natural. "And I suppose you make your own."

"O-Of course." When he licked her ear, it took her a moment to go on, in a rather breathy voice. "Perfumers are m-merely chemists with . . . different ingredients at their . . . disposal."

"Like French chefs making salads," he murmured.

"I-If you w-wish."

What he wished was to touch her in more intimate ways, no matter how his mind screamed it was unwise. She felt so bloody good in his arms. Still, Grey would never forgive him if she took umbrage and left the estate in a huff.

But Thorn didn't think she would. Leaving in a huff wasn't her mode of behavior.

So he raised the hand he'd placed on her waist until it rested on the side of one breast. And when her only reaction was to sigh, he took the daring next step of covering her breast with his hand.

"Good . . . heavens . . ." she whispered.

He fondled her breast gently, shamelessly. "You like that, do you?"

"Oh, *yes*." Then she paused. "That is . . . what I meant was . . ."

"Never deny that you enjoy pleasure. Unless you truly don't."

Her redingote gown was lighter than most dresses of that fashion, but between it and her stays, he couldn't feel her nipple. And he badly wanted to. So he began unbuttoning her redingote where it was closed in the front.

She stiffened. "Wh-What are you doing now?"

"I want to caress you inside your gown." He lowered his voice. "If you'll allow it."

After a moment's hesitation she whispered, "All right."

His blood leapt at her answer, and then leapt even higher when he delved inside her gown and then inside one flimsy cup of her stays to cup her breast. As he began to fondle her through the thin linen of her shift, she gasped. He kneaded her breast, then thumbed her nipple, reveling in how it knotted up. And the little broken sigh she gave was almost as erotic as the feel of her ample breast in his hand.

God, he was growing hard. He hoped she couldn't feel his thickening cock against her backside. Then again, it wasn't as if he could hide it.

Her bosom was so responsive to his touch that he craved even more. A chance to taste her.

Now in a fever to cross that new threshold, he turned her to face him. Then he lifted her onto the table and sat her right down on the journals.

"Thorn!" she cried. "Be careful!"

"I will, sweeting." He spread the upper part of her redingote open. "I'd never hurt you, you know."

"That's not . . . what I meant." Her breathing quickened as he lowered one cup of her stays. Then he untied the gathered neckline of her shift so he could ungather it, so to speak, and drag it down to expose her bare bounty to his eyes and fingers.

And mouth.

Oh, God, yes. He bent his head to suck her and thought surely he'd died and gone to Paradise. She smelled of jasmine here, too, and he feared he might come right in his trousers. Which were becoming painfully tight at the moment.

He shifted her a little, and she caught his shoulders. "When I said 'be careful,' I meant . . . I meant . . ."

The words left her brain, apparently, once he began flicking his tongue over her bare nipple and lightly pinching the other one through her clothes. At this moment, it wouldn't take much for him to lift her skirts and explore her lovely quim, too.

God save him, but he desired her most powerfully. It was madness, he knew, yet he couldn't get the thought of bedding her out of his randy brain.

No, it wasn't his brain doing the thinking right now, but his cock. And damn, if he didn't want to give it free rein.

Chapter Seven

A thousand thoughts rushed through Olivia's head, but only one kept pushing its way to the front.

More. Now. Yes. Good.

If her brain would stop chanting that, she might remember why she'd been cautioning him. But that seemed impossible at present. Because he was treating her breasts to such sucks and nips and astonishing licks of his tongue that she wanted to swoon.

She never swooned.

And all the while that he was devouring her naked breast, he was fondling the other one through her clothes. It drove her to distraction.

Was this *supposed* to feel so wonderful? Or was he simply that good at being a rakehell? Because if this was what he'd been learning to do all this time, it was a pity she'd stopped going into society to avoid him. She might have run into him and had this sooner.

"You taste delicious," he rasped against her breast. "I could fondle and suck you for hours."

"That would be . . . unwise."

"*This,* right now, is unwise." He lazily traced her areola with his tongue. "Hasn't stopped me, though."

She paused at the other end of the room to right her clothing. "From now on, I can't have you in the laboratory, Thorn." She would never get anything done if he continued to come with her. "It's too dangerous."

"It was merely an accident," he said. "Next time I'll be more cautious."

"It doesn't matter. I simply can't have you here."

"Why?" he drawled. "Afraid I'll see something I shouldn't?"

"Oh, for pity's sake, you'll force me to say it, won't you? You distract me, all right? You can't help yourself. You enjoy flirting and dallying with women, and I happen to be handy." Olivia finished buttoning up her redingote before forcing herself to look him in the eye. "But these experiments are too important for me. I refuse to make a hash of it simply because you are . . . being yourself."

"You didn't enjoy what we did?"

His eyes had gone cold, and she knew she had once again been too blunt in her speech. But she couldn't figure out how she *should* have said it. "Of course I enjoyed it." More than she could possibly have expected. "That's not the point."

"It's the only point," the dratted fellow said. "Unless you're looking for that impossible dream—love and happiness in marriage."

Thinking of what she'd seen between Grey and Beatrice today, she murmured, "What if I think it *is* possible? Your brother and sister-in-law seem to be happily in love."

"They're lucky." He sounded bitter. "But the odds are against it. Most of the time, love is an illusion."

"All the more reason not to indulge in . . . activities that can only lead nowhere."

"They don't have to lead anywhere. They just . . . need

to be enjoyable. As long as we're discreet when we meet in the laboratory—"

"A lack of discretion isn't the problem!" Huffing out a breath, she fought for calm. "From what I understand, you rarely worry about discretion or you wouldn't have gained your reputation. But I'm not one of your mistresses or a soiled dove, no matter what you may think. If I let you stand about in my laboratory, keeping me from my work, then I'm precisely the fool you tried to make me out to be to your brother."

He dragged his fingers through his hair. "I wasn't . . . I didn't say . . ."

"I will never get as good an opportunity as this to test my method on human remains. Grey is giving me a chance to make history. I cannot repay him by squandering that chance to have stolen moments with you."

As delicious as those moments might be.

She shook off that dangerous thought. He was the glittering brightness of phosphorus, and she was the mundane, everyday air. Together they created toxic smoke. And she simply couldn't allow that.

He was eyeing her with new interest. "Is that the real reason you refused me years ago? Because—"

"The duchess sent me to fetch you," came a voice from the door. "Dinner will be served soon, and she thought you both might wish to change clothes."

Taken off guard by the footman, Olivia felt heat rise in her cheeks.

"Are you ready to return, Miss Norley?" the footman asked, holding his lantern high.

"Yes," she said.

"We both are," Thorn put in, his voice as icy as a duke's should be.

Because of her frank remarks? Or simply because he'd

realized that he had gone too far and now wished to recoup? Either way, she was grateful for the reprieve from being alone with him.

"Just give me one moment to see to something," she said, and hurried back to the hearth.

She'd known there would probably be no more phosphorus under the sand, but she pretended to search for it while also checking herself for any lingering signs of her recent . . . adventure with Thorn. She'd die of mortification if she arrived at the main hall looking like a slattern just come from a man's bed. Although if the footman had arrived while she and Thorn were . . .

Heavens, that didn't even bear thinking on. No one would ever take her seriously as a chemist if she got caught doing such a fool thing. Certainly no man would ever marry her.

She blinked. Since when did she care about marriage? This was what came of letting the man tempt her to distraction—she began craving things she'd never even wanted. Curse him for that!

Gathering her defenses about her, she marched back to where the two men stood waiting for her.

"Is everything all right?" Thorn asked, seeming to have thawed a bit from before.

"It's fine. We can go."

They left then, pausing only to secure the door with a heavy lock. That was another reason his lordship's choice of the dairy was excellent. Dairies were sometimes locked to prevent thieves or animals from stealing or eating the cheeses stored there.

As they set out down the path, the light died enough so that the footman's lantern was welcome. Fortunately, it also prevented the two of them from having another private conversation.

They walked in silence a good way before Thorn spoke. "Tomorrow is the exhumation. Do you mean to witness it?"

"Oh, Lord, no," she said. "Your brother knows what I require, and the local coroner will be there to help him . . . er . . . harvest it."

"You don't wish to make sure it's done properly?" he asked.

"My field is chemistry, sir. I know nothing of that science, I'm afraid, and have no desire to learn it. I can complete my experiments perfectly well from the comfort of my laboratory."

"I think I shall go," Thorn said. "I've never seen an exhumation. And after this, I may very well have to—" He caught himself for the second time since the footman had arrived. "It doesn't matter. Suffice it to say, I have a personal interest in what happens."

"Then by all means you should attend, Your Grace."

Thorn lowered his voice to a murmur. "So we're back to 'Your Grace,' are we?"

"I think that's best," she whispered.

"Like you think it's best if I don't go to the laboratory with you?"

"Precisely."

"Best for whom?" he asked.

She didn't answer. The truth was, she had no idea, and that wasn't likely to change anytime soon.

Thorn had hoped to get Olivia alone after dinner, but as soon as she and Beatrice went to the drawing room to await the men, they'd apparently spent a short while talking and then had gone up to their respective bedchambers. Or so the footman said.

That left him and Grey to drink and smoke and discuss nothing of consequence. Until . . .

"You like her, don't you?" Grey asked as he poured himself another glass of brandy.

"Of course," Thorn said. "Your wife is delightful, which I seem to recall telling you last year before you even married her."

Grey arched one eyebrow. "I wasn't speaking of my wife, and you know it."

With a stony stare Thorn set his empty glass in front of Grey. "I'd rather not talk about Miss Norley. It will only lead to an argument."

"Actually, I'm beginning to come around to your view of things concerning her." Grey poured some brandy for Thorn. "I don't know if she can do this work. The footman I sent to call the two of you in to dinner said there had been some broken glass and a smell of burning in the air at the laboratory. And she hasn't even begun her experiments."

Damn Grey's chatty footman. "That . . . um . . . wasn't her fault. While helping her put things away, I knocked off a jar of something called phosphorus. Apparently, it bursts into flames when it's not kept under water."

Grey eyed Thorn closely. "Then she shouldn't have put the jar where it could be knocked off."

"She didn't." Thorn took a large swallow of brandy. "That too was my fault. I pushed some other items around on the table, which moved the jar to the edge and then off."

"Some other items, eh? Let me think what those might be—perhaps Miss Norley herself?" When Thorn's gaze shot to Grey, his brother burst into laughter. "I *knew* you liked her."

"Very amusing," Thorn muttered. "You're a regular Punch and Judy, you are."

"Don't forget. I've been where you are, and I know how

easy it is to get carried away with a woman." Grey sobered. "But I must remind you that she's not to be dallied with. She might not have her stepmother around to look after her, but Beatrice and I are happy to step into the breach and make sure you don't get her into trouble."

"Trust me," Thorn grumbled, "she can take care of herself."

"No doubt that's true in a chemistry laboratory. But I'm not so sure she can do so in the rarefied world of rakehells. You do have a way with women."

"Oh, for God's sake, I wish people would stop saying that. And I don't have a way with Olivia, trust me. She refused my offer of marriage, remember?"

"So it's *Olivia* now, is it?" Grey probed.

Thorn glared at him. "Think what you want, but what I told you last year is still true: I would never ruin a woman. You were the one to warn me years ago that one must beware of matchmaking mamas and scheming daughters. And I learned my lesson—avoid getting the scheming daughter into a compromising position."

"I see. So the accident in the laboratory showed how you'd learned your lesson."

"Damn it, Grey, I told you I don't want to discuss Miss Norley." Thorn set his half-empty glass on the table and stood. "I'm tired. I think I'll retire early."

Grey merely laughed. "Coward."

"Sapskull."

His brother narrowed his gaze. "Roué."

"Bloody arse."

"Well, if you're not going to play nice," Grey drawled, "good night."

"Well, if 'good night' is the best you can do . . ." Thorn headed for the door, then paused there. "By the way, I'm going with you to the exhumation. I'd like to see how it works in case I should need to exhume my own father's body, though I doubt it could tell me much about *his* accident."

"You never know. And it's fine if you want to come, but I'm meeting the coroner at ten, so don't sleep too late, slugabed."

"I won't, scapegrace." He fully intended to be up with the chickens, if only to see if he could catch Olivia at breakfast.

But the next morning when he came down at a much earlier hour than was typical for him, Thorn discovered Olivia had already headed off to the laboratory. Devil take her. Was it asking too much to have a few moments alone with her?

Apparently it was, because after Grey and Beatrice came down, the footman informed them all that Miss Norley had asked for a tray to be sent to the laboratory that evening for dinner. She said she would be too busy with her work to join them.

Thorn told himself he wouldn't have time for her anyway with the exhumation going on. But the truth was, he'd spent half the night digesting everything she'd said and done, both yesterday and at their first meeting years ago, and he'd realized he might have been hasty in his assumptions. It was time they had a frank discussion about what her stepmother had held over his head years ago. But how could he do that when she avoided him?

At least the exhumation proved more interesting than he'd expected. The body of Grey's father had been remarkably well-preserved in the tomb, partly because of the thorough job someone had done of embalming him, and partly because of the limestone tomb his coffin was in. Or so the coroner had explained.

Although unburying the dead was a grim task, he and

Grey had been relieved to find that certain organs of Grey's father had been preserved in lead-lined chests. Apparently that was sometimes done for the interment of nobility, especially those of very high rank.

Since the organs were the most important of the items required for Olivia's tests and since they might also need preservation in event of a trial, the coroner divided each into halves to be stored in other lead-lined chests. The coroner also gathered samples of hair, skin, and nails, since Olivia had said she was interested in those as well.

Grey said he'd take the first half to the estate's icehouse, where they were to remain until such time as a trial commenced. He gave the other half to Thorn to carry to Olivia.

"I'd use a footman," Grey said, "but if anything happened to the items while they're being moved, I'd never forgive myself."

If Thorn had hoped his macabre offerings would lead the way into Olivia's laboratory, he was quite wrong. She opened the door, accepted the chests, and then shut the door in his face even as he loudly protested.

He was certainly doing a bad job of keeping an eye on her work. Not that he felt the need for that anymore. It galled him to admit it, but Grey had proved to be right about her and her abilities. That had become abundantly clear yesterday.

He still had to talk to her. Because once she did enough tests to confirm whether Grey's father had died by poisoning, there was nothing to keep her here. Beatrice clearly didn't need a companion, and Olivia had no desire to go into society, so the only person to whom Olivia would need to explain her early return home would be her stepmother. Undoubtedly, Olivia could figure out a way to make that sound believable.

But once she departed from here, she had no reason to

see him again. Ever. And that disturbed him. They'd left too many issues unsettled between them. At the very least, he wanted to learn the truth about certain matters. He deserved that, didn't he?

Fortunately, the upstairs drawing room overlooked the path to and from the old dairy. So he set up watch by the window after dinner, with a glass of brandy in one hand and a newspaper in the other. The lights were now on in the building, and he felt fairly certain she'd never leave lamps or candles to burn down in her laboratory.

Sure enough, close to ten o'clock he saw those lights go out one by one. Eventually Olivia, enveloped in a cloak, emerged and headed down the path.

Thank God.

After one last swig of brandy, Thorn headed to the stairs to waylay her.

Chapter Eight

Olivia let the sleepy footman take her cloak as she entered the house, with the journals and notebooks she wanted to review clutched in one hand. Then she climbed the stairs in a daze of anticipation. The first crucial element of her plan had gone well. Tomorrow she would tackle the one that mattered to Grey. She'd left everything prepared for it in her laboratory. How could she even sleep? She was far too excited.

The chemist in her wanted to press on tonight. But a lack of sleep could easily cause one to make a mistake, and she wanted nothing to stand in the way of her doing this properly. Besides, she suspected that the tests would take more than a few hours anyway. So it was better to read over her materials rather than to make a crucial error in her experiments.

Still musing about the tests—how best to perform and document them and which one she should tackle first—she didn't even see Thorn at the head of the stairs until she was almost upon him.

She jumped. "Don't startle me like that!" She scowled

at him as she took the final steps. "Why are you up so late, anyway?"

"I wanted to talk to you. And since you refused to let me into your laboratory . . ." He finished with a shrug so typically him she couldn't help but shake her head.

"Has everyone else retired?" she asked.

"Everyone but us."

"Then I'm glad you're up. I have to tell *someone* how everything went, and I don't think I can sleep until I do."

"By all means, let me be your confidant," he said. "Just remember that I don't know a damned thing about chemistry, which I think I illustrated quite well yesterday."

A laugh escaped her. "True, but then I don't know anything about being a duke. So I suppose we're even."

"Here, let's go into the blue drawing room," he said. "No one's awake to see, and I promise to behave."

She wasn't sure she *wanted* him to behave. But telling him that was obviously unwise. He'd made it clear in London that he would never offer for her, and she refused to let him tarnish her reputation for the sake of a little fun.

Even if a little fun did sound delicious after her long day in the laboratory.

As he ushered her inside, fortunately leaving the door open, she said, "Oh, I didn't even know this room was here! How beautiful it is." Majestic delft tiles surrounded the fireplace, and everything else seemed designed to complement it, from the simple sofa of cobalt-blue brocade to the elegant writing table and the curtains of a blue-and-white toile fabric.

He lit candles to give them a bit more light. Then taking a seat on one end of the sofa, he gestured for her to sit at the other end.

But she was too excited to do so. After setting her journals and notebooks on the writing table next to a tray with two glasses and a crystal decanter of what looked like brandy, she began to pace before the fireplace.

He chuckled. "What's got you so energetic at this late hour? Don't tell me you've already found arsenic in what I brought you earlier."

"No, not yet. The important thing is what I *didn't* find arsenic in."

A frown creased his brow. "I don't understand."

"You know that Grey's father was embalmed, right? Well, I got lucky and was able to extract embalming fluid from the heart. And it contained no arsenic."

"So he wasn't poisoned."

"I don't know that yet." She stopped in front of Thorn. "You see, some embalmers use a fluid that has arsenous acid as an ingredient. But the embalmer of Grey's father didn't, thank goodness."

He still looked perplexed.

"Arsenous acid is . . ." She paused, trying to think in a layman's terms. "It's like a variant of arsenic—if it's in the embalming fluid, it would turn up as arsenic in any test. A good chemist would know that, too, so he—or she—might try to claim in a court trial that the arsenic came from the embalming fluid, not from poison. But now we can test for arsenic in the other organs, and if we find any, then there's no doubt it came from poison."

"Ah, I see." He leaned forward to rest his elbows on his knees. "You're already thinking ahead to proving your results."

"I'm already thinking ahead to a trial, yes." She began pacing again. "And honestly, given the description of his father's death that Grey got from his mother, his relations, and their old servants, it sounds like a case of *acute* arsenic poisoning. So the arsenic trioxide wouldn't even have had

cially after your stepmother worked so hard to blacken
reputation."

he crossed her arms over her chest. "She merely said
t everyone else was saying."

Actually, no. Until then, I hadn't had much of a rep-
tion for anything except being more German than
glish in my habits. Your stepmother had to figure out a
y to keep you from being blamed for jilting a duke, so
e told people you refused me because of my rakehell
ays. Thus our . . . indiscretion was seen in a different
ght."

His tone turned sarcastic. "I became the wicked whore-
ound taking advantage of a naive young woman, and you
became the virtuous virgin who stood up to me. It was a
brilliant strategy on her part." He sipped his brandy. "And
in a way, it worked in my favor, too, since society loves the
wicked. The rumormongers have to have *someone* to talk
about, after all. Your stepmother made sure they weren't
gossiping about *you*."

Olivia stood there, stunned. "*What?* I—I had no idea."
he stared hard at him. "Wait, I know I've read tales of
ou and your conquests of opera singers and merry
dows, of wives you seduced and brothels you frequented.
t yesterday, you mentioned having a mistress, for good-
s' sake. Not only that, but you wanted us to . . . indulge
uch activities without fear of the consequences. So
reputation wasn't all created out of whole cloth by my
other."

never said it was. But once she invented the role for
didn't see any reason not to step into the character. I
d if I had to endure her spurious gossip, I might as
joy myself while doing it. That way I could choose
adventures." His tone flattened. "But I would have

time to affect the hair and nails. The previous duke died
within a day of contracting his ague. If there's arsenic, the
stomach might still contain traces of it. The intestines
almost certainly will."

"I now know more about the anatomy of Grey's father
than I ever wanted to know," he said dryly.

"And I don't know enough." She sat down on the sofa.
"I can't believe you're not excited about this."

"I can't believe you *are*." He shifted to face her, bringing one leg up so he could rest his knee on the sofa. "I
mean, I recognize the implications your discovery has for
doing the arsenic testing, but it . . . doesn't thrill me as it
seems to do you."

"That's because you're not a chemist."

"Thank God." He stared at her. "I'd make a very bad
chemist."

"But you make an excellent duke, I'm sure."

"I don't know about that." He sucked in a heavy breath.

That reminded her . . . "I'm sorry, but I forgot you said
you had to talk to me about something. What was it?"

His lips tightened into a thin line. "I wanted to ask you
about our first meeting."

She stifled a sigh. It was long past time they discussed
it. She wished he hadn't waited until when she was exhausted, but she *had* been avoiding him, and that wasn't
his fault. Perhaps it was better to deal with it and be done.

"As a matter of fact," she said, "I've been wanting to
ask you about that, too." Her heart began pounding. "But
you go first. I've already regaled you for too long with the
intricacies of my favorite subject."

"Very well." He rose and went over to the writing table.
After refilling the glass he'd obviously been drinking from
before, he took the other glass on the tray and waved it at
her. "Would you like some brandy?"

"You know ladies aren't supposed to drink brandy neat."

"Yes, but *chemists* can drink whatever they please."

"Are you trying to ply me with strong drink so you can have your wicked way with me, Your Grace?" she asked, with a lift of one eyebrow.

A lazy grin crossed his face. "Now, would I do something like that?"

"You know you would." And she wouldn't mind it either.

Oh, dear. Working so late had clearly muddled her brain.

"Still, I should like to taste it," she told him. A little bit couldn't hurt, could it? And something about being recklessly alone with him made her wish to do other reckless things.

He set down the empty glass and came toward her. "Then you can taste mine." He handed her his glass. "Here you go."

Her first sip went down like fire, making her cough. But it was a warming drink in the chill of the room, so she sipped again. "It's . . . um . . . strong." And it made her feel thoroughly naughty, which was as heady a sensation as the drink itself. She handed the glass back to him. "Too strong for me."

He took a rather large swallow. "You get used to it."

"You're stalling," she said softly.

"You caught me," he said with a rueful laugh. Then he stared down into his glass. "That night at the Devonshires' ball, did you intend for us to be caught kissing?"

She frowned. "I don't understand what you mean."

"Grey warned me that night to be careful of matchmaking mamas and scheming daughters. And in the years since then, I've found his advice to be sound." He lifted his gaze to bore into her. "But . . . I was never sure about you and what you'd intended."

The crushing pain in her chest was like when he'd made his cold offer the morning

"So you thought that I . . . that I . . ." She cou

"You thought I schemed to trap you into mar

"At the time, I did. You're the one who g You're the one who encouraged me to remove waistcoat."

Anger welled up in her, sudden and fierce. " one who kissed *me*."

"True. That's one reason I've been rethinkin sumptions."

She jumped up. "If you had bothered to stop and me on the way out of that library, I would have exp that I never intended that."

"I probably wouldn't have believed you, anyway."

"But surely my rejection of your offer the next day m have told you I'd never meant to do anything so deceitfu

"It told me you had changed your mind after kiss me. Perhaps I was too forward or—"

"Your kissing was fine," she muttered. "But you posal could have used improvement."

"Right." He searched her face. "Because I was ' in showing I didn't wish to make it in the first pla what you said the other night, at any rate."

"It's true. You clearly wanted to be anywher father's town house, offering for my hand. know why you came at all." She stared at him question. You were a duke. You could have entanglement with just a word or two, and have dared gainsay it."

"I might point out that if I *had* used purpose, you would have been ruined. B offer and you refused it, you were onl preferred being myself instead and not the character in someone else's play."

What an odd way to put it. Then again, he did enjoy the theater. And she could see how it would feel like that to him, poor man.

Her skeptical side reasserted itself. Poor man, ha! He might have told himself he hadn't enjoyed his reputation as a rakehell, but obviously he'd had his fun all the same. Mama hadn't needed to push so *very* hard to get him playing that role. "I didn't know Mama's gossip had such an effect on you. All I ever saw of that night was her anger at me for refusing you and your hurt pride over it. Which, quite honestly, didn't make sense to me. And still doesn't. I was only doing what you and I both wanted."

"Being refused wasn't what I wanted. I wanted not to be forced into offering for you in the first place. I wanted your stepmother and I to smooth things over, so that no one's reputation was . . . harmed. Unfortunately, she could only see one way out. So she forced my hand."

"But how? You still haven't told me that."

He narrowed his gaze on her. "You really didn't know your stepmother was blackmailing me with a secret about my family?"

Blackmail! A chill skittered down her spine. "Of course I didn't. How could you even think it? Besides, what could Mama have possibly known about you that you felt was worth hiding?"

"Not about me. About my mother."

Her heart dropped into her stomach. "Y-Your *mother*? The lovely woman I met at your sister's ball?"

"Yes. That lovely woman had her debut at the same time as your stepmother, remember? And according to your 'Mama,' they were good friends back then. It's why she knew what to blackmail me with."

Her knees wobbled at that. She lowered herself to the sofa. "I felt sure there was something more to your offer. I heard you mention a bargain there at the end, but—"

"You were listening at doors, were you?"

"Not on purpose. I just happened to drop into a chair near the door." She steadied her shoulders. "I had too much to absorb all at once and had to . . . to sit down."

His voice softened. "Exactly as you're doing now." He took a seat next to her on the sofa. "Here. Have another sip of this."

When he tried to press the glass into her hand, she shook her head no. "Tell me about the blackmail."

"Well, if *you're* not going to drink it . . ." He sipped the brandy, his eyes dark in the candlelight. "If I tell you, you must swear not to say a word to anyone about it. I haven't even told my siblings. Mother would be terribly hurt if she ever got wind of it, and I don't want that."

"Nor do I." Without thinking, she covered his hand with hers. "You must believe me."

"I do." When she started to withdraw her hand, he caught it in his. "You may not be aware of this, but just before Gwyn and I were born our father died in a carriage accident on his way to London from Rosethorn, our family seat. That was all we'd ever known about it until your step-mother claimed he'd been on his way to meet his mistress. She didn't say how she knew, but she threatened to tell the world about it if I didn't offer for you."

The enormity of that sank in, and she stiffened. "You must have misunderstood. She wouldn't . . . she couldn't possibly have . . ."

"She did. Ask her."

"I did! Well, I asked her what you meant when you said she'd threatened you. And she . . . she said she had threatened to ruin you in society." Her gaze shot to him. "Though I wondered—"

"How she could manage that feat when I was a duke and the half brother of another duke? She couldn't have. But if I'd allowed her to spread tales about Mother, it wouldn't have hurt only me, but the whole family. At the time, my stepfather was an ambassador and considered above reproach. Hell, he used to lecture me about how I should behave. And Gwyn . . . well . . ."

He squeezed Olivia's hand. "Mother had always told us that our father was the love of her life. Gwyn believed it. *I* believed it. And I truly think Mother believed it. So if my father had kept a mistress, it meant their entire marriage was a lie. I couldn't let my mother suffer such gossip when it might have been false. I certainly couldn't let *Gwyn* suffer it."

"Of course not. But . . . but you were willing to marry a woman you barely knew just to prevent it?"

After setting his glass on the carved wooden stool, he twisted a bit to face her, so he could hold her hand in both of his. "I liked you well enough before your stepmother discovered us together. I thought I could learn to tolerate marriage to you, if only because you and I had a clear attraction to each other. At least we were honest about *that.*"

"But then I refused your offer." She caught her breath as his thumb began to trace circles on her hand. "You must have thought us all quite mad."

Forcing a smile, he pulled his near hand free, only to stretch his arm out along the top of the sofa behind her. "Your stepmother said you just needed courting. And perhaps she was right."

His fingers were now very close to her neck.

She tried not to notice. "I didn't want to be courted; I wanted to be a chemist." Something he'd said earlier sank in. "If you had 'ruined' me by refusing to propose, I would actually have been delighted. It would have enabled me to do nothing but chemistry for the rest of my life."

He eyed her askance. "You wouldn't have been the least bit insulted by my refusal to save you from ruin?"

"Perhaps for a day or two." When he leaned closer, her breath quickened in spite of herself. "I—I would have forgotten about it once my first . . . significant article on chemistry was published."

"Would you have? Truly?" When he ran his finger lightly over the nape of her neck, her heart thundered in her chest. As if he could tell, his voice dropped to a husky murmur. "Chemistry and courtship don't have to be mutually exclusive, you know. Take your Mrs. Fulhame. Unless the 'Mrs.' is just for show, she clearly manages both chemistry and marriage."

Olivia fought the thrill that his words—and his intimate gestures—were sending through her. "Her husband is a physician. In rank and situation, they're equal." *And he doesn't spend his nights with a mistress or at his club gambling.* When Thorn brought his devilish finger around to tip up her chin and keep her from looking away, she added shakily, "It's hardly . . . the same situation as you and I."

"And yet, you aren't slapping me. Or storming from the room. Or crying out for my sister-in-law."

He was right, curse him. "Because you promised to behave," she pointed out.

"I break my promises all the time," he said with a thin smile. "I'm a whorehound, remember?"

"But I'm not a whore." And she was no longer sure about his wicked persona either. What he'd said about Mama's blackmailing him made Olivia question everything she'd thought she knew about him.

"No, you're not," he said. "More's the pity."

"Is that what you want? A whore?"

"Hardly." One corner of his lips crooked up. "As usual, I want what I can't have."

The words heated her through and through. Indeed, if her blood ran any hotter, she would erupt into fire. "You're not alone in that. Except that *I* want what isn't good for me."

"Is that so?" His eyes were the molten blue of copper chloride burning. "Then we'd be equally culpable if we should happen just to finish where we left off yesterday."

At last he kissed her, in that slow, sensuous way he had of making a woman feel needed, wanted . . . *desired*. And even though she still feared it was an illusion created by a man used to getting what he wanted from women, she couldn't help hoping she was wrong.

While he continued to kiss her, he laid her hand on the hard bulge in his trousers and then used his hand to start sliding her skirts up her legs.

She tore her mouth free to whisper, "The door is still open."

He chuckled. "Leave it to you, sweeting, to notice that. No one is on this floor at this time of night. I dismissed my valet for the evening, your maid is probably dozing while she waits for you in your bedchamber upstairs, and Grey and Beatrice are in their bedchamber upstairs, also. So you need not worry."

"I'd still feel less uneasy if the door were closed, given our propensity to be caught." She rose. "I'll do it."

She hurried over to look out in the hall, and seeing no one there, shut the door. But when she turned back toward the sofa, she found he was already right there in front of her.

"Now, where were we?" he rasped.

Backing her against the door, he kissed her with such passion that it melted her very bones. As she felt his thick flesh press into hers, she remembered what he'd wanted and covered his prominent bulge with her hand.

"Oh, God, yes," he whispered. "Stroke me there. Please, sweeting."

When she began to do so, he returned to kissing her but with a savagery he'd never shown before. It should have alarmed her, but all it did was make her want him more. Then he dragged up her skirts so he could slide *his* hand up under them to between her thighs where she was utterly naked. She gasped, not in outrage but in anticipation of what he might do. And when he cupped her there and began to rub her slowly and sensually, she thought for sure she would disintegrate beneath his hand.

It felt so *good*. Impossibly pleasurable. She undulated against his hand in a frank request for more, and he chuckled against her lips.

What he fondled down there felt slick and wet, though how her body had come to be in that state was anyone's guess. But his caresses stoked the flames already searing her, and made her crave satisfaction, though she knew not what kind.

Apparently he knew what kind, for he parted her curls with one finger and then delved inside her. *Inside* her!

And it was delicious. Maddening. The most exotic sensation she'd ever experienced.

"Hold on," he muttered, and reached down with his free hand to undo the fall of his trousers and unbutton his drawers. Then taking the hand she'd been caressing him with, he pulled it inside so she could stroke his bare flesh as he was stroking hers. "Grab it, I beg you."

So she did. And his aroused member became even stiffer in her hand.

He groaned, and she let go, sure that she'd caused him pain. "I'm sorry," she whispered.

Putting her hand back, he said, "You're not . . . hurting me, I swear. Just keep pulling on it. Not too hard. Yes, *yes*! Exactly . . . like that." He pressed a kiss to her ear. "That feels incredible, sweeting. So bloody . . . incredible. You have no idea."

"I have . . . some," she gasped because his finger had grown bolder, having found a hard little spot to fondle that drove her out of her mind.

"You like that . . . do you?" His breathing was erratic now, too, and growing more so by the moment.

"You can't tell?" she choked out. She thought she might explode any minute, though she didn't know exactly how. "It's . . . you're . . ." She had no words for it. "Yes, I like it."

With a strangled laugh, he nuzzled her neck.

Suddenly a boom sounded, so loud it shook the room.

He jerked back, dropping his hand from between her legs. "What the hell was *that*?"

For half a second, she thought perhaps *she* had exploded. But of course that was absurd. Struggling to regain control over her wayward impulses, she pulled her hand out of his drawers. "No one is setting off fireworks around here, are they?"

"In October? No."

She yanked her skirts down as he fastened up his trousers. They both hurried to look out the window, and her heart sank.

Her new laboratory was no more. Flames engulfed the dairy, leaping up to the sky. Occasionally another chemical would break free, only to burn blue or green or purple. Olivia would have thought it beautiful . . . if it hadn't meant death to all her hopes.

"My samples!" she cried, and ran for the door.

But she only got as far as the hallway before Thorn caught up to her. "No, it's not safe. You know as well as I do that all the chemicals in there may not have burned yet. If the saltpeter erupts or—"

"It's not the saltpeter you have to worry about. There are things like sodium hydroxide, which shouldn't be allowed to burn at all, but is probably already burning. The fumes of *that* are toxic, too."

"What's sodium hydroxide?" he asked.

"You would know it as lye."

"Damn. Even I know that lye on fire can't be good."

They could hear noises from downstairs that said the servants had been alerted.

"Stay here," Thorn told her. "I'll tell the servants just to let the fire burn itself out. It's far enough from the house and high enough on that hill that it shouldn't ignite anything else."

He hurried down the stairs and she rushed after him. Whether he admitted it or not, he didn't know what he was doing, so he needed her.

As she approached the bottom, one of the servants cried, "Miss, that fire is already so hot we can't get near to it. You must have left coals burning in the fireplace or something."

"I didn't start it, I swear," she protested. "I'm always careful to douse the coals with water, and I never leave a candle burning—"

"That's what we need—water!" another footman called out. "Buckets and buckets of water!"

"No!" she screamed, trying to be heard over the sudden clamor of servants making suggestions. "That could make it worse!"

But no one could hear her. When Grey and Beatrice appeared at the top of the stairs, the servants called out to their master to do something. Judging from Grey's crookedly buttoned banyan and mussed hair, he had just awakened and still hadn't figured out what was going on, so he wasn't going to be any use to them.

Then Thorn moved higher on the stairs and let out an ear-piercing whistle that got everyone's attention. When the noise quieted, he said, "The fire is made up of burning chemicals. So we should listen to Miss Norley, since she's the chemist and it was her laboratory that exploded. She knows better than anyone how to handle things."

Stepping aside in clear deference to her, he then hurried up the stairs to apprise Grey and Beatrice of the situation.

"I beg you," Olivia said, "don't try to douse anything with water. Some of those chemicals are harmless in fire but explode in water. Others explode in air. If you *must* go near the fire—and I wouldn't advise it, frankly—use salt or sand to extinguish it."

"Why must we not go near it, miss?" one footman asked her.

"Because depending on which chemicals are burning, poisonous gases will be rising from those flames, and you don't want to breathe any of those."

Another fellow cried, "Why are we listening to *her*, anyway? She's the one what started the fire in the first place."

Olivia bristled. "I swear I did not—"

"The miss didn't start it!" another man called out. "It was that boy who did."

That shocked everyone into silence.

"What boy?" Thorn asked the man. He and Grey hurried back down the stairs, leaving a clearly pregnant Beatrice standing at the top in her nightdress and wrapper.

"I was outside getting some air, Your Graces, when I saw a boy—couldn't have been more than fifteen—running from the old dairy. I called out to him to stop, but then the whole place exploded, and I lost sight of him."

When the servants began murmuring among themselves, Grey turned to Thorn and lowered his voice. "Do you think perhaps we're getting too close to the truth? That someone would go so far as to blow up Miss Norley's laboratory to prevent that?"

Thorn paled. "It's possible, I suppose."

Olivia shook her head. "They'd have to know which chemicals to ignite and—"

"They wouldn't have to know a damned thing," Thorn said in a low voice. "I started a fire in your laboratory just by knocking off a jar, remember?"

"Good point," Grey said.

Her cheeks reddened as she glanced at Thorn. "Wait, you didn't tell him about—"

"I told him I accidentally knocked off a jar, which is true." Thorn ran his fingers through his hair in obvious frustration. "Olivia, could this fellow, whoever the hell he is, have started an explosion simply by smashing jars and throwing things about?"

"Absolutely. But that would be very stupid of him, given the sort of chemicals one would find in a working laboratory."

"We're not dealing with chemists here, sweeting," Thorn said, not even realizing he'd used the endearment in front of his brother. "I mean, it's unlikely the boy knew that much about what he was doing."

Thorn headed out the front door and onto the steps to gaze toward the laboratory with its still burning fire. She followed him.

"If we do nothing, will it burn itself out?" he asked her.

"I think so."

He shot her a hard look. "You don't know for sure?"

"How can I? I've never seen a laboratory explode before."

"Right," he said hastily. "Of course not. But you do believe our best course of action is to leave it alone."

"Yes, definitely. There's little wind tonight, thank heaven, so there's not much likelihood of having sparks blown onto the roofs of other buildings. The fire shouldn't take too long to die out, and Grey doesn't need his people choking to death on toxic fumes in an attempt to make it happen sooner."

"I certainly don't," Grey said as he came up behind them. "But there are two things that can be done at least."

Turning to his servants, he ordered several to search the grounds for the lad who might have destroyed the laboratory and a few others to take turns keeping watch that the fire didn't ignite anything beyond the dairy.

Then he told everyone else to go to bed.

Grey turned to her as the servants drifted off to do their several duties. "That includes you, Olivia. I know you must have stayed up late in the laboratory because you were still out there when Beatrice and I retired. But you need your sleep like everyone else."

"Listen to him," Thorn said.

"How can I sleep when we've lost everything we worked for?" she said. "The samples are gone, and I don't think we can use what was left of the remains."

"We still have that set of samples in the icehouse," Grey said soothingly.

Hope sprouted inside her. "I don't know what you mean."

"Damn, I forgot to tell you," Thorn said. "The coroner split everything in half in case we needed fresh samples for a trial. You only received one half. I meant to say something when I brought the samples this afternoon, but . . ."

"I wouldn't let you in," she said.

"I'm sorry I didn't mention it tonight."

She beamed. "I don't care. That's marvelous news! I can still do the experiments! Of course, we may have to set a man to keep watch over the laboratory at night, and we'll have to send for fresh chemicals and equipment." Her mind jumped ahead to what needed to be done. "I should make a list right now while I'm thinking of it. Ooh, and my journals and notebooks are upstairs—thank heavens *they're* safe—so I can refer to them if—"

"We'll discuss all that in the morning." Thorn shot Grey a somber look. "For now, you should rest, Olivia."

She thrust out her chin, trying not to be flattered by his concern for her. "Only after I make my shopping lists."

"*Before*," Thorn said sternly. "Or I swear I'll lock up your journals and notebooks until tomorrow."

He would do it, too. The two of them were up to something. She could tell.

"Oh, very well, if you insist," she muttered. "But only if you promise to fetch me if the fire worsens."

"I swear it," Thorn said. "Now off with you."

She sighed. But there was really nothing else she could do until the fire was out. Besides, as Grey had guessed, she was exhausted, not only from the long day but from the wild swings her emotions had taken. Much as she truly wanted to start picking items for the new laboratory, her exhaustion had begun to take over.

So she would put off everything until tomorrow morning.

Chapter Nine

Thorn stood at a distance, surveying the remains of the fire that had raged nearly until dawn. Here and there a pile of something either smoldered or flared up briefly, and there was the occasional wisp of smoke. But the flames seemed mostly banished, although he couldn't be sure of anything until he spoke to Olivia.

As if he'd conjured her up, he suddenly felt her at his side. Her scent, faint as it was, alerted him to her presence. Knowing how much the laboratory had meant to her, he could only imagine how the sight of its destruction must be affecting her.

"You're up early," she said with a catch in her voice.

He faced her. "So are you."

Like any other typical young miss, she wore some gossamer muslin gown, beautiful and fragile. But the sturdy shawl of green wool she'd draped around it showed her to be more resilient than the typical young miss. Here she stood itching to go on, even after what had happened to her laboratory . . . even with the destruction laid out before her.

It reminded him of the first time they'd met . . . and last

night's revelations about that first meeting. She was never exactly what she seemed. Best to remember that.

"Did you get any sleep?" he asked.

"A little. Did you?"

"Some," he lied. He and Grey had stayed up quite a bit longer figuring out what to do, and now he had to tell her what they'd decided without her. He wasn't sure she'd go along with their new plan. But before he revealed it . . . "What do you think? Is the fire mostly out?"

"It seems to be."

"Is it safe to go near? Grey has a bag of salt over there," he said, pointing to a spot a little way from the fire, "but sand isn't easy to come by here. We'd have to send to the coast."

"No need for that. The salt should be enough to extinguish the last bits if Grey wants his footmen to spread it over what's still smoldering."

"Good."

She stared at the embers a while, then straightened her shoulders. "Now that Grey knows the dangers, does he have any other buildings on his property I could use for a laboratory? When I couldn't sleep last night, I made a list of chemicals and laboratory equipment, but I was careful to pare it down now that I know precisely what to test and how, so—"

"We're not staying," he broke in.

She looked stricken. "What do you mean?"

"Someone clearly wants to make sure you don't do these tests," he said. "Grey and I think that the lad who smashed up your laboratory, whoever he is, was hired by the person who poisoned Grey's father. So as long as you stay here, you're in danger."

"I don't see why *I* am—"

"You could have been inside when that devil broke in," he said hoarsely. The thought of anybody daring to murder her turned his blood to ice. "You could be lying in those embers right now."

She laid her hand on his arm. "Yes, but I wasn't, and I'm not."

"Not yet. But after finding out that you mean to continue, this . . . this *arse* may decide to do worse than destroy your laboratory. He might decide to destroy *you*." He caught her by the shoulders, barely resisting the urge to shake her. "And that's a chance neither Grey nor I wish to take."

Hurt glinted in her eyes. "You'll put an end to my experiments just like that, without giving me a say in it?"

It took him a minute to realize how she'd taken what he'd said. "I'm sorry. I didn't explain myself very well. We're not putting an end to anything. We're simply spiriting you away to do the experiments elsewhere."

Her face cleared. "Oh." She walked over to view the destruction more closely. "And you're sure the explosion was caused by some villainous 'lad'? That it wasn't anything I failed to do properly or some residual chemical I overlooked in my tests that ignited on its own?"

"We're sure. Although the broken glass and emptied containers could conceivably have resulted from the explosion, the dairy's lock, found beneath the intact door and door frame, was clearly busted apart by a sledgehammer *before* the explosion. We know that because we found the hammer in the wreckage. Apparently, the lad left it behind in his hurry to escape with his life. He probably saw a chemical catch fire and then ran out, in fear that the whole place might burn. I doubt he had any idea that it would explode."

"Neither did I."

"We realize that."

"Thank heavens it wasn't my fault." Then, as if realizing how callous that sounded, she grimaced. "I—I only meant—"

"I know what you meant. No one wants to be responsible for this level of destruction . . . or for possibly exposing innocent people to caustic chemicals. And you would never behave so recklessly."

He hoped not, anyway. Because she had *no* idea how dangerous this whole venture could turn out to be. He and his brothers already believed that four men might have died to serve the villain's purpose, whatever it was. One woman more would mean nothing to this scoundrel.

Shoving his hands into his greatcoat pockets, he added, "That's why we've found a better place for you to do your work. Somewhere safer that no one knows about."

She eyed him skeptically. "And where in creation would that be?"

"My estate. In Berkshire."

He'd expected surprise and perhaps resistance to the idea. Not the bitter laughter that erupted from her. "I can only imagine what Mama would think of *that*," she said.

"She won't think anything, because she won't know about it. No one will. That's the point. Since plenty of people were aware that you were coming here for a visit, anyone could have done this. So, until your work is finished, the only safe place for you is somewhere no one expects you to be."

She crossed her arms over her chest. "And you think your estate is best for that."

"Yes."

"Oh, come now, Thorn, that's—"

"Trust me, Grey and I have thought through our whole

plan. I'll take Grey's phaeton to London later today. You'll leave tomorrow, ostensibly to head home. Everyone will see Grey and Beatrice making a big show of packing you off in Grey's carriage, accompanied by a maid. We'll make sure the news is spread in Sudbury in case our villain is hanging about, hoping to try again if we decide to set up a new laboratory."

He paced in front of the ruins. "But you'll really be meeting me at Gwyn's town house in the city. Gwyn's husband, Major Wolfe, is an investigator of sorts so I'll send him up here to see what he can discover about the lad who did this." He gestured to the destruction. "Meanwhile, in London I'll personally oversee the purchase of more materials and equipment for your laboratory. With any luck, we can leave for Rosethorn in Berkshire, south of London, in a day or two."

Her lips tightened into a line. "You realize that if anyone finds out I'm traveling with you, let alone staying at your estate, I'll be ruined."

"Did I forget to mention that Gwyn will be coming with us to chaperone? That's the beauty of our plan. There's no risk to you. Well, except the usual risk of exploding chemicals."

She ignored his half-joking remark. "Have you asked *either* Lady Gwyn or Major Wolfe to do this?"

"Not yet, but I know them. They'll help."

"And if they don't? Or can't, for some reason?"

"Then I'll ask another member of my family—Heywood's wife, perhaps. I don't want to ask Mother if I can avoid it. We haven't even told her we're doing this and why."

Nor had they told Olivia everything about their investigation. There was no reason to do so. Once this part of the investigation was finished, they wouldn't need her.

In fact, while he was in Berkshire and she was doing

her experiments, he planned to ask around about his father's carriage accident. It had happened close enough to the estate that it had still been under the jurisdiction of the local constable. Until a year ago, he'd had no reason to look into it. Thirty years ago, no one had suspected foul play. Thorn still wasn't sure it had been murder. But it was time to rule that out.

And perhaps that would keep him from spending every waking moment trying to seduce her.

"Anyway," he told Olivia, "I'm certain Gwyn will travel with us and chaperone you. I'm family, and she knows you're important to—" Thank God he'd caught himself before he'd said "me." "To Grey and Beatrice."

He could feel her eyes probing him.

"*Only* to Grey and Beatrice?" she asked softly.

God, she *would* ask him a question like that. He stared out over the destruction. "And to the rest of the family, of course."

Coward. But he knew better than to let anyone get too close, especially a woman whose favorite pastime was dancing with danger. If she had been inside the laboratory when that fellow had broken in . . .

Instantly tensing, he swung his gaze back to her. "Grey and I can think of no other way to protect you from whoever is trying to prevent you from doing your work. As long as the villain thinks we've given up, he'll leave you alone. And that's what we all want. Obviously you struck a nerve, and now the killer is focused on *you*."

"Wonderful," she said dryly. "Just what I require to make my life complete."

"I'm sorry," he said, and meant it. "I'm sure Grey never expected this to be a hazardous proposition. I know I didn't."

"It's fine. I knew what I was agreeing to." She shivered. "Mostly, anyway."

He searched her face. "Are you sure you're ready to start all over again with a new laboratory? Or has this rattled your resolve?"

A faint smile crossed her lips. "You don't know me very well if you think *that*. There's very little that rattles my resolve."

"Nonetheless, we intend to put the laboratory closer to the house this time and post a guard."

"Aren't you afraid I'll set fire to your expensive manor? You're very brave, letting me play with chemicals so close to where you live."

"I'm not brave at all. Every time I think of some chemical accidentally mixing with another and going 'boom,' my heart falters." More for her than for any part of his "expensive" manor. "But since you seem determined to continue—"

"Which I am," she said stoutly.

"Which I knew you would be," he countered, "there appears to be no point to arguing with you on the subject."

"You know me better than I thought."

Her minxish smile reminded him that he'd spent half of last night in an agony of unfulfilled desire. Combined with the time he'd spent worrying over the threat to her from some unknown villain, he'd had no sleep at all.

With a glance around to make sure no one was near, he lowered his head to kiss her. Just to reassure her, of course. That was all.

But before he could, his damned brother strolled up the path toward them. "I take it that you're discussing our plan with Olivia? Has she agreed to go along with it?"

"Yes," she told Grey. "Provided that Thorn can coax

Lady Gwyn into being my chaperone, and that he can acquire everything I need to set up my second laboratory."

"I've already sent someone to London to invite Joshua here and to inform Gwyn that Thorn is on his way there," Grey said. "And fortunately, I kept that list you gave me of what was needed in your laboratory. Thorn will have that to refer to when he starts overseeing the purchase of the materials. So, by tomorrow or the next day, you should be able to leave."

"And what if Mama gets wind of this sudden change in plans? What if she happens to run into me in London or hears of it from someone local?"

"Is she still in London?" Grey asked. "Surely, she's returned to the country by now."

Olivia's face brightened. "That's true. I forgot it's not really the Season. Mama came into London only to join us all at Lady Gwyn's ball."

"What's more," Grey said, "I can't imagine who would tell your stepmother that you've left Carymont for London. Everyone around here, including my servants, will be informed you went home to Surrey, so why should they mention anything to Lady Norley?"

"Good point," she said. "I do hope you're right."

So did Thorn. Because if the baroness caught him with Olivia again, he knew exactly what she'd do. And this time he might be tempted to sweeten his offer of marriage to Olivia so that she'd actually accept it.

No good would come of that. Olivia had certain expectations about marriage, and one of them was that it meant a great deal more than just a civil union. She seemed to want love and all that it entailed. And he simply couldn't offer her that.

* * *

Olivia had expected to miss Thorn during the day and night they were apart. But Beatrice and Grey had kept her so busy with preparations and packing for the trip that she'd had no chance to even think about him.

Not until she was on the road with the maid they'd sent with her did she realize that the carriage seemed much less cheery without him. And without her friends, too, of course. She amused herself by going over her notebooks and the journal articles in preparation for what she'd be doing once she *did* have a laboratory to do it in. But she was relieved when they reached London in record time. She only hoped that after all the trouble Grey's family was taking to protect her she would finally be able to confirm or rule out arsenic poisoning.

Fortunately, she'd already been to Lady Gwyn's town house for the ball last week and had felt wholly welcome. Still, the house her parents generally rented for the Season was in a less fashionable—and less expensive—part of London, so it was quite a change to be in Mayfair. She felt decidedly out of her element in the neighborhood, with its elegant facades and costly carriages, although she knew better than to show it.

As soon as the footman helped her down from Grey's carriage, however, Lady Gwyn was at her side, greeting her with a broad smile. "I'm so glad you're here at last, Miss Norley."

"Please call me Olivia. Everyone does."

"Well then, since everyone calls me Gwyn, you should, too. It sounds as if we'll be spending a great deal of time together."

"It does, indeed."

"But I had to deduce that on my own. When Thorn told me of your arrival, he failed to explain the reason for your visit. I had to wrestle it out of my husband."

"Oh, dear," Olivia said. "I hope I didn't cause any strife between you."

"Don't worry yourself over that for one moment. Joshua enjoys having me wrestle things out of him. And he would confirm that if he were here." She tucked Olivia's hand in the crook of her arm and led her up the steps. "But he isn't, of course, because he's on his way to Carymont to help Grey find the man who blew up your laboratory, isn't he?"

"Oh, yes, and I'm sure—"

"He'll put everything to rights, trust me," Gwyn went on, as if Olivia hadn't spoken. "Though you must have been in a terror the whole time it was happening!"

"Well, it was rather—"

"I cannot believe that Thorn and Grey took such a chance in the first place." She shook her head. "They should have asked Joshua to join them from the beginning. You've met my husband, right?"

"Yes. He seemed very—"

"But of course you met him. At the ball here last week. I don't know where my mind is."

Just as they reached the top step, a new voice sounded from behind them. "I don't know where your mind is either, sis. Perhaps back with all the questions you keep asking poor Miss Norley without waiting for an answer."

"Thorn!" Gwyn said as she turned on him. "I thought you were planning to be here when she arrived."

"I got a bit caught up buying dangerous chemicals and funny-looking glass-bulb things for her laboratory. But it's finally all on its way to Rosethorn, so we can leave tomorrow." He met Olivia's gaze and smiled. "Unless you need some time to rest from your journey, Miss Norley?"

"No, indeed. I'm eager to get started again."

Thorn winked at her before telling his sister, "That's

how it's done, Gwyn. You ask a question and then you *wait* for the person to answer you." When she lifted her eyes heavenward, he said to Olivia, "Gwyn talks very fast when she's nervous. Give her a little while to get to know you and to settle down. Then she'll behave more normally, I swear."

"Or as normally as I can," Gwyn said saucily, "when dealing with Mr. Know-It-All."

Olivia laughed. She was certain she and Thorn's sister would get along just fine.

The three of them entered the foyer through the open front door. As two footmen scurried to take both Olivia's cloak and Thorn's greatcoat, Thorn asked Olivia, "How was your trip?"

"Dull," she said. "But I read my journals and took more notes, so it wasn't a complete loss."

He smiled at her. "Admit it—you missed having me there to keep the conversation lively."

"Lively!" Gwyn said. "Is that what you call it when you go on and on about the latest plays and such? And that is a rhetorical question, Thorn. No need to answer." She stopped short. "Oh, dear, I almost forgot—your friend Mr. Juncker has been waiting almost an hour for you."

That knocked the wind right out of Olivia. Mr. Juncker? *Here?* She'd never even seen her favorite playwright, much less met him. And he was here? Dear heavens! She had to remind herself to breathe.

But Thorn's face had turned a peculiar shade of gray. "In *your* house, Gwyn? He's waiting just down the hall?"

"Of course," Gwyn said, apparently as surprised by his reaction as Olivia. "How would I know about it otherwise? He's in our drawing room." When Thorn muttered a curse under his breath and changed direction to head that way, Gwyn said, "He didn't make advances toward me or anything, if that's what worries you."

"Not a bit. I'm just surprised he knew I'd be here."

Gwyn hurried to keep up with Thorn's long strides. "I offered him tea but he said he wouldn't be staying long."

"He won't," Thorn said grimly. "I'll get rid of him quick enough."

Olivia must have made some sound of disappointment because at that moment, Thorn and Gwyn apparently realized she wasn't right behind them and halted to stare back at her.

"Are you quite all right, Olivia?" Gwyn asked.

"Not . . . entirely." Olivia thought she might actually faint.

Thorn took one look at her and groaned. "I forgot you're an admirer of Juncker's plays."

"Is she really?" Gwyn smirked at her brother. "How intriguing."

"I—I don't suppose it would be . . . possible for me to meet him, would it?" Olivia asked.

"I can't imagine why not." Gwyn lifted an eyebrow at Thorn. "You can introduce them, can't you?"

Thorn uttered a heavy sigh. "Certainly. Just . . . give me a moment alone with him, all right?"

Olivia bobbed her head. She would give him an *hour* alone with Mr. Juncker if that was what it took. Because for the first time in her life, she was actually excited about meeting someone who wasn't a chemist.

Now if only she could keep from making a fool of herself in front of him.

rn wanted to throttle his friend. Especially when
ker shot him a taunting smile.

"I've seen them all, sir, and found them to be most
rtaining," Olivia said in a breathy flurry of words.

"And which is your favorite?" Juncker asked.

"Oh, don't make me choose!" she cried. "I like them all
ally. Although if I *were* to choose one, it would proba-
be *The Wild Adventures of a Foreign Gentleman Loose
London.*"

"Ah," Juncker said. "The one where they steal fire-
orks on Guy Fawkes Day, only to have them all go off in
inn yard in the middle of the night because someone
rew a smoldering rush light into the wagon."

"That one, yes. Although that wasn't my favorite part,
be honest, since the chemistry wasn't correct."

Thorn bit back a laugh. He'd forgotten about that scene,
hich Juncker had written. Thorn had wanted to have a
al chemist read it to be sure, but Juncker had said there
as no time, so they'd fudged it as usual.

Now Juncker was eyeing Olivia askance. "And what
uld you know about *chemistry,* Miss Norley?"

"Quite a lot, actually," Thorn put in. "Miss Norley is a
emist. So trust me, she knows the chemistry firsthand."

"I see," Juncker said, though it was clear he was still
fed. "If I may be so bold, madam, what *was* your
orite part?"

Oh! Well, the part about the farmer going to gather the
eggs and finding billiard balls in their place."

horn nodded. "And then the fellow thought the hens
laid billiard balls because of an attack of the pox." It
his favorite scene of all the ones he'd written. "I like
part myself."

livia cocked her head at him. "For a man who at first
ned not to have seen any of the plays, you certainly

Chapter Ten

After Thorn entered Gwyn's drawing room and shut
the door, he wasted no time coming right to the point.
"Why are you here, Juncker? How did you even know
where to find me?"

Juncker, wearing his usual "romantic writer" attire, was
sprawled unrepentantly across the settee. "I heard you
were in town, so I went to your house, where your servants
told me that you were over here. And you *know* why I
came. Vickerman blistered my ears for not having the play
finished. So, did you get any writing done during your
travels?"

"Keep your voice down." Thorn walked over to sit across
from Juncker. "Gwyn doesn't know about my writing, and
neither does her guest."

"I could remedy that if you like," Juncker drawled.

Thorn scowled. "And I could cut off all your funds. Just
try me. See how you like not being able to use credit at
half the taverns in town."

"Fine." Juncker straightened on the settee. "But you
still haven't answered my question. Did you finish the
damned play?"

"I have the final scene mapped out in my head," Thorn said truthfully. "But I haven't had a chance to write it."

"Your sister said you and she and your mysterious guest are off to Berkshire tomorrow. Is there any possibility you can write it there?"

"Perhaps," Thorn said. "Give me a few days, and I swear I'll try to have it to you. But after this one, we need to start a new sort of play with new characters. And that's all I'll say about that for now." He rose. "I do have one favor to ask of you before you leave."

Juncker eyed him suspiciously. "What sort of favor?"

"Our mysterious guest is an admirer of the plays. She's seen every one performed, and probably more than once, given her extensive knowledge of them. She wants to meet the author."

"You mean me." Juncker laughed. "That must really gall you."

"If it does, it's only because she's a fetching young woman whom I don't want to see you take advantage of."

"You think *I* will take advantage of her more than *you* would? Talk about the pot calling the kettle black. You must be getting prudish in your old age."

"I'm a year younger than you," Thorn said dryly.

"Still prudish. A fetching young woman, eh? She's not a friend of Vanessa's, is she?"

"Grey's cousin Vanessa? As far as I know, they've never met. Why?"

"Just making sure." With a broad smile, Juncker stood and smoothed his trousers. "Vanessa will be the death of me. The chit's got some fool notion that if I marry her, she'll be able to manage my writing life the way she manages her mother's household. And God forgive me, but even though she's rich as Croesus and a pretty little thing, I am not ready to be managed by her."

"If it's any consolation," Thorn sai[...] probably break you in half if he thought yo[...] his beloved cousin. She's like a sister to h[...] you, I'd keep my hands off her."

"Ah, but you're not me, are you?" Junck[...] wink. "That's the trouble, old chap. So bring[...] damsel. I'll decide if she's fetching or not."

God help him. If Thorn wasn't careful, th[...] very badly. But the look of awe and antic[...] Olivia's face when she'd heard that her idol w[...] He had to do this, even if it meant risking her fi[...] who'd really written the plays.

He *could* just tell her the truth. Ask her to ke[...]

Right. As soon as he did she'd realize that [...] boots was meant to be her, and it would wou[...] deeply he'd probably never get near her again.[...] might not even do those tests for Grey if she kn[...] certainly not go with him to his estate.

So it was best to continue as he had unti[...] opened the door to let both women in.

Gwyn wasn't swayed by Juncker's suppos[...] all, but Olivia stared at the chap with the smi[...] sion women often wore with Thorn. He didn[...] bit. Which was ridiculous, considering that th[...] was smitten by was *him*!

Not that Juncker cared about that fine di[...] sooner had Thorn performed the introd[...] Juncker began flirting, damn his hide.

"I am so very pleased to meet you, M[...] Juncker said as he took Olivia's hand. "T[...] you're quite the admirer of my plays." He k[...] Continental style.

When Olivia, who rarely blushed, did so[...]

know a great deal about them." She set her hands on her hips. "I think Grey is right—you *are* jealous of Mr. Juncker."

Thorn snorted. "You said it yourself in the carriage— why would I be jealous of a playwright?"

"Ah, but I believe Miss Norley has hit upon the truth," Juncker said, with a grin as wide as his stupidly big head. "You're utterly jealous of my success. Aren't you, Thorn?"

Thorn glowered at him. "Didn't you tell me you had somewhere to be, Juncker? At the theater perhaps?"

"No, no, I don't think so," Juncker said gleefully. "I would much rather chat with Miss Norley for a while about *my* plays."

At the moment, Thorn would much rather shove a manuscript down Juncker's gullet. But that would probably just reinforce Olivia's ridiculous idea that Thorn was jealous of Juncker's success.

"Actually," Gwyn put in, her eyes suspiciously gleaming, "I thought we might invite Mr. Juncker to stay for dinner. You would enjoy that, wouldn't you, Olivia?"

"Very much so," Olivia said, and beamed at Juncker.

She'd never beamed at Thorn like that, except for when he'd told her they'd preserved extra samples in Grey's icehouse. What would it take to have her beaming at him because she was excited about being with him? What would he have to do to gain *that*?

He grimaced. Now he was being absurd. Go to extremes just to get a woman to smile at him? Never. He'd seen his brothers and his brother-in-law do it, and that was all well and good for them. Personally, he was cynical about how long their cream-pot love would last, though he supposed they might get a few good years out of it.

But he knew instinctively that gaining such devotion from a woman required exposing one's many foibles and flaws. The very idea made him shudder. Bad enough that

Juncker knew exactly how to use his flaws against him. Thorn didn't have to live with Juncker, thank God.

"That settles it," Gwyn said, jerking Thorn from his depressing thoughts. "And you'll join us for dinner, too, right, Thorn?"

Damn, he should have paid better attention. They'd set up the entire evening without consulting him.

"I wouldn't miss it," Thorn said. "But I'm a bit worried about Miss Norley." He stared hard at Olivia. "Are you sure you're not too tired for dinner? We do have a long journey ahead of us tomorrow."

Either she was enjoying tormenting him or she seriously didn't care what he said on the matter, because she shook her head. "I'm not tired at all. I could use a relaxing dinner with a lively discussion among friends."

Friends. Wonderful. Thorn had already been relegated to the category of "friend." He'd rather hoped for a chance at a kiss and a caress or two this evening, if they could break away from Gwyn. Clearly, that would not happen.

It was just as well. Because if he didn't watch it, he would end up traveling down the road to ruining her, which was unacceptable.

Olivia hadn't laughed so hard since the last time she'd attended a production of Mr. Juncker's plays. It made sense, since the man would need quite the sense of humor to write such funny characters and situations. But oddly enough, it was Mr. Juncker and Gwyn together who kept her amused throughout dinner, while Thorn vacillated between scowling at her and scowling at Mr. Juncker.

Now she was *sure* Thorn was jealous. But she was growing less sure it was Mr. Juncker's success in writing that made Thorn jealous. Because every time Mr. Juncker's gaze fell on her silk bodice, which *did* show more of her bosom than her other dinner gowns, Thorn made a sort of growling noise deep in his throat that only she seemed to hear. It was rather intriguing.

They'd finished dessert when Gwyn started a funny story about a visit the king of Prussia had paid to the residence of her stepfather, the ambassador, which His Majesty had apparently done from time to time.

Gwyn leaned forward in her chair. "Then the king asked Thorn, as my brother was dashing through the parlor, 'Where are you running to in such a hurry, young man?' And after performing a perfect bow, Thorn answered the king in German, with all the formality of a diplomat's stepson, 'Forgive me, Your Majesty, but I must find an acceptable place wherein to deposit my excrement.' He was serious, too."

Thorn groaned.

"He didn't really say that word, though, did he?" Olivia asked, torn between laughter and shock.

"I'm afraid he did," Gwyn said.

"The word is the same in German as in English," Mr. Juncker explained.

"And Thorn is nothing if not honest about his needs, even his unsavory ones," Gwyn added.

Mr. Juncker snorted. "Ah, yes, scrupulously honest. That's our Thorn."

Thorn glared at both him and Gwyn. "This is hardly appropriate dinner table conversation."

"We're done with dinner," Gwyn said.

"Then you and Miss Norley should repair to the drawing room so Juncker and I can have our brandy," Thorn said.

"Not on your life," Mr. Juncker said. "No one is leaving until I hear the rest of this story. Actually, if anyone is repairing to the drawing room, it should be all of us." He shot Thorn a taunting look. "I'm enjoying the company of the ladies." Then Mr. Juncker turned to Gwyn. "Do go on, madam."

"You must consider the fact that Thorn was only six at the time," Gwyn said. "And since we were all in the garden, it was easy for him to slip away from our nursemaid when she was dealing with three other children—two of whom were still in swaddling."

"*Three* other children? Not four?" Olivia asked.

"Grey had a tutor by then." Gwyn looked pensive. "Or perhaps that was after he'd returned to England. I can't remember. I was only six, too, you know."

"Well, don't leave us hanging," Olivia said. "How did the king respond?"

"He laughed heartily, thank heavens," Gwyn said, "or I daresay Papa would have punished Thorn for it. From then on, our nursemaid was ordered to take us for a long walk during any visit from the royalty of Prussia. Frederick the Great died a couple of years later, I believe. And Thorn cried when he heard of it. The king did seem like a nice man."

"He certainly always treated me better than I deserved," Thorn said, and the look of affection that passed between him and his twin made Olivia envious. She would so have enjoyed having a brother or sister.

"The stories you and your siblings must have about growing up in Prussia in a large family," Olivia said. "My childhood was so dull by comparison. It was just Mama and I most of the time. Indeed, since this is the longest I've ever been away from Mama, I worry she might get lonely while I'm gone."

"Your mother is a widow?" Mr. Juncker asked.

Olivia could feel Thorn's gaze on her. "She might as

well be. Papa is always in London for some reason or another, it seems. Except during hunting season, when he tramps the woods every day. And even when we're in the city with him, he's at his club or Parliament or . . . who knows where else." She didn't want to know, honestly. The possibility that her father might have a mistress always bothered her.

"Yet you enjoy plays about men who get into trouble in the city," Thorn pointed out.

"Not *men*," Olivia said. "Bachelors. Mr. Juncker's plays are all about unmarried men and the scrapes they get into. But the plays mock those married men who act like bachelors."

"Do they?" Mr. Juncker asked, with a glance at Thorn.

"Don't look at *me*," Thorn drawled. "You're the one who writes the things."

"Yes, but I don't recall any part about mocking married men," Mr. Juncker said.

Olivia frowned. "Like when Felix and his friend try to steal the mistresses of the married men? Or joke about the husbands' big paunches? Or use the latest slang to poke fun at the men because they're too old to know what the words mean?"

"Ah, right," Mr. Juncker said. "Those parts."

"So those scenes aren't based on your experiences as a bachelor?" Olivia asked.

"A few are," Mr. Juncker said. "Not as many as people think."

Olivia stared at him. "Then where did you get your comic characters, like Lady Slyboots and Lady Grasping?"

Mr. Juncker tapped his head. "From here, my dear. They came from right up here. The best writers don't work from real life, you see. They get their ideas from dreams and fancies and the merest whispers of the universe in their ears."

"What rot," Thorn muttered. "You only blather such nonsense when you're trying to impress the ladies."

"Someone must, since you're making no effort to do so yourself," Mr. Juncker said.

"I don't need to make an effort," Thorn snapped. "They already know me."

"And what they know of you doesn't seem to impress them," Mr. Juncker said.

Olivia stifled a gasp. There was decided tension between the two gentlemen, and Mr. Juncker was definitely fanning the flames of it. But why?

"To be fair, Mr. Juncker," Gwyn said, "Thorn sees no need to impress *me* because I'm his sister. Which is fine because I don't feel a need to impress *him,* either."

"And I prefer that gentlemen be themselves around me," Olivia said. "I don't need to have gentlemen flattering me. Not to mention that there's nothing more worrisome than a gentleman who is obviously keeping secrets."

"So you'd rather have the plain truth always, even if it might hurt your feelings?" Thorn asked.

Thinking of her father, Olivia met his gaze evenly. "I would."

"Don't be silly, my dear," Gwyn said. "No woman *really* wants to hear from her husband that she talks too loudly or her eyes look puffy first thing in the morning."

"That's a brother's task, not a husband's," Thorn said with a smirk. "I do my best to tell my sister the unvarnished truth."

Gwyn thrust her tongue out at him before turning to Olivia. "Trust me, there are some things a husband should keep secret from his wife for all time."

"If you say so," Olivia said. "As an unmarried lady I

don't know about that. But Mama would probably prefer that Papa be more honest with her about where he spends his evenings."

"Oh, in such a case as that, I agree," Gwyn said. "Joshua knows if I caught him doing anything he shouldn't with his evenings, I would hand him his head on a platter."

Thorn chuckled. "The only person Major Wolfe is afraid of in this world is my sister. Actually, she's the only person *I'm* afraid of."

Mr. Juncker shuddered. "Precisely why I'm still unwed."

"As am I." Thorn met Olivia's gaze. "Although I begin to see the advantages of having a wife."

"Do you?" Mr. Juncker said. "You never did before."

He'd taken the words right out of Olivia's mouth.

Thorn eyed his friend askance. "Feel free to leave whenever you please, Juncker."

"Thorn!" Gwyn said. "You're being very rude."

"It's all right, Lady Gwyn." Mr. Juncker stood. "I'm used to your brother's unfeeling treatment."

He struck a dramatic woe-is-me pose, making both Gwyn and Olivia laugh, although Thorn only raised an eyebrow.

"But honestly," Mr. Juncker continued, "I fear I've overstayed my welcome. Besides, there are women to be wooed, cards to be dealt, and brandy to be drunk. The night is young, and I intend to suck the very marrow from its bones." He stared at Thorn. "Feel free to join me."

"No, thank you," Thorn drawled. "I have several matters to attend to before we leave for Berkshire tomorrow, and marrow-sucking isn't one of them. But I assume I'll see you next time I'm in London?"

"Certainly." Mr. Juncker gave an elaborate bow to Olivia and Gwyn. "'Good night, good night! Parting is such sweet sorrow / That I shall say good night till it be morrow.'"

"I hope not," Thorn said. "We're leaving on the morrow. So I'll show you out."

"Good Lord, *I* will show him out," Gwyn said. "It's my home, after all."

"Forgive me, sis," Thorn said. "I didn't mean to over-step my bounds."

"Of course you did. It's what you do." Gwyn rose and headed for the door with Mr. Juncker. But as she reached it, she turned and made a face at her brother before she and Mr. Juncker walked out.

Olivia laughed.

Thorn merely rolled his eyes. "You'd think she was five."

"I'd think *you* were five." Olivia sniffed. "You were so rude to Mr. Juncker, baiting him all night."

Leaning forward, Thorn fixed her with a dark look. "You seem terribly concerned about Juncker's feelings. Were you hoping he might stay longer? Shall I call him back so you can flirt with him some more?"

"What? I wasn't flirting, for pity's sake. Clearly your jealousy is overriding your common sense."

"I am not jealous of that . . . that buffoon!" He crossed his arms over his chest. "You're the one who claimed I couldn't be because I'm a duke."

"I was talking about you being jealous of his play-writing. But tonight you're showing yourself to be jealous of his interest in *me*, too, although why that should be the case, I have no idea. You've always made it clear I'm good for only one thing . . . and it isn't marriage."

Thorn raked his fingers through his hair, mussing it thoroughly. "I never said that. I never even implied it."

"Right." She rose and tossed down her napkin. "I'm

going to bed. Would you please let your sister know I've retired?"

She rounded the table, but she wasn't quick enough to avoid Thorn, who met her at the end to catch her by the arm.

He scoured her attire with blatant impudence. "Did you wear that gown to tempt Juncker? Or to torment *me*?"

"I wore this gown because I like it," she said sweetly. "The fact that it makes you jealous is merely icing on the cake." Then she added, just to see how he would react, "And apparently Mr. Juncker likes it as well. He certainly stared at it enough."

Thorn's thunderous expression gave her pause. "He wasn't staring at the gown; he was staring at *you* in it." Checking to be sure he was blocking the footman's view, Thorn took one finger and dragged it down from her neck to between the swells of her bosom, then dropped his voice. "He was wondering how these taste, and what the nipples would feel like in his mouth. He was wondering if he dared get you alone to find out."

Despite the delicious shivers his words and caress were provoking in her, she managed to sound marginally calm. "So now you can read Mr. Juncker's mind, can you?"

"Oh, yes." He leaned in to whisper in her ear. "Because I can promise he was thinking the same things I was throughout dinner. That he wanted to engage in very wicked acts with you. Repeatedly. Often."

Struggling not to let his words turn her to jelly, she moved his finger away from her bodice. "You seem to have gleaned a great many naughty ideas from one look. But not everyone has your predilection for . . . sordid behavior."

"I can assure you that Juncker does."

"By the way you speak of him, I'd never have guessed

you two were as good friends as Grey said you were, Your Grace."

He shook his head. "You're the only person I know who can make 'Your Grace' sound like an insult."

"And you're the only one who takes insult from a perfectly appropriate honorific."

"Because you use it to put me in my place," he said.

"Now you can read *my* mind? Perhaps you should join the mesmerizers, sir. I'm sure they would love to have a man as brilliant as you."

"Ah, but would *you* love to have me?"

She took a sharp breath. "As what? Entertainment?"

"Olivia," he said softly. "That's not what I—"

A new voice sounded from the door. "Is my brother bothering you?" Gwyn asked. "Because he too has overstayed his welcome." Gwyn approached them as they took a step back from each other. "Come, Thorn, you have your own house. You should probably go stay in it. Especially with our 'long journey' ahead of us tomorrow."

"Of course," Thorn said, though his eyes were still on Olivia. "Very well, I'll be here at ten in the morning. Make sure you're both ready and packed."

"Fine." Gwyn pushed him. "Now go. Unless you want to hear me snoring in the carriage tomorrow, you must allow me and Olivia to get some sleep. So 'good night, sweet prince.'"

Thorn lifted an eyebrow. "You do realize that line is spoken by Horatio to a dead Hamlet, right?"

"Is it?" Gwyn remarked, a decided glint in her eye. "I had no idea."

"I'm merely saying I hope you're not wishing me dead."

"Certainly not." Gwyn winked at Olivia. "I'm just wishing you gone so Olivia and I can have some peace at last."

"Hmm." He kissed her cheek. "I'll see you in the morning."

Then he bowed to Olivia. "Unlike Juncker, I won't say good night until it's morrow. But I *will* wish you a good sleep, 'perchance to dream.'"

As he walked out, she sighed heavily. She'd rather *not* dream tonight. If she did, it would be of him. And she couldn't let him keep playing with her emotions. On the one hand, he seemed to have softened toward her a great deal. On the other hand, he didn't seem to have changed his feelings about marrying, and he'd told her very firmly at Gwyn's ball that he would never propose marriage again. So she should step carefully if she didn't want to end up walking off a cliff into ruin.

Because this time he clearly had no intention of making even a cursory attempt to rescue her.

Chapter Eleven

They left London at a decent hour the next morning. But although Thorn had hoped to have a pleasant chat with Olivia on the way, she and Gwyn had made that impossible. Endless discussion about Gwyn's upcoming confinement had lulled him into sleeping much of the way, especially since they'd ignored his attempts to change the subject.

Once they'd arrived at Rosethorn, he'd shown Olivia around the building he'd selected as the best location for her laboratory. But she'd insisted on having a footman—rather than him—help her set everything up.

Over the next three days, she'd also refused to let him enter the place while she was working, and when he'd protested, she'd reminded him of what had happened the last time he'd "invaded the sanctuary of my laboratory." It was hard to argue with that, especially now that he'd seen how much damage could truly be done if one behaved heedlessly in a chemistry laboratory.

Besides, he had plenty of work to do himself—meeting with tenants, consulting with his estate manager, and, at night, trying to finish his play. He'd also attempted to meet with the constable about his father's accident, but the man's wife had said he was in London and wouldn't return for a few days.

Yet, despite how Thorn filled his time, he still wished for dinners with Olivia. Or cozy meetings with her in his study or the library.

Obviously, after he'd acted like a jealous fool at Gwyn's, Olivia was determined to make him reap the consequences of his actions. Although honestly, he couldn't be sure if she was avoiding him or just thoroughly absorbed in her work. Whichever it was, he didn't like it.

So when he entered the breakfast room on their fourth day at Rosethorn to find no sign of Olivia yet again, he'd had enough.

"Aren't you up a bit early for you?" he growled at his sister.

Gwyn sipped her coffee and continued to read the newspaper. "Aren't you up a bit late for *you*?"

"I suppose. It took me a while to fall asleep." But only because he'd been trying to write. He nearly had his play done—it was only that pesky last scene that eluded him.

He filled his plate with toast and bacon, then took a seat opposite her. "I don't suppose you've seen our guest this morning."

"No," Gwyn said. "Nor have I been overly concerned about it. Last I checked, Rosethorn is a fairly safe place."

"That's what we thought about Carymont, too."

"But you took care of that here by posting a guard. So you have no reason to worry about her."

He bit back a curse. He wasn't worried. He was annoyed about not being able to see her. "Is she planning on eating *any* of her meals with us?"

"Does it matter? She's not here to be sociable. You made that perfectly clear when you asked me to chaper-one." With a sigh, Gwyn set down her paper. "How did you put it? Ah, yes. 'Don't expect her to be tramping about the countryside or going riding or talking about architecture with you. She has a task to complete and must not be disturbed.' Perhaps you should heed your own advice."

"I just didn't think she'd be quite this unsociable. And for this long, either."

"Three or four days?" Gwyn snorted. "That isn't so long. And I suspect you didn't think at all. Honestly, given how you behaved at dinner with Mr. Juncker, I don't blame her for wanting to keep to herself."

"He was being an arse," Thorn grumbled.

"Because he was using his celebrity to flirt with her?"

Thorn had to bite his tongue to keep from telling Gwyn that Juncker had no celebrity. But then he'd also have to tell her the whole story about his writing, and he didn't want to risk her revealing it to Olivia.

"You'd do the same in Mr. Juncker's place," Gwyn added with a sly grin, "and you know it."

"I suppose I would."

Apparently that settled the matter in Gwyn's head, for she returned to reading her newspaper. Sometimes he wondered if Gwyn had already guessed he was writing the Juncker plays. But surely she would tell him if she did.

Thwarted in his attempt to get information from her about Olivia, he picked up a paper Gwyn had already discarded and began to read as he ate. They sat there a long while in companionable silence.

Then Thorn's butler came in. "The parish constable is here to see you, Your Grace. He said you left a message for him at his home?"

"I did indeed. Please show him in here."

As the butler walked out, Gwyn narrowed her gaze on him. "Why are you speaking to the parish constable?"

"Because if Olivia determines that Grey's father was

poisoned, then our next step is to determine if our father's accident was something more."

"Oh, right."

Just then Constable Upton, a wizened old man with huge ears and bushy white eyebrows, was ushered in. With hat in hand, he bowed and said, "Your Grace. You wished to see me?"

"Yes, Upton. Thank you for coming."

"I'm sorry I couldn't do it sooner. Had business in London, y'see, and I only just got back late last night."

"No need to apologize. Indeed, we much appreciate your attending us so soon after your return home. Please, help yourself to some breakfast."

Upton relaxed now that he could tell he wasn't in any trouble. "I already ate this morning, Your Grace, but I wouldn't mind a cup of that coffee."

"Would you prefer tea?" Gwyn asked. "We have both."

"Coffee's fine, my lady."

As she poured Upton a cup of coffee, Thorn gestured to a chair. "Do have a seat, Constable."

Upton shot a wary glance at Gwyn as he sat down across from Thorn.

"Don't worry," Thorn added. "My sister knows all about what I wish to discuss with you, although I suppose we should close the door. It's probably unwise to let anyone else hear."

After determining how the constable wanted his coffee, Gwyn doctored it accordingly and handed it to him. Meanwhile Thorn rose to shut the door, then debated how to begin.

Might as well be blunt. "We have some questions for you about the carriage accident that took our father's life. You were constable then, too, weren't you?"

Upton thrust his chest out. "Aye, Your Grace. I've served as constable for forty years."

"When you're not running the blacksmith shop in town. Is that correct?"

"Aye, along with my boy. Got to make a living somehow, Your Grace."

"Of course," Thorn said. "No one questions that." The constabulary was unpaid, so most constables had to do it alongside their regular work. "Here's the thing. It has come to our attention that someone may have purposely damaged our father's carriage in order to cause the accident that killed him."

The constable frowned. "I don't know nothing about that, Your Grace."

Gwyn cleared her throat. "You understand, sir, that no one is accusing you. We are simply trying to get at the truth. After all, it wasn't just our father who was killed. Two footmen died in the accident as well, and the coachman was gravely injured. It was quite a tragedy."

"Exactly," Thorn said hastily, grateful to have Gwyn there since she had a way of putting people at their ease. He wasn't quite as good at that. "And you're the only person who might be able to tell us anything. The estate manager who ran Rosethorn while Gwyn and I were abroad with our mother and stepfather died a few years ago, so we can't ask him. But I thought you might have examined Father's carriage after the accident. That you might remember how it looked."

"Anything you can tell us would be appreciated," Gwyn added, casting the man a kindly smile.

The constable drank some coffee, then set the cup down. "The carriage ended up as kindling on account of it being so mangled in the accident that it couldn't be repaired. But the coachman's perch was found a ways behind the carriage, and we did think at the time as perhaps it came off first, spooking the horses into bolting and causing the accident."

A chill skittered down Thorn's spine. "So the screws holding the perch on might have been loosened?" he asked. When Gwyn's husband had determined a few months ago that someone had tried to damage Thorn's own carriage, that was exactly how the person had done it.

"I suppose it's possible. Whatever was done, the carriage rolled not too far down the road and broke open, crushing His Grace beneath it and dashing the footmen against a boulder." He shook his head. "Forgive me, Duke, but I hope you're wrong about the cause of it. Your father was a good man and an excellent landlord. His tenants loved him. I can't think of nobody who'd have wished him dead."

"Thank you for saying so, Constable," Gwyn said. "Since neither of us were even born at the time of his death, we must rely on good people like you to tell us about him. Mother doesn't like to talk about him. They were so very happy that his death nearly broke her heart, or so she has always said."

Thorn held his tongue. Perhaps it was time he pressed Mother for the truth. After he pressed the constable, that is. "I do have one question regarding what happened that day. Someone who knew my parents said that Father was in a hurry to get to London, and that his urging the coachman to a reckless speed was why the accident happened. Do you know if that could have been the case?"

He felt Gwyn's gaze on him. He might end up having to tell *her* what information Lady Norley had blackmailed him with, but perhaps that was just as well. As Shakespeare once wrote, "truth will out." And he was tired of keeping his late father's secrets.

"Begging your pardon, Your Grace," the constable said, "but that don't sound right. His Grace wasn't the reckless sort of young man. And knowing he was to be a father very soon would have kept him from recklessness anyway."

Thorn forced a smile. "I'm sure you're right." He toyed with the handle of his empty coffee cup. "One more question before you go. Why *did* my father head off to London that day? Mother said he had urgent business, but she didn't seem to know what it was." Or she hadn't wanted to say, which was more likely. "And as you pointed out, he was expecting to be a father any day. So why rush off and leave our mother with only servants to attend her?"

The constable was already shaking his head. "He didn't leave the duchess by herself. There was a house full of people—his family, her family, some of her friends who wanted to be here for the birth. . . . She wasn't alone, in any case."

Thorn and Gwyn exchanged glances. Their mother had never said anything about houseguests. Then again, she didn't like to talk about that day at all.

"You don't happen to know who exactly was here, do you?" Thorn asked.

"No, Duke, I don't. I'm sorry." He pushed his cup aside. "But as for why your father left, the gossip in town was he hurried off to London to fetch some famous accoucheur to deliver the babe. It was looking like you were coming early, and everyone was worried about that. Of course, once you proved to be twins, that explained the early birth. And our local midwife did just fine in delivering you both."

Because Mother hadn't had a choice. By the time she'd gone into labor, Father had already died trying to bring back that "famous accoucheur." Thorn preferred that explanation of Father's sudden London trip to the one Lady

Norley had offered. Perhaps she'd been wrong. Perhaps she'd even lied. It did seem odd that Father would have gone off to visit a mistress while they'd had a houseful of guests at Rosethorn.

And why hadn't Mother ever mentioned that, anyway? Perhaps because it hadn't signified when compared to the awful circumstances surrounding Father's death.

In any case, the constable had told them more than they knew before. It was nothing concrete, but it did support the idea that Father might have had good reason for hurrying to London. And the fact that there had been so many guests around meant that in both cases—the death of Grey's father and the death of his and Gwyn's father—there'd been a sort of house party going on. So they should pursue that angle.

Thorn stood. "Thank you, sir. You've been invaluable in giving us a place to start." As the constable rose as well, Thorn held out his hand. "We appreciate your candor and the information you did have to offer."

The constable shook Thorn's hand. "I only wish I could have been of more help, Your Grace." He picked up his hat and headed for the door. Then he paused. "But if you're still curious about the accident, you ought to pay a visit to your late father's coachman."

"He's alive?" Gwyn said. "We understood that he hadn't survived his injuries."

"Well," Upton said, "he didn't entirely. His head ain't quite right, and his legs don't work. But he still might remember something of use to you. Your mother made sure he received the best of care and a pension, too, so he's to be looked after for the rest of his days. Just keep in mind that he was in his forties at the time of the accident, so now he's in his seventies. Lives over in Newbury with his daughter."

Another surprise. But Thorn should have known. He paid the funds for that pension, yet he'd never asked who the man was that received it. It was a sobering realization. What else did he not know about the past?

"I best be getting on then," the constable said. "Let me know if you wish me to bring you over to visit the coachman, Your Grace." He nodded to Gwyn. "And thank you for the coffee, my lady. You grew up to be as gracious as your mother."

Gwyn smiled warmly. "You couldn't have paid me a higher compliment, sir."

After he left, Gwyn took a seat at the table once more. "Well! That was interesting."

"To say the least." Thorn sat down and poured himself more coffee. "Did you know about that house party? Because I didn't."

"That was the first *I'd* heard of it, to be sure." She tapped her chin. "We should ask Mother who was here."

"Absolutely. I'll leave that to you. You're better at not rousing her suspicions."

Gwyn rose to go look out the window. "I wonder if we're making a mistake in not telling Mama what we're investigating. She's the one whose husbands were quite possibly murdered. Shouldn't she at least know that? She might be able to give us information that we require."

"Yes, but if we're wrong, then we've roused her painful memories for nothing."

Gwyn shook her head. "Mama isn't as fragile as you fellows seem to think. Besides, from what I gleaned from Lady Hornsby during my debut, Mama barely tolerated Grey's father. He married her for her fortune, which he then looted as soon as the wedding was over. She never speaks of him with any kind of affection."

"True, but he also gave her a son. Whom she loves dearly."

"My point is, her only memories of Grey's father are bad ones, so rousing those won't be a problem. I suspect she's happy he died when he did."

"Probably." Thorn drank more coffee. "Especially since she found our father as a result. Things were different between her and him than between her and Grey's father, though." For the first time in nine years, he could almost believe in that again.

"I think they truly were in love," Gwyn said.

"Or they truly believed they were, anyway," he said.

"Are you still so cynical?" Gwyn asked. "Hasn't Olivia changed your opinion about love in the least?"

He snorted. "Certainly not." And surely Olivia was too practical to believe in love.

But Gwyn was wrong about it being time they told Mother their suspicions concerning the deaths. It was too soon. They didn't even have enough evidence to prove the murders or who might have done them.

Telling his half brothers, Sheridan and Heywood, on the other hand, was another matter. When Sheridan had first pointed out that the two most recent dukes of Armitage, including their stepfather, might have been murdered, Grey, and later, Thorn, had been skeptical. Now both of them were less so. And since the current Duke of Armitage was Sheridan, Thorn could no longer afford to ignore the possibility that Sheridan might be next.

That thought rolled around in his head throughout the day. While he was riding out to speak to a tenant farmer about switching to growing barley next year. Or when he was talking to the master of the hounds about buying a few more retrievers to fill out their kennel. Or even after dinner while he relaxed in his banyan and hunted through the printed copies of his plays to see if he'd ever done a final scene like the one he was preparing to write.

Thoughts of Sheridan and Heywood were still at the back of his mind when he strolled out into the hallway to find Olivia coming up the stairs with brisk steps and bright eyes. Her gown—a coarse one of bottle-green fustian with cap sleeves—seemed to be the one she preferred for working with chemicals. To that was added a white apron.

For some reason, he imagined her in nothing but that apron, and his pulse leapt into double-time. He wanted to strip everything from her. He wanted to see her naked.

Damn. "Up late again, I see." Thorn closed the door to his study behind him. It wouldn't do for her to wander in and see his work in progress spread out across his desk.

"So are you. But I'm glad." She smiled as she paused outside his study. "How is it you always guess when I've made an important discovery I'm just itching to tell you about?"

"Perhaps I really can read your mind."

"I doubt that," she said with a lilting laugh. "Because if you could, you'd know I have done it!" She continued up the stairs at a slow pace that invited him to follow.

So he did. "Done what? Is this another of those remarkable developments in chemistry that I can't even understand when you explain them?"

"No, indeed. This is the culmination of everything we hoped for. I found arsenic exactly where I'd postulated that it might be—in his stomach, which means his food had been poisoned with a large dose. And the fact that I didn't find any in his other organs only confirms that the poison had been fed to him."

"That's impressive. Congratulations. So that means your method works just as you had expected?"

"It does. I can write an article about it as soon as you and Grey are comfortable with that."

"You're sure it can be trusted as evidence in a court of law?"

"I am. Isn't that amazing?"

"It is," he said as they reached the next floor. He found her excitement amusing, considering what had caused it. "You've proved that Grey's father was murdered. Amazing, indeed."

Her face fell. "When you say it like that, it sounds *awful*." Slowly, she headed toward the suite of rooms she'd been using, across from Gwyn's bedchamber. "I shouldn't be excited over any man's death."

"I'm just teasing you. He died long ago." He prayed his sister was asleep by now. Otherwise, their voices might impel her to come chaperone, and he was enjoying having Olivia to himself. "Forgive me, but I find it funny the way you get so delighted about the results of your experiments."

"Well, I've always been more comfortable in the laboratory. I don't understand people very well. I try to, but sometimes their behavior just isn't logical."

"I agree with you there. People are peculiar beings."

She nodded. "As Shakespeare said, 'For man—'"

"'—is a giddy thing.'"

"Yes! I do love that line."

"And I do realize your success in finding the arsenic is quite an accomplishment, not just for you, but for all of us. It means we haven't been imagining things."

She paused outside her sitting room. "You mean about Grey's father being murdered?"

He glanced at the door to his sister's bedchamber. "More than that. But it's a long story, which we can discuss in the morning. I don't want to wake Gwyn."

"Of course." She lowered her voice. "Why don't you come into my sitting room for a bit? Unless you're too tired to talk."

The chance to be alone with her outweighed any weariness he might be feeling just now. "I'm fine," he said, and opened the door for her.

Once they'd both entered, he closed the door behind them. She didn't seem to notice or care. But after what had happened between them the night of the explosion, he wasn't taking any chances on their being caught, not by Gwyn and not by one of his servants. He wanted to at least kiss her, and for that he needed privacy.

"Give me a moment." She walked through the connecting door to her bedchamber.

He heard her dismissing her maid for the night, and his blood roared through his veins. Clearly he wasn't the only one who craved privacy.

When she reentered the room, she met his heated gaze with a defensive one. "I don't want her waiting up half the night for me. She's done it enough as it is."

"I'm sure that's true."

Now that they were alone, she wouldn't meet his gaze. "I suppose you're the one I must thank for this lovely suite." She swept her hand to indicate the sitting room with its settee upholstered in emerald-green damask and its matching curtains.

"Not me." He stared her down, willing her to look at him. "I would have put you in the bedchamber adjoining mine downstairs."

That startled her. "Very amusing, but unlikely. Your sister would have protested, *I* would have protested, and even you know you can't be that blatant."

"Can't I?"

Her cheeks pinkened. "Anyway, it's a lovely suite. You may not realize this, but green is my favorite color."

He practically bit his tongue off to keep from saying that anyone with eyes would know that. "It should be. You look beautiful in it."

"I never . . . That's not why." She swallowed hard. "I . . . I just like the color." She steadied her shoulders. "But we're supposed to be talking about the murder of Grey's father and how it means you aren't 'imagining things.'"

Damn. She really *had* only dismissed her maid out of kindness for the servant and not out of any eagerness to let him bed her. Meanwhile, he was in a fever pitch of excitement at just the possibility of taking her to bed.

"I'd rather talk about what happens next," he said.

"I took some hasty notes about my methods, so I'll have to get those in order tomorrow. And we *must* write Grey to tell him the news."

"That's not what I was referring to. I meant what happens next for *us*. You and me."

Her gaze shot to his. "I—I haven't really thought about it."

"You should. Because this might very well be our last night together. You've done what Grey asked, and now there's little left for you to do until the trial. And since I haven't encountered you in all the years since that morning I proposed to you, it's unlikely we'll be seeing each other again. Is that what you want?"

She tipped up her chin. "I think I should be asking that question of *you*."

"All I know is the thought of never seeing you again . . ." *Drives a spike through my chest.* No, that revealed far too much. "Doesn't sit well with me."

"Nor me," she said breathlessly.

"Are you sure? When we first met, you didn't seem to like me all that much."

"Because you were behaving like an arse." She softened. "Although you showed yourself to be . . . more appealing once I got to know you."

"Nine years later."

"And even nine years ago." She wandered to the window to look out over the lawn. "Our first kiss was . . . was . . ."

"Special?"

"My first kiss ever."

That surprised him. "Really? You took to it rather . . . well."

She shot him a sly look over her shoulder. "Men aren't the only ones with desires, you know. For me, our kiss was magical."

He snorted. "Not magical enough to coax you into marrying me." When she shook her head at him, he held up his hand. "I know, I know. My proposal left much to be desired. But you did say when we were at Grey's that you probably wouldn't have married me even if I'd proposed more . . . courteously."

"Nine years ago. But you and I have both changed since then. You've become more cynical, while I've learned there are certain advantages to . . . being around a man like you."

His blood roaring in his ears, he walked toward her. "Such as?"

"Companionship, for one. I find it stimulating to talk to a fellow who appreciates my accomplishments in chemistry even if he doesn't understand them." She faced him fully as he approached her. "Who shares my interest in the theater, among other things."

"You find talking to a man about chemistry and the theater stimulating, eh?" He came near enough so he could smell her erotic scent, see her eyes darken with desire. "I find it stimulating to be this close to you." He cupped her cheek in his hand. "To touch you." He lowered his lips to within a half inch of hers. "To kiss you. You have a mouth made for kissing."

So he did precisely that.

Chapter Twelve

Olivia could hardly think when he was distracting her with his lips and tongue and teeth. Why must he kiss so divinely, with an angel's sweet tenderness and a devil's hot urgency? The combination turned her knees weak.

She wanted more of everything . . . his mouth, his hands . . . his hard body hot against her. His loose banyan of cobalt-blue silk whispered over her arms, as if even the fabric wished to caress her, arouse her.

He drew back to say hoarsely, "I've missed you."

"Me? Or *this*?"

"Can't I miss both?" Without warning, he hoisted her up to sit on the wide windowsill and tugged out her fichu so he could kiss and suck and tongue her bare skin, from her throat to the upper swells of her breasts. The mere rasp of his evening whiskers against her skin made her eager for more of him.

She clutched his shoulders and let the pleasure of having him against her wash over her like a warm bath. "Thorn, what are we doing?"

"I don't know what you're doing, but *I'm* taking advantage of you." As if to emphasize the fact, he slid his fingers slowly through her hair, which was still in the chignon she always used for working, and let her hairpins fall where they may. "My God, but your hair is lovely. It shines like a sunny summer day . . . or a field of barley in autumn."

He was as poetic as Mr. Juncker. She wondered if he realized that.

"Thorn, be serious."

His gaze burned into her. "I'm always serious about hair."

She shook her head, making her hair fall even further. "I mean, don't you think perhaps this isn't . . . very wise?"

"Yet here I am doing it anyway." As if in a trance, he spread her hair out over her shoulders. "That's what we rakehells do, you know." He nuzzled her breasts, making her yearn for more.

She kissed his temple, then his hair, and made a last ditch protest. "My dear reckless rakehell, aren't you worried someone will happen upon us?"

"Not at this hour."

The reminder that everyone else was in bed, that they could behave with impunity, was enough to rouse her. And why shouldn't she be with him? It wasn't as if she needed to save her virtue. After this, she meant to be a chemist her whole life. To be alone.

The thought depressed her, making her throw herself even more into their . . . activities.

He untied her apron and tossed it over the settee, then dragged her skirts up above her stockings so he could move between her legs. The thickness of his arousal pushed at the part of her already eager for him, making her sigh and ache. The contrast of his heat there and the cold of the window against her back made her shiver.

"Let's move somewhere warmer, shall we?" Thorn said. "Put your legs around me."

When she did, just to see what he would do, he carried

her away from the window and into her bedchamber through the door she hadn't meant to leave open. Or had she?

Just the movement of his body against her bare privates turned her molten. Was it wrong that she always felt wet down there when he did these things? Was that normal?

She didn't care. Dear Lord, but he was driving her dangerously, thoroughly mad.

He set her down on the high mattress of her bed, then cupped her head in his hands and gazed down into her eyes. "I want you. And I believe you want me. Am I wrong about that?"

"No." She kicked off her shoes, already eager to begin. "But I don't wish to simply be one of your many conquests."

"There's nothing simple about this. Or about you. You couldn't be a mere conquest of mine if you tried."

The words oddly reassured her. She knew she ought to beware them. Supposedly, a man like him would say anything to get a woman into bed. Yet this felt . . . different somehow.

Or was she just being terribly naive?

Either way, she knew in her heart she'd already made her choice. Him in her bed. Tonight. She might never get another chance to find out what being with a man was like. What being with *him* was like. In all this time she'd never met any other man who even remotely appealed to her. Thorn had spoiled her for the rest of them.

He shrugged off his banyan, then bent on one knee in front of her to slide her skirts up again, so he could untie her garters and draw down her stockings. Slowly. Seductively. The very motion made her want to pull them back up just so he could slip them back down again.

"So I assume this is a yes," he choked out as he ran his

fingers over the smoothness of her thighs. "That you mean to share a bed with me tonight."

"And here I thought you were merely playing lady's maid," she teased him.

He eyed her askance. "I fear I'm not the right sex for that."

"Let me just make sure." She unbuttoned his waistcoat and pushed it off, then undid the three buttons of his shirt so she could pull it off over his head to bare his chest.

"My, my," she said. "Definitely not a lady's maid." How magnificent his chest was! A few years ago, she'd seen a line drawing of Michelangelo's *David*, and ever since, she'd imagined Thorn as that sculpture, but in full living color. Still, she hadn't thought to add, in her imagination, sprinklings of dusky hair across his upper half and a narrowing line of hair leading down to his navel.

She ran her hands over his muscles, which were every bit as sculpted as the statue's. Except that Thorn's flesh was warm and responsive, the muscles flexing beneath her touch in a most gratifying way.

A guttural groan sounded low in his throat when she thumbed his nipples, then pressed a kiss against the hairy flesh between them. He smelled so good she wanted to rub herself all over him. What an odd notion!

But when she slid her hands down to the buttons of his trousers, he growled, "My turn." Then he pushed her skirts up to her waist and bent his head a little to bury his mouth between her thighs.

She couldn't believe it! Was he actually licking her there?

He soon had her in a frenzy of excitement, then pulled back to fix her with a hungry look. "You taste like heaven, sweeting. Shall I do more?"

"Yes, oh, yes." She caught his head and urged him back, and with a chuckle he complied.

Then he put his tongue inside her the way he'd put his finger a few days ago. Oh, dear Lord, how marvelous! How intoxicating. This was a drug she could easily come to crave.

He started flicking his tongue over a spot that felt tender and needy with each lash of his tongue. She found herself making strange mewling noises and undulating against him until suddenly he drew back.

"Not yet, my dear. I want you fully naked first." Using his handkerchief to wipe his mouth, he stared down at her mons. "Lovely as this is, I want to see the rest of you—every inch laid bare for me."

Even the words made her frantic for more of whatever he'd just been doing to her.

As if he knew he'd made her legs too wobbly for her to stand, he got up off the floor so he could sit beside her. Then he turned her so he could undo her gown where she sat.

Between the two of them they got it and her corset off. Then it only took mere seconds for him to have her shift off, too, leaving her with nothing but her hair to hide her from his gaze.

He ran a hand down her back to her bottom. "You're a goddess, sweeting." He brought his hands around her from behind to cup both her breasts, fondling them shamelessly. "From these lovely ladies"—he skimmed one hand down her belly to cup her privates below—"to this pouting beauty. Look in the mirror. I want you to see what I see."

The mirror? She glanced around and realized that the two of them were perfectly captured in the looking glass opposite her bed. Part of her wondered if that was his purpose, if he'd brought other women here for this.

Part of her just reveled in his expression of pure, savage need as he rubbed the nipple of one breast while using the fingers on his other hand to arouse her below. Merely seeing him caressing her made her slick and wet.

"When do I get *my* turn?" she asked. "I want to see you naked, too." She was curious about the thickening bulge in his trousers that she'd only had a few minutes to fondle the last time they were this intimate.

"Oh, God, yes," he rasped.

He kicked off his slippers, then stood to unbutton his trousers and drawers before shoving them off along with his stockings.

"There," he said as he stood before her with his hands resting impudently on his hips. "Look your fill. But don't take too long, or I'll embarrass myself."

She didn't know how he could possibly do that, given that he was already standing naked before her, but it was most enlightening to see him in his full glory. The line drawing of *David* had a much smaller, much tamer bundle of a man's privates.

Thorn's thick rod of flesh thrusting boldly toward her from a nest of dark hair, with large ballocks hanging down, was another thing entirely. He was no statue for certain.

She swallowed hard. That *thing* of his was supposed to go inside her, the way his finger and his tongue had?

Dear Lord.

She reached out to touch it, and it twitched as if it had a mind of its own. Thorn caught her hand. "Not now, sweeting, or I won't be able to do this right, I swear."

"There's a right way and a wrong way?"

"Yes. Sort of." He moved closer. "Lie down, Olivia, and I'll show you the right way." He added, under his breath, "Assuming I can survive that long."

So she did as he bade, and the next thing she knew he was kneeling between her legs and looming over her.

"You're sure that you want this?" he asked.

"How can I be sure if I've never done it?"

He groaned. "I can stop now before anything happens, if that's what you want."

Too much had already happened. She refused to go back. "Don't stop," she whispered.

"Thank God," he said hoarsely, then pressed the tip of his . . . his *member* inside her and began to inch his way farther in.

At first it was maddening. It didn't seem to fit at all.

He must have thought the same thing. "You're so tight, sweeting. So warm and wet and tight."

"Are you certain this is the *right* way?"

"Oh, yes, trust me," he choked out. "It's as right as it can be . . . for me. But I don't imagine the first time . . . feels wonderful to a virgin. I'll try to make . . . it better for you."

Grabbing a pillow, he then lifted her hips enough to get it under her. She wasn't sure why, but the change in position did improve matters.

"Better?" he growled.

She nodded. She couldn't speak, consumed by the sensation of having him so intimately joined to her. He seemed to grow bigger inside her the farther he went. But then he reached down to rub the hard knot that seemed to hold all her enjoyable sensations, and like a dam bursting, pleasure flooded her.

With a gasp, she arched against his finger, while he began to pull out, then thrust in, over and over in an exquisite, unfamiliar rhythm. This was out of her realm of experience, and all she could do was clasp the well-wrought arms that held him above her and pray he took her with him to wherever he was going.

Because he was definitely going somewhere, what with his muscles straining and his face flushing. Now she began to feel as if she too was going somewhere. His quickening strokes drubbed that knot of pleasure even more, and his eyes burned into hers with such intensity that she was soon gasping and sighing and arching up to meet his thrusts, eager for every delicious feeling searing its way through her.

"Ah, my . . . lovely dear. You're killing me. You feel . . . so *damned* good."

"So do you," she answered, and realized it wasn't a lie. "This is . . . amazing."

It was. Shocks of heat radiated through her, growing bigger, stronger, hotter until suddenly they arced inside her, making her cry out from the intensity of her ecstasy.

As if that set off his own release, he drove into her with a hoarse cry of his own, then spilled himself inside her. As he lay atop her, his body still joined to hers and his head cradled in the bend of her neck, a contentment stole over her that was beyond anything she'd ever felt. She belonged here, with him. He might not realize it yet, but she did.

That was enough. For now.

Thorn lay beside her, his heart no longer thundering and his body replete with satisfaction. Yet he wanted her again. And again and again and again.

It made no sense. Nine years ago, he would have been panicked, knowing that a marriage was now in his future. Hell, he'd been panicked back then after they'd been caught kissing. Instead, he felt nothing but contentment. And a faint echo of his earlier desire.

If he made love to her again, he could do it with less urgency and more care. But that was a mad train of thought. It implied that he . . . *needed* her. And he didn't need anyone.

He looked down to where her naked body was curled against him, and his blood roused at just the sight. God, he was in trouble now. He reached over to grab the other side of the coverlet and, for the sake of his sanity, pulled it over the parts of her he found tempting. Although honestly, if he followed that logic, he'd be covering her from head to toe.

Her response was to lay her head on his bare shoulder. "That was not what I expected."

He didn't even have to ask what "that" referred to. "Worse? Or better?"

"Oh, better, most definitely."

She toyed with the hair on his chest, and he felt a stirring in his cock. He willed it to go away, even though that had never worked before, especially around her. But he had to try.

"What were you expecting?" he asked, hoping for something to get his mind off the fact that he wanted her again.

"You know—what they always tell young ladies." She fixed her gaze somewhere beyond him. "That once you're married, you'll have painful relations with your husband, but it's all right because he'll gift you with jewels and furs and such."

Good God. *That* certainly dampened his arousal. "In other words, they tell young ladies they'll be whores after they marry."

Her gaze shot to him. "That's what *I* always said! Why do you think I wasn't keen to marry? I mean, how is a society marriage any different than being a man's mistress?"

"For one thing, your children won't be born bastards." He smoothed out a lock of her disordered and highly erotic hair. "If 'painful relations' was what you expected, why did you let me . . . I mean . . ."

"Because I wasn't sure *what* to believe. And when I'm not sure, I always want to experience things for myself."

"Like an experiment."

"Exactly!" She beamed at him.

So *that* was what it was like to have her beaming at him. No wonder Juncker had been so pleased with himself. Just seeing her like that made Thorn's chest swell.

He chuckled. "I much prefer that sort of experiment to the kind you've been doing."

"It's certainly more . . . enjoyable in some respects." Her expression turned pensive. "And speaking of those experiments, do you think Grey will be *terribly* upset to learn the truth about his father's death?"

"I doubt it. He has suspected it for some time. Besides, he never knew his father, and given what he'd heard from others about the man, the late duke wasn't a very nice person."

"That's rather sad. Forgive me for asking, but if he never knew his father, why does he care if the man was murdered?"

Thorn debated how much to tell her about Grey's father, but at this point she might as well know the whole of it. At the very least, she'd be testifying at the trial of the murderer, assuming they could learn who the man was. Besides, she might have some insight into the other deaths, too. She was, after all, a clever woman.

"Grey is afraid that the person who poisoned his father may also have murdered my and Gwyn's father and our stepfather, not to mention Sheridan's late uncle."

Her eyes widened. "But . . . but I thought your father died in a carriage accident."

"He did. I spoke to the local constable this morning, however, and he said it was conceivable that the accident came about because someone damaged the carriage beforehand. Perhaps even loosened the screws on the coachman's perch, since it was found at a distance from the carriage."

"Dear heaven. How awful!"

"This is all conjecture, you realize. So we may have trouble proving it. But I'm willing to look into it to see what I can learn."

"What about the other deaths? Did *those* people die of poison, too?"

"Afraid not. That would make everything simple. The death of Grey's father was actually the easiest to prove, which was why we were investigating it first. The manner of death for the others is different. But their deaths did seem suspicious—all were accidents and the like. That's why this is important to us. Because none of us can feel safe without being sure of the reasons for the deaths of our fathers . . . and for two of Beatrice's and Joshua's uncles, one of them being our stepfather."

She hugged him closer as if to protect him. "That does seem to be a lot of deaths."

"Especially when all four were dukes. And two of them died relatively young."

"How shocking! And your poor mother, to be widowed three times. How does she bear it?"

"For one thing, we haven't involved her in this investigation, as I mentioned before. We don't want to say anything to her until we're certain they were murdered."

"That's wise. No point in alarming her unless you're sure."

"Precisely."

"But what I meant was how does she bear the loss of three husbands? That has to have been difficult."

"It was. It is." He smiled. "Thankfully, she has all of us to lean on."

Olivia shifted to lie on her back, staring up at the canopy. "Oh, but that's not the same, and you know it. I can't imagine being used to having a husband, and somehow having him torn from me through no fault of my own. Even once would be awful. But three times? That would be horrible."

She had a point. And he did know Mother had suffered. It was a vote for never marrying, in his opinion. Yet Mother obviously didn't feel that way.

"To be honest," he said, "our mother only truly loved one of her husbands—in the grandiose sense of a romantic love for the ages, that is."

Olivia turned to stare at him. "Your father, you mean. The one Mama said had a mistress."

"Yes. Though I'm not entirely sure I believe your stepmother on that score anymore."

"But you used to, apparently. Is that why you don't put any stock in love and happiness in marriage?" she whispered. "Because of what Mama said about your parents?"

Damn. They'd wandered into a subject he'd rather not discuss just now. He knew he must make an offer for Olivia's hand, but he wasn't ready to do so.

You're afraid she'll turn you down again, his conscience whispered.

That wasn't true. He wasn't afraid of anything.

Yet here he was, talking around the fact that she deserved better. He shook off that thought.

"Well?" she persisted. "Is that why you don't believe in love and happiness? Because of what Mama told you?"

He sighed. "Partly. But partly because I've seen first-hand how unhappy a marriage can be." He turned the tables on her. "And so have you. You said yourself that your stepmother might as well be a widow given how often your father leaves her alone."

"Yes, but I don't think their marriage is unhappy. They don't fight. They just . . . don't do much of anything to-gether. Neither did Papa and my mother, to the extent that I can recall. He's just . . . not the marrying sort. I suspect *he* has a mistress. Or a string of them. Although honestly, I don't know for certain. He would never be so foolish as to flaunt them." She met his gaze steadily. "So whose un-happy marriage did you witness 'firsthand'? Your mother's to your stepfather?"

"Not them. Like your parents, they weren't unhappy exactly. But neither were they in love. They made a practi-cal match, and it served them well. I think they had true affection for each other . . . just not the sort of romantic love the poets praise." He smoothed a lock of her hair over her shoulder. "In fact, I would hazard a guess they were happy precisely because love did *not* enter into their marriage."

"So, once again, not an 'unhappy' marriage you've 'seen firsthand.' I wager you're just using that as an excuse for why you continue as a carefree bachelor."

He tensed. *Offer for her, you arse. That's what she wants.*

Damn his conscience. Instead, he said, "Trust me, I've witnessed plenty of unhappy society unions from the viewpoint of various married women's beds. They thought being bedded by me would make up for the misery of their marriages. They thought wrong."

"'Various married women's beds'?" A pained expression crossed her face. "How many?"

Why must he keep blathering things that only made the situation worse? He definitely didn't want to talk about how many women he'd bedded. Not with *her,* anyway. "Enough to make me skeptical of my prospects for happiness with the typical society bride. The young ladies trying to capture my affections only wanted me because I'm a wealthy duke. They never cared about me in particular. For that matter, neither did any of those married women. I was always just a means to an end."

She eyed him askance. "How can you be sure of that? With the young ladies, I mean."

"I just am." He shifted to lie on his side, facing her. "Must we talk about this now?" Slipping his hand over her breast, he pressed a kiss to her lips. "I can think of any number of things more enjoyable to do."

Despite his fondling of her bountiful breast, she seemed to hesitate. Then with a forced smile, she slid her hand behind his head to pull him back for another kiss.

He was safe. He *would* offer for her, just not at this very moment. Not while they still had these few hours alone.

Scoundrel. Blackguard. Reprobate.

Yes, he was all those things. And he meant to be them a short while longer. There was plenty of time later for offering marriage.

Chapter Thirteen

As she awakened, Olivia looked for Thorn, but he'd left her bed. And judging from the bright sunshine flooding the room, that was probably wise of him. Still, there was no reason for *her* to rush around, now that he was gone.

She pulled the covers up to her chin with a sigh of pure contentment. Thorn had made love to her *twice*. And though he'd left her rather sore after the second time, she still couldn't help feeling like a woman. Not a girl anymore, although obviously she hadn't been a girl in some time.

A woman, yes. *His* woman.

With a quick pang, she turned her head to look at his pillow. That's when she remembered that somewhere during their second time, they'd climbed under the covers. But now it was almost as if he'd never been here.

She thrust out her chin. Nonsense. He'd been here, and he'd behaved as if she was special to him.

You mean, like last time? When your mother had to blackmail him into offering marriage?

"Hush," she said aloud to her saner self. "Let me enjoy this a while longer, will you?"

Suddenly, her temporary lady's maid burst into her bedchamber. "Oh, thank heaven you're finally awake, miss. Your stepmother has come, and she's spitting mad. She's with His Grace right now in the drawing room and asking for you."

It took a moment for that to sink in, but when it did, panic replaced her delicious haze of satisfaction. Mama, here?

Dear Lord. Something must be wrong. Otherwise, how had Mama known that Olivia had come to Rosethorn? And Thorn was *with* her mother? This just got worse and worse.

Olivia was about to leave the bed when she realized she was completely naked, which the maid was bound to find suspicious.

So she told the young woman, "Would you mind calling for a pot of coffee? I'll never make it through a conversation with my mother otherwise."

"Of course. But you should probably hurry, miss. His Grace seems a bit . . . um . . . annoyed at Lady Norley."

"No doubt," Olivia muttered.

As soon as the maid had gone out into the hall, Olivia leapt from the bed, found her nightdress, and dragged it on. Then she froze as she spotted last night's clothes draped over a chair. She knew *she* hadn't done that, which meant that *he* had.

She ran into the sitting room to look at the windowsill where he'd undone her chignon. There was nary a hairpin to be seen. He must have gathered them all and put them somewhere.

Sure enough, when she returned to the other room, she found them on her dressing table. Her heart sank. He'd gone to great pains not to have her caught doing something that might ruin her for good.

She could take that one of two ways. Either he was being scrupulously courteous to the woman he meant to marry. Or he was covering his tracks so he wouldn't *have* to marry her. No doubt that was something he'd done countless times before with his married lovers.

The maid returned to announce that the coffee was on its way, and Olivia thanked her. Then the young woman walked over to the bed and started as she saw something.

"Miss," the maid said, pointing to the coverlet. "There is . . . um . . . blood here."

Oh, dear, Thorn had missed one crucial indication of their . . . indiscretion. Olivia thought fast. "I came in so late and was so exhausted that I barely had time to disrobe before I had to lie down on the bed or risk falling down. When I woke in the night, I realized my menses had begun. I was too tired to do more than change out of my shift into my nightdress and grab some rags. I didn't realize I had bled on the coverlet. I hope it doesn't prove too difficult to clean."

Olivia knew she was babbling, but she was desperate to hide what had happened. Because if Thorn had gone to such great lengths to do so, he might have had a reason, and she didn't want to be truly ruined just because she couldn't lie convincingly.

Though the maid blushed, her suspicious expression had vanished entirely. "Oh, no, miss, don't you worry your head about it in the least. We women know how that happens. If you'll just give me your soiled shift, I'll make sure it's taken care of."

"Thank you."

The maid helped her dress and didn't say another word about Olivia's menses. Olivia could only hope the young woman had believed her.

But Mama was here. Olivia found that more reassuring than she should have. It would be nice to have a shoulder to cry on if Thorn proved to be as much of a rakehell as he'd seemed last night.

Even if he did offer marriage, he'd already as much as said he would never offer her love and happiness. And he probably meant it. She wasn't sure how she felt about that.

Once she was dressed, she gulped some coffee, then hurried downstairs to the drawing room. She walked in to find both Gwyn and Thorn trying to hold her stepmother at bay.

"I swear on my life, Lady Norley," Thorn said, "I haven't hidden your daughter or whisked her away somewhere. I'm sure she'll be down any moment." He glanced over at the doorway and saw her. "You see? Here she is. She must have been sleeping deeply. I do know from the servants that she worked in her laboratory until very late."

Olivia's stepmother walked over to kiss her on both cheeks, concern clear in her eyes. "You're all right, aren't you? I was so worried!"

"I'm fine, Mama."

Gwyn said, "How about I call for some tea and coffee for all of us?"

"And perhaps a bit of toast and butter for me?" Olivia was starving after her late night activities.

"Of course," Gwyn said with a smile, and left the room.

Reluctantly, Olivia turned her attention to her stepmother. "How did you even find me, Mama?"

Her stepmother pursed her lips. "Don't remind me that you didn't tell me the real reason you were going to Greycourt's estate. And you certainly made no attempt to let me know you agreed to come here with"—she shot Thorn a chilling look—"with a man who nearly ruined you once before. And is obviously not trying to keep from ruining you again."

Thorn was unusually silent on that score.

"Mama!" Olivia protested. "The duke has been nothing but kind and courteous. Besides, as you can see, his sister, Lady Gwyn, has been here the whole time as my chaperone. Everything is perfectly proper."

Her stepmother snorted. "You never cared about things being proper before. But you don't realize how quickly a woman can go from being a diamond of the first water to being the subject of ruinous gossip, and all with one heedless act." She glared at Thorn. "*I*, however, know precisely how that can happen. I've seen it plenty of times in my years in society."

"All I have done, Mama," she lied, "is to practice my profession. Greycourt and his wife were very courteous hosts who gave me a chance to be a real chemist. To do something important instead of . . . of embroidering cushions and enduring courtships from men who had no interest in me beyond my modest fortune. The only reason we had to come here later on was—"

She caught herself too late, judging from how Mama was frowning.

"Was *what*?" her stepmother said.

"Something . . . er . . . happened to my laboratory there. Someone broke in and destroyed a few things—"

"You mean, by blowing the place up? I would call 'destroyed a few things' an understatement," Mama said with a hint of hurt in her tone. "You, young lady, are still keeping things from me."

Olivia surprised herself by saying, "And you, Mama, are doing the same. For one thing, you still haven't explained how you learned I had left Carymont."

When her stepmother hemmed and hawed, Thorn stepped in. "It's important that we know, Lady Norley."

"Very well." Mama straightened her posture. "I received an anonymous letter at home, saying I should look to my daughter because she was no longer at Carymont. The letter did *not* say where you had gone, but I went to Carymont to find out. Then I came here straightaway."

"Do you have the letter with you?" Thorn asked.

"I'm sure I do." Her stepmother hunted around in her large reticule until she found it. "Here you go, Your Grace," she said as she held it out to him. "Though I don't know what more you can discover from it."

He examined it, envelope and all. "Did it come through the regular mail?"

"No. It was left with the butler at our house in Surrey."

"May I keep this?" he asked.

"Of course," her stepmother said, though she was clearly bemused by the question.

Olivia watched a frown cross his brow. "What are you thinking?" she asked. "Who do you believe sent it?"

"The same lad who blew up the laboratory, most likely." Thorn turned to Mama. "Did you spot anyone following you on your way here?"

"*Following* me? Good heavens, no! Mind you, I wasn't looking out the window to watch for anyone behind us, but I'm sure our coachman would have noticed someone following us and would have informed me."

Olivia focused on Thorn. "So you think the fellow sent a letter in order to see where Mama went? In hopes of finding *me*?"

Thorn shrugged. "We've already established he'll stop at nothing to keep you from determining if Grey's father was poisoned."

"Poisoned!" Mama exclaimed. "Oh, my." She began rooting around in her reticule. "Where's my smelling salts? I need my smelling salts."

Olivia walked over, searched her reticule, and handed her the smelling salts.

"Thank you, my dear," Mama said, and wafted them under her nose, probably more for effect than for any real need to stave off a fainting fit.

"I'll have men posted on the road just in case," Thorn said.

"No need," her stepmother said as she continued to sniff the smelling salts. "Olivia and I are leaving right away. I shan't allow her to stay here with you and be ruined for good."

"Mama—" Olivia began.

"I have no intention of ruining her," Thorn said, as if Olivia hadn't spoken. "I mean to marry her."

Olivia froze. Had he really just said that?

Meanwhile, her stepmother wasn't pacified in the least by his offhand proposal. "Over my dead body," she said, startling Olivia and Thorn both.

He narrowed his gaze on her stepmother. "Perhaps you and I should speak privately, Lady Norley."

"Absolutely not," Olivia put in. "The *last* time you two spoke privately, Mama blackmailed you into making a lackluster offer for me."

"You knew about the blackmail?" her stepmother squeaked.

"Not until recently," Olivia said. "And that's yet another matter you kept from me."

"I didn't want to hurt your feelings," Mama said.

"I'm sure you had noble intentions. Everyone seems to have noble intentions when they leave me out of things."

At just that moment, Gwyn returned with servants bearing tea and coffee, a number of delicious-looking cakes, and toast and butter. While they were setting out the trays, Gwyn urged Olivia, Thorn, and Olivia's stepmother to take a seat.

Olivia ate her toast while waiting for the servants to leave. Once they were gone, however, she told Thorn, "The only way I will even consider marrying you, Your Grace, is if you make me a genuine offer."

Gwyn looked startled by the comment, but wisely didn't try to be part of the conversation.

Thorn, who'd taken the seat opposite Olivia's, flashed her a tender smile. "This *is* a genuine offer, sweeting. I truly wish for you to be my duchess."

A million questions entered Olivia's head. But first . . . "Mama, would you go out into the hall for a few minutes? His Grace and I need to have a private conversation."

Mama glanced from Olivia to Thorn. "You're not marrying him, not a man with his reputation. I've learned my lesson when it comes to Thornstock. And you, dearest, can do better."

Olivia seriously doubted that, but that would require a longer explanation than she had time for. "Please, Mama. Let me speak to the duke alone."

Gwyn stepped in at that moment, rising from the settee to hold her hand out to Mama. "Lady Norley, have you seen my brother's beautiful gardens? It's a lovely day outside, and I know you would enjoy touring them."

Mama appeared apprehensive, but she rose at last and let Gwyn guide her out. They were barely out the door when Thorn changed seats so he could sit next to Olivia.

He took her hand. "Tell me what your objections are, sweeting, and I will try to address them."

Her main objection was he didn't love her and didn't have any intention of changing that state of affairs. But she was too much a coward to say that, especially since she still wasn't sure if she loved *him*. Besides, she had plenty of other objections to voice.

Steadying her gaze on him, she said, "You told me at your sister's ball in London that you would never offer for me. So what changed your mind?"

"Everything is different now."

She lowered her voice. "You mean, because you bedded me."

"I mean, because I have come to know you. Once I realized you had no idea that your stepmother was blackmailing me, I was able to look at you more clearly, to see the lovely and principled woman I was so enamored of nine years ago."

"'Enamored of'! You weren't enamored of me."

He leaned closer. "Did you really think it was usual for me to kiss women I had just met? I assure you, it was not. But you and your interest in chemistry fascinated me. Why else do you think I got so angry once we were caught? I was sure you had conspired with your mother to entrap me, that you had somehow pulled the wool over my eyes."

"Oh, for pity's sake," she muttered, and started to stand.

But he pulled her back down. "My point is, as far as I'm concerned, things have changed between us. Or we've merely taken off our blinders so we can see each other as we really are. Don't you agree?"

"Perhaps."

"And there are practical reasons for us to marry. However you feel about it, I have taken your innocence. Some anonymous person has already learned that you left Carymont and has informed your stepmother of that fact, so what's to keep him from telling the rest of society? And if he followed your stepmother here, he'll know you're with me. Just a whisper of a possibility that you and I are alone together would ruin you."

"That doesn't matter to me." She dropped his hand to

pour herself some coffee. "I don't care if I'm a pariah. I never did belong in society anyway. Why do you think I like the Juncker plays so much? Because he mocks those who will do anything to fit in and lauds those who have minds of their own. Sometimes it seems almost as if he writes the plays for *me*. I know that sounds silly, but that's how I feel."

A pinched expression crossed his face, reminding her he didn't much care for his friend Juncker's plays.

"My point is," she said hastily, "it doesn't matter if I'm ruined."

He stared intently at her. "But having scandal surround you won't help you establish yourself as a legitimate chemist."

"Chemists don't care about society and scandal. They merely care about isolating new elements, doing experiments to prove their hypotheses, and finding new chemical compositions that would help people. Besides, it's not as if you'll let me be a chemist once we marry, anyway."

"Why wouldn't I?"

She sipped her coffee. "You would let me do experiments that might lead to dangerous situations?"

"Your experiments don't *usually* blow up in your face, do they?"

"Not as a general rule, no. But they could."

"I see." He poured himself some coffee, too, and took a sip. "That's something we would have to work out—what you do in your laboratory." He stared down into his cup. "And honestly, you and I both have hobbies we enjoy, so we'll simply have to agree on how far we would allow each other to take those hobbies."

That was certainly a curious way of putting it. "I don't consider what I do a 'hobby.' I take my work very seriously."

"Fine. Then call it a pastime."

"A profession," she said.

"Duchesses don't usually have professions," he pointed out.

"You're certainly not reassuring me that I'll be able to continue as a chemist if I marry you." She eyed him closely. "And what hobbies do *you* have, anyway?"

Alarm flashed over his face. "Nothing that would bother you, I'm sure. Just the usual gentlemanly pursuits."

"Like drinking, gambling, and whoring?" she asked pointedly.

He fixed her with a dark look. "I would be faithful to you, if that's what you're asking."

That was one of the things she was asking. "You already know what *my* 'hobby' is. Why can't you tell me what yours is?"

"As I said, it's nothing as concrete as yours." His shuttered expression belied that. "I enjoy going to the theater and going to my club, that sort of thing."

"Much like my Papa."

"*Not* like your 'Papa,'" he said fiercely. "I intend to be around for you and our children. I mean to be a proper husband, not a selfish arse." He caught himself. "Not that I'm calling your father an arse, mind you, but—"

"He is one, trust me," she said dryly.

And clearly she wasn't going to get a better answer from Thorn. Perhaps she could live with that, too. As long as he let her practice her chosen profession.

"Speaking of children," he said, "what if you find yourself with child?"

"That would be a different matter entirely. I'd certainly marry you then. I shan't make any child of mine suffer the ignominy of being a bastard when it was *my* reckless behavior that brought him or her into this world."

"And mine. If anything, I'm more culpable. I seduced you."

She shrugged. "I *wanted* to be seduced."

He took her hand again. "And now that you have been, you will almost certainly wish to do it again. Assuming that you enjoyed it."

"I did," she admitted.

A faint smile tipped up his lips. "So that's an argument in favor of our marrying, don't you think?"

"I suppose." She gazed at their joined hands. "I just . . . don't want you to marry me out of some noble impulse to save me from ruin. Or because you think you must protect me from the villain or villains you and your family are trying to find."

"I'll admit I'd prefer to keep you close, partly because I *do* worry about the 'villain or villains' who might have you in their sights. But the rest of the truth is more selfish—I want to marry you out of a thoroughly ignoble impulse to have you in my bed whenever I wish. Does that make you feel any better about my marriage proposal?"

She arched an eyebrow. "It sounds more like you, at least."

He turned serious again. "I think we could make a good go of it, Olivia. We prefer each other's company to that of good society. We want the same things out of life. And we make sense together. That's enough for me. Isn't it enough for you?"

A pang seized her that she fought to ignore. No, it wasn't enough for her, but only because she still yearned for love and happiness and all that those entailed. Unfortunately, he did not. And she wasn't sure he ever would.

Could she live with that?

"Yes," she said. "It's enough."

For the moment, anyway. She would simply have to take each day as it came, and hope that in time they would learn to love each other.

But now came the most difficult part. Telling Mama.

Chapter Fourteen

"Have you lost your mind?" Olivia's stepmother cried. "That man will be the ruin of you if you marry him."

"Mama, please," Olivia said.

They'd been going round and round about this in the drawing room, while Thorn had been in the hall telling his sister about their engagement. Her stepmother was being unreasonable.

"I mean it!" Mama said. "Do you know his reputation? The women he has seduced? You'd be better off marrying nobody, and I have never said that before, as you well know."

Olivia eyed her stepmother askance. "You're not making any sense. Years ago, you resorted to blackmail to try and get him to marry me, and now you don't *want* him to marry me?"

"Years ago, I wanted to be a good mother to you. And that meant finding you the best gentleman to marry, as far as I was concerned. At the time, I thought that was Thornstock. He was a duke, for one thing. For another, he'd been caught kissing you, so he clearly liked you." Her voice hardened. "But back then he wasn't who he is today—a roué and a rogue."

"Don't speak ill of him to me," Olivia said firmly. "I want to marry him, and he wants to marry me. So you will just have to accept it, Mama. I'm old enough that I don't need your permission." She softened her voice. "But I should like to have your blessing, all the same."

Her stepmother dropped onto the settee with a heavy sigh. "I want to do right by you, dear heart. But sometimes I don't know what that is."

"Sometimes *I* don't know what that is." Olivia sat down beside her to take her hand. "But I appreciate your efforts, and I know you have my best interests in mind."

"When I married your father, he made it quite clear he was marrying me for two reasons only: to give him an heir and you a mother. I failed at the first, but I have tried very hard at the second. I wanted to be a good mother to you."

"And you have been, Mama. Truly."

Mama clasped her hand tightly. "I fell in love with you the moment I saw you, you know." Tears welled in her eyes. "You were such a little waif at eight years old, still grieving the loss of your real mother, and you needed me so much. But now . . ."

"Now I need you even more. There's a wedding to plan and this house to set to rights." Privately, Olivia thought the house didn't really need anything, but Mama was always looking for things to change in their own house, so she would probably have suggestions for Olivia's house, too.

It dawned on Olivia that she was to have her own household: a place that was hers to run as she saw fit. Granted, Thorn had a housekeeper and a butler and probably a million other servants doing this and that. But someone at the top had to be in charge and tell them what to do. That person would be *her*. What a heady thought!

There were clearly some advantages to marriage she

hadn't considered. *I want to marry you out of a thoroughly ignoble impulse to have you in my bed whenever I wish.*

Her cheeks flamed. That was another advantage—sharing Thorn's bed.

"You're blushing," her stepmother said.

"It's rather warm in here, don't you think?" Olivia said, pressing her hands to her cheeks.

Her stepmother's gaze narrowed on her. "You're blushing over *him.*"

"What's wrong with that? Shouldn't I find my future husband attractive?"

Mama sighed. "Of course you should. It just means you're more enamored of him than I realized." She stared down at her hands. "I suppose he was the one to tell you about the blackmail?"

"He was. He wanted to explain why he was so angry when I refused his offer the first time." Olivia gazed across the room and through the window, where she could see Thorn and Gwyn walking in the garden, and the tightness in her chest grew painful. The blackmail was a sore subject for her. "Did you really assume I was so incapable of attracting a husband that you had to blackmail one into offering for me?"

"No, indeed, dear heart! Is that what you thought?"

"I thought you wished to get rid of your ungainly chemist of a stepdaughter before you were saddled with her for all your days." A bitterness several years in the making crept into her tone. "You must have been very disappointed in me when I turned him down after you'd gone to all that trouble to secure him."

"No, indeed. There is naught you could do to disappoint me, dear heart." Mama patted her hand. "And I never meant for you to know about my bargain with him. I assure you I was simply trying to do my best by you. It was certainly never about getting rid of you. Why do you think I'm here? To save you from a bad marriage."

"I don't need saving this time. Or rather, I can save myself if I must." She smiled at her stepmother. "So do I have your blessing?"

Mama stared earnestly at her. "Do you love him?"

The question caught her off guard, probably because she'd avoided thinking about it once he'd voiced his cynicism about love and happiness in a marriage. So she told the truth. "I don't know. If I let myself love him, I fear he'll break my heart in the end."

Saying it out loud made it feel even more possible.

Her stepmother nodded. "I understand your fear, though marriage was different for me. I knew, when I married your father, that it wasn't a love match, and I accepted that. I hadn't had any other offers of marriage, you see, so I took my chances." She chucked Olivia under the chin. "I don't regret it one bit, because I've had you to make me happy, *you* to love. And though I may not understand your passion for chemistry, I do finally accept your need to do it. Why, you have the great Duke of Greycourt relying on your knowledge! That's more than most male chemists have. I'm very proud of you."

"Oh, Mama," she whispered, and hugged her hard, tears filling her eyes. "That means a lot to me." More than her stepmother could possibly know.

Mama drew back to stare at her with concern. "But, my dearest, just be sure of what you want. You know his reputation."

"I do. But I also know he came by some of it unfairly." Still, the conversation she'd had with him about hobbies was a little disconcerting, especially since she was almost certain he'd been holding back something about *his*. But she wasn't about to tell her stepmother about that.

"Well then, if you love him, do it with your whole heart. I daresay it's better to risk rejection than to spend the rest of your life as you have the past nine years, not loving anyone at all. He seems to truly wish to marry you this time. And if you want him"—she let out a heavy breath—"then you have my blessing."

"Thank you, Mama."

Olivia rose from the settee, but her stepmother grabbed her hand before she could move away. "With one caveat. If you have *any* concern, any reason you have changed your mind about him, just tell me and your father and I will stand by you, no matter what."

"You mean, even if it requires watching me jilt the same duke twice?"

Her stepmother laughed. "Even then. But let's hope you don't have to."

"Let's hope not."

Because she wasn't certain she could survive that again.

Thorn paced the hall outside the drawing room, waiting for Olivia and Lady Norley to finish their conversation. Olivia's stepmother had better not talk her out of marrying him. If the baroness meddled with him and Olivia a second time, he would . . . would . . .

What would he do? What *could* he do? He held Olivia by the merest thread, and nearly anything might make that thread snap.

"It's odd to see you so flustered over a woman," Gwyn said as she sat coolly on a hall chair. "Or perhaps in love for a change?"

"Perhaps," he said noncommittally. Although he wasn't about to tell his sister, he knew better than to fall in love. That way lay madness.

Olivia's words last night leapt into his mind: *I wager you're just using that as an excuse for why you continue as a carefree bachelor.*

Not in the least. He was using it as an excuse for why he stayed sane.

Or he tried to, anyway. The fact that he found the possibility of losing her to be alarming wasn't a good sign. He told himself he was only worried about her safety, about the possibility that the arse who'd blown up her laboratory might show up here and try to harm her.

But the truth was, he didn't want her to leave with her stepmother. In the course of telling Gwyn about his offer of marriage, he'd grown used to the words "engaged" and "betrothed." And especially the word "wife." Mad as it might be, he rather liked the idea of having Olivia as his wife.

The drawing room door opened to reveal Lady Norley with her arm around Olivia's shoulders.

Thorn walked in, his heart hammering oddly in his chest. "Well? Will I be making a trip to London to meet with the baron or not?"

"You will," Olivia said, rather smugly.

Thank God. "In that case, Lady Norley, would you be so kind as to join us for dinner this evening? Gwyn and I would also be happy to have you—and Miss Norley, of course—as our guests for the night, assuming you've brought sufficient clothes for that."

"I'd be delighted to stay." Lady Norley patted Olivia's shoulder. "I've missed having my dear girl around for the past several days."

He nodded to Gwyn, who hurried off to consult with his cook about that evening's menu.

Olivia smiled at her stepmother. "Now that I've finished my experiments, Mama, I can go home with you tomorrow." She looked at him. "If that's all right with His Grace, that is."

"Whatever you wish to do is fine. But I'll accompany you both to London." When Olivia shot him an odd look, he added, "So I can gain the baron's permission to marry you, of course." There was no way in hell he would risk having Olivia caught in their villain's snare, especially since he still had no idea who their villain was.

"Lady Norley," he went on, "I do need to discuss one more matter with you while my sister is out of earshot." He walked over to the settee. "Please, have a seat. You too, Miss Norley."

Soon to be the Duchess of Thornstock. *His* duchess. How odd was it that those words sounded amazingly satisfying?

When they were all three seated, he said, "When you told me years ago about my father's mistress, to whom were you referring? And how reliable was your source of that knowledge?"

Lady Norley colored deeply. "I'm afraid I may have . . . er . . . exaggerated a bit about how much I knew."

"What do you mean?" he asked, leaning forward.

"I mean it was plain old gossip. Something bandied about in society that no one had proof of."

"Mama!" Olivia said. "You trumped up false information just to blackmail Thorn into offering for me?"

The baroness thrust out her chin. "I don't know for sure that it was false, just that it wasn't necessarily . . . well . . . true."

Olivia shook her head, obviously none too happy with her stepmother's answer.

Thorn was, however. He sat back, feeling his heart lighten for the first time in a long while. But he couldn't bask in it. He still had to uncover the truth. "So you didn't get the information from my mother."

"No," she said firmly. "Your mother wouldn't ever have said a bad word about your father. She adored him."

"That's not in question," Thorn said. "What I need to know is did *he* adore *her*?"

"I believe he did. It's difficult for me to say for sure," she said archly, "given that I've never experienced such a thing, but he did seem to adore her."

Thorn let out a breath. All these years of thinking his mother had either outright lied to him or had been deceived, and it was based on nothing but rumor and innuendo. Coupled with what the constable had told him, it solidified his conviction that his father had done nothing to deserve whatever nonsense the rumormongers had been spreading about him in his final days on this earth. "Can you tell me who the gossips believed was his mistress?"

This time Lady Norley looked positively mortified. "She's a friend of your mother's, actually, and was at your sister's ball. Eliza. Lady Hornsby."

"Lady Hornsby," he repeated. "With my *father*? Did you . . . ever see anything between them that might have lent credence to the rumor?"

"Not really. He did court her briefly when she was still Miss Rundle and your mother was preparing to marry the Duke of Greycourt. That was the seed of the rumor, I believe, that began growing once Eliza and your mother had married their respective husbands. In fact, I think Eliza might have introduced your mother to your father a few years later. But beyond that, I don't know."

"It's unusual for such a young, respectable woman to be rumored to be anyone's mistress, so why did people even believe it possible?"

Lady Norley shrugged. "Eliza was always rather fast.

I mean, there's a reason people call her a merry widow behind her back. But she doesn't care. She does as she pleases. Always did."

"An admirable trait," Olivia muttered under her breath.

Thorn stifled a laugh before turning to Lady Norley. "So you really don't think there was anything going on between her and my father."

"I doubt it. Eliza was already married to Lord Hornsby by then, and I don't think he would have tolerated any misbehavior on the part of his wife, if you know what I mean. Though she didn't have to put up with the old devil for long. He died only a few years into their marriage as I recall."

Thorn looked at Olivia, whose quick glance told him they were thinking the same thing: that it was odd how Lady Hornsby's husband had died so soon after their marriage.

"What did he die of, Mama?" Olivia asked.

"Oh, I don't recall." She waved her hand. "An ague perhaps?"

"There was a lot of that going around, I take it," Thorn said dryly.

"Honestly, I'm not sure," Lady Norley said. "But he was quite old when he married Eliza. She was his second wife, you see. He was in his seventies, I believe."

"And she was twenty-something," Olivia pointed out. "Poor woman, to be married to a man fifty years her senior."

Poor woman, indeed. Unless she made a habit of getting rid of husbands—sometimes not her own.

"In any case, Duke," Lady Norley said, "I hope you realize what a good woman you're gaining for a wife. Olivia may be an unusual young lady, but she will be loyal to you."

"Rather like a basset hound," Olivia said, the corners of her eyes crinkling with merriment.

Her stepmother snorted. "That wasn't what I meant, dear, and you know it."

"I'm just teasing you, Mama."

She was teasing *him*. But he didn't care. He'd gained her hand in marriage. And he found that more satisfying than he'd expected.

He was just basking in that knowledge when he heard a commotion in the hall.

"I won't do it!" a young man shouted. "And you can't make me!"

"I can bloody well make you do whatever I please if you want to escape the gallows."

Thorn recognized the second voice as that of Gwyn's husband. Before Thorn could do more than rise from the settee, Major Wolfe was entering the drawing room with a young man whose hands were tied together behind him.

"We found the villain you were looking for, Thorn." Wolfe shoved the lad forward. "This is Elias. He's the fellow who blew up Miss Norley's laboratory."

Chapter Fifteen

Olivia stared at the culprit in disbelief. The man had to be younger than she—a fellow barely the age to shave, much less blow up anything.

She rose from her seat. "Why would you do such a thing, sir? I've never even seen you before, and I certainly haven't done anything to you. So why would you try to kill me?"

"This, Elias, is Miss Norley," Major Wolfe said. "The woman whose laboratory you destroyed."

Elias paled. "I swear I didn't try to kill nobody."

"But you do admit you were the one to decimate her laboratory," Major Wolfe prodded.

"I don't know about no decimating, whatever that is," Elias said hastily. "I was only told to throw things about and make it hard for the lady to keep on with her experiments. Nobody warned me some of them things could catch fire all by themselves. I got out right quick when that happened. But I barely got shut of it before all hell broke loose. Then 'twas like Guy Fawkes Day behind me, with explosions and flames up to the sky."

Mama jumped to her feet to wag her finger at Elias.

"You awful creature, you! That's my daughter you nearly murdered!"

Olivia took her by the arm. "Perhaps, Mama, you should go upstairs and get some rest. You traveled far this morning, and I'm sure you could use a nap. I daresay His Grace has already ordered your room to be made ready, and his servants are in the process of bringing up your trunk."

"Absolutely," Thorn said. "It's being handled as we speak. All you need do is walk in." When her stepmother hesitated, Thorn added, "We promise we'll tell you everything we learn. But I fear this scoundrel's tale will only upset you."

"To say the least." She glanced from Olivia to Thorn, then muttered, "Although I *am* tired after all this excitement," and allowed Thorn to call for a servant to take her to her room. But before she left, she fixed Thorn with a dark look. "You make sure that wicked chap gets what's coming to him."

"Don't worry, I have every intention of doing so," Thorn told her. "His deeds will not go unpunished."

Apparently, Thorn had thought Olivia would go, too, because he looked surprised when she didn't accompany her mother and the servant upstairs. When he made some token protest, Olivia said, "The lad destroyed my laboratory and could have killed me and Lord knows who else. I'm staying."

Thorn acquiesced, but he looked none too happy about it. At the moment Olivia didn't care. This was *her* life, and she had to make sure nothing like this ever happened again—to her or to anyone.

"Like I said," Elias told Olivia, jutting out his chin, "I wasn't looking to kill nobody. And I damned well know you weren't in or about there, miss, when I first broke in, on account of I waited until you left."

A chill swept through her. "You mean, all the while I was working, you were *watching* me? How dare you?" It was enough to make her want to lock herself in her home and never leave. She marched up to poke him in the chest. "You had no right, curse you!"

Frowning at her, he rubbed his chest where she'd poked him. "P'raps not, but that's how I know you weren't in no danger of being blowed up."

With fire in his eyes, Thorn stalked over to put himself between Olivia and Elias. "You got lucky, that's all," he growled at the young man. "If that laboratory had been closer to other structures, we could still be pulling bodies from buildings."

The words made Olivia shiver. Because if Elias had been heedless enough to try and destroy the laboratory here, too, he very well could have set the entirety of Rosethorn on fire.

"I could've put the lady in danger if I'd wanted," Elias protested. "I was told to destroy the place whether or no she was there, but I'm no murderer, and I waited till she were gone."

Her heart missed a beat. Whoever was behind Elias's machinations hadn't even cared if she were killed in the destruction? Dear Lord.

Thorn loomed over Elias, his face filling with the fury of an avenging angel. "So who hired you to destroy the place? Who *is* this mysterious devil?"

Elias visibly flinched. "Can't say, mister."

"It's *duke*. I'm the Duke of Thornstock, and the lady chemist is my fiancée. So if you don't tell me who paid you, I'll become your worst nightmare up until the time you hang from the gallows!"

Major Wolfe looked momentarily startled by the news that Olivia was now Thorn's fiancée. Olivia was merely surprised to hear Thorn use rank to intimidate someone, but if ever there was a situation that required it, it was now.

With an unrepentant expression, Elias stared up at Thorn. "What I did ain't a hanging offense. It's damage to property, it is, and the most they'll give is transportation. More likely they'll give me a few years in Newgate. I can serve that in my sleep, and that'd be better any day than me endin' up with a slit throat. Or worse."

"What's worse than having your throat slit?" Major Wolfe asked.

Crossing his arms over his chest, Elias got a stubborn look on his face. "A long, slow death by poison, that's what. And that'll be what I'm gettin' if I talk."

"Poison?" Thorn murmured to Major Wolfe. "At least now we know we're on the right track."

At that moment, Gwyn entered the room. "I heard that Joshua—You!" When everyone turned to eye her in confusion, she said to her husband, "He's the fellow who tried to cause Thorn's carriage to have an accident in Cambridge a few months ago, when you and Thorn and Mama and I went to London for my debut."

The alarm on Elias's face instantly implied guilt.

"Are you sure?" her husband asked.

"Absolutely. How could you not remember him?"

"I didn't get as good a look as you did."

"Well, I never forget a face." Gwyn glared at Elias. "And I certainly have never forgotten *his*. We could have been killed!"

"Weren't trying to kill nobody," Elias muttered. "I keep sayin' that."

Major Wolfe shook the young man until his teeth rattled. "Then what *were* you trying to do, you little bastard?"

"Stop you from goin' to London is all. That's what I was told—make it so the carriage ain't able to run. Didn't know why and didn't care."

"There had to be more to it than that," Major Wolfe said. "If you were just supposed to disable the carriage, what was to stop us from hiring another? Or waiting an extra day at the inn so Thornstock could send for another of his own? It makes no sense."

"Only know what I was told," Elias said.

Major Wolfe shoved the lad into a chair, then motioned to the others to join him in the corner. "What are we to do with him? He has confessed to the destruction of the laboratory, but that carries a minor sentence at best."

"Couldn't they charge him with attempted murder?" Olivia asked.

"They could," Major Wolfe said, "if they could prove he knew that the destruction of the laboratory might kill someone. But he didn't know it could even blow up."

"Yes," Olivia said, "but since I've proved definitively that Grey's father was poisoned—"

"You *have*?" Major Wolfe and Gwyn said in unison.

"She has," Thorn told them with a pride in his voice that touched Olivia. "And I think what my fiancée is getting at is there's more here than damage to property. It was an attempt at perverting justice. Surely that can carry a heavier sentence."

"*If* you can prove that the lad knew that was the intention. We can't. Nor did he seem to intend to cause murder when he loosened the screws of the perch, so he can't be charged with attempted murder for that either."

"Which, by the way, I found out was how our father had his own accident," Thorn told Gwyn.

"So . . . so *that's* a murder," Gwyn said.

"Not one *he* did," Olivia pointed out. "Look at the lad.

He was only a gleam in his mother's eye when your father was killed."

"True," Thorn said. "But whoever is paying him might have done it, and then told Elias how to do it as well. We could charge *that* man with murder."

"Or woman," Gwyn put in. "If we could find out who the wretch is, we could still discover it to be a woman."

"I suppose," Thorn said.

"And there's also the deaths of my uncles," Major Wolfe said. "We may only suspect that someone killed Uncle Armie, but we're fairly certain that whoever delivered that fake note from me summoning Uncle Maurice to the dower house also shoved him off that bridge."

"We can't prove that this fellow was part of any of that." Thorn glanced over at Elias. "There's one other thing we *might* be able to prove, though." He looked at Major Wolfe. "Would you untie him for a moment, if you please?"

Although Major Wolfe looked apprehensive, he did what Thorn asked. Meanwhile, Thorn strode over to a writing table and drew out some paper, an ink pot, and a quill. Then he placed them on the table and gestured to Elias to approach.

Wary now, Elias rose and headed that way, rubbing his wrists. "I ain't much for writing, sir."

"I'm offering you a chance to save yourself a longer term in Newgate or the hulks."

The mention of the hulks made Elias go pale, and rightfully so. The hulks were old naval ships that had outlived their usefulness on the high seas and been turned into floating prisons on the Thames. They were notoriously damp, crowded, and unpleasant places to serve out one's sentence.

Thorn set the quill and ink in front of Elias. "You already confessed to accidentally blowing up Miss Norley's laboratory. So write that down in your own words, will you? Explain how you were unaware that breaking jars and tossing chemicals around would end up setting fire to her laboratory."

Elias cocked his head. "You sure it'll help me not go to the hulks?"

"I can make it so, if I like what I read." He waited as Elias scratched away, but the boy hadn't written more than a few sentences, when Thorn said, "That's enough," and took the paper from Elias. Then Thorn pulled a sheet of paper out of his pocket and compared the two.

He looked at Olivia. "The letter to your stepmother about you leaving Carymont was definitely written by Elias. And it could go to prove intent to harm you." He scowled at Elias. "That *is* what you were planning, isn't it? To follow Lady Norley here and then destroy *this* laboratory? Or worse, harm Miss Norley herself?"

Elias glared at him and crossed his arms over his chest. "I ain't saying nuthin' more, sir. You'll just have to haul me off to gaol."

"Which I intend to do right now," Major Wolfe said, swiftly retying the fellow's arms behind his back. "Perhaps a few days in Newgate or the hulks will loosen your tongue, lad."

"Wait!" Gwyn said. "You're leaving *again*? We haven't seen each other in days!"

"I'd take you with me, dearling," Major Wolfe said, a decided softness in his voice, "but we came by a two-seat post chaise, and there's no room."

"We'll carry Gwyn back," Thorn said. "I already promised Lady Norley and Olivia that I would accompany them to London tomorrow, so Gwyn is welcome to join us."

Olivia smiled at Gwyn. "I would enjoy having more of a chance to chat."

Gwyn smiled back. "That sounds wonderful."

Then she walked Major Wolfe and his prisoner out, probably so she could spend a few more precious minutes with her husband.

"Your sister and Major Wolfe seem very much in love," Olivia said, now that she was alone with Thorn once again.

Will that ever be us? Are you even capable of that? She knew better than to ask questions she might not like the answers to.

Thorn pulled her close. "What they're in is lust." He brushed a kiss to her lips. "I know the feeling."

She did, too, but she was hoping for both love *and* lust from him. Which really wasn't fair, given her uncertainty about her own feelings. "You don't think it's more than lust?"

"I think *they* think it's more than that. And they're entitled to their delusions."

He tried to kiss her again, but she was having none of it. "The way your parents were entitled to theirs?"

His face clouded over. "I'd rather not talk about my parents right now. Not when my sister will return any minute and prevent me from stealing a kiss."

"Too late," Gwyn said cheerily from the door. "I'm back. And now that you two are engaged, I think it's high time we discuss the wedding." She walked in. "Although perhaps we should wait for Lady Norley."

"Absolutely not," Olivia said. "I love Mama, but she does much better if you offer her a fait accompli. Otherwise, she dithers forever over each decision and ends up with nothing to show for it."

"Here's what I discovered from planning my own wedding not that long ago," Gwyn said. "You should start with the guest list. Then we'll know exactly how large or small the wedding is, and where we wish to have it."

"Here," Thorn said. "It will be here. I'll acquire a special license tomorrow when I'm in London, and then we can have it as soon as possible. But here."

Gwyn eyed him and Olivia suspiciously. "Is there something you're not telling me about why you have to marry so hastily?"

Thorn blinked like a fox caught in torchlight.

Olivia shook her head. "Your brother hasn't considered that his demand sounds questionable when weddings usually take weeks to plan." She smiled at Gwyn. "But no, there isn't a reason for haste. Just the fact that your brother is the impatient sort."

"Oh, you mean, he's a *man*," Gwyn said.

"Precisely," Olivia said. "And like a man he just assumes that what his bride-to-be wants is the same as what *he* wants."

"I can hear both of you, you realize," he said sourly.

"Trust me, we do," Olivia said.

"We just don't care," Gwyn added.

They both laughed. Oh, how Olivia was enjoying being able to join Thorn's sister in teasing him.

"But getting back to the guest list," Olivia said, "shouldn't we decide where we want it first? Because if, for example, all the dukes of Thornstock have been married at Rosethorn, then I wouldn't want to go against tradition, and there would be plenty of room for a large wedding and breakfast. But if Mama truly wants me to marry from our parish church and have the breakfast at home, then I couldn't have as many people."

Gwyn tapped her chin. "If I remember what my mother said, her wedding to our father did take place here. I wonder how many people attended."

"Just ask her when you ask who was invited to the house for our birth," Thorn said dryly.

"Oh!" Gwyn cried. "I just figured out how to learn who went to that house party as well as who was at Grey's christening. And we don't even have to tell Mama the truth about why we're asking. We'll just say we want to invite those same people to your wedding!"

Olivia frowned. "But I don't know any of those people, and some of them are likely to be dead, anyway."

"She's not talking about actually inviting them to our wedding, sweeting," Thorn said. "She's talking about using that as a ruse to gain the guest lists from the two house parties without alarming our mother needlessly. Then we can compare the lists to figure out who attended both parties. Because that could seriously narrow our suspect list for who killed Mother's first two husbands. Assuming it's the same person for both."

"That's brilliant!" Olivia said.

"Why, thank you," Gwyn said.

Olivia frowned. "But if your villain paid someone like Elias to do the actual poisoning and the tampering with the carriage, we might not find ourselves any closer to the truth."

"I don't know," Gwyn said. "I suspect that whoever this is probably wouldn't have trusted a henchman for the actual murdering. It could too easily come back to him or her. After all, Elias might have told us who'd hired him if he'd been afraid of being charged with murder. But since Elias knew he probably wouldn't hang for what he'd done . . ."

"Good point," Thorn said. "So, I'll add that to my list of what I must do while in London: ask Mother for the guest lists for both house parties—and hope her memory isn't too faulty to reconstruct them."

Gwyn snorted. "I'm sure she has them all written down somewhere in a box labeled 'Wedding to Duke of

Thornstock' and a corresponding box labeled 'Wedding to Duke of Greycourt.' You know Mama—sentimental to the core. I think she still has her debut gown somewhere in the boxes in Rosethorn's attic."

"Does she?" Olivia frowned. "How odd. It's not as if she could wear the gown again, what with the changes in fashion over the years."

"Olivia is *not* sentimental, is she?" Gwyn asked her brother.

Thorn chuckled. "Not that I've noticed."

Olivia had an odd feeling the twins were poking fun at her. But she didn't mind. She was finally about to gain siblings who teased her. And stood up for her. And included her in all their schemes.

Although it didn't make up for Thorn not being able to tell her he loved her, it still made up for a lot.

Chapter Sixteen

Thorn's pleasure at having gained Olivia's hand began to dim the longer his fiancée, his sister, and his future mother-in-law spent at dinner discussing his upcoming nuptials. Actually, his pleasure was becoming more of a panic.

Part of it had to do with the transformation Olivia had made while planning their wedding. She'd become as excited about it as the other two women. He'd expected that of his sister and Lady Norley, but not of Olivia, who didn't seem to have a girlish bone in her body. Why should she care, when their marriage would be more a way to satisfy their mutual desires than any sort of . . . romantic union? It was incomprehensible.

Yet here she was with the other two, discussing who would be her bridesmaids, which foods they should serve at the wedding breakfast, and what she should wear. Personally, he'd prefer she wore nothing, but he suspected her mother wouldn't approve of such depravity. Though Olivia might.

He smiled a little at the thought.

Gwyn pounced on him. "So you agree with me and Olivia."

Damn. They wanted his opinion. He didn't have one. He just wanted to get the wedding over with so he could get right to the wedding night. Because every time he thought about the solemnity of wedding vows, a strange tightness gripped his chest. He wasn't ready.

He wasn't worthy.

Nonsense. Worthiness wasn't an issue.

"Agree with you about what?" Thorn asked.

Olivia took up the fight. "Gwyn and I think it's always better to have a head covering for a wedding in church, and a silk bonnet with ribbons and lace would be best." She cast her stepmother a pitying glance. "Mama thinks I should just wear orange blossoms in my hair."

That his fiancée and his twin already got along well pleased Thorn enormously, but there was such a thing as getting along *too* well. He disliked being left out of the plans entirely.

"Since we're *not* marrying in a church," he said, "I don't see that it matters. We're marrying at Rosethorn by special license, which I will—"

"Special license!" Lady Norley exclaimed. "That would be wonderful, Your Grace. And very kind of you."

Ah, he had an unexpected ally in Lady Norley. "Yes, by special license, so we can marry as soon as we please wherever we please. And we're only inviting family. God knows my family alone is large enough to fill the dining room, but we can squeeze a number of others in there from your own family."

"It sounds as if you've made many of the decisions on your own already, without consulting your fiancée," Olivia said archly.

Bloody hell. "You did say that if the dukes of Thornstock had all been married here, you wouldn't want to break with tradition. Why, did you really want to marry in a church—have the banns read for three weeks and all that?"

"I don't know," Olivia said. "But I'd like to keep the possibility open, if you don't mind. And it might take me three weeks to get a gown made up that's suitable."

"I'm sure my husband would prefer that she marry in our parish church, Your Grace," Lady Norley added. "He's friendly with the local vicar, you see, who comes to hunt on our land sometimes. But all you need to say is 'special license,' and I imagine he will come around to your way of thinking."

Thorn frowned. "I'll have to take your word for it. I've yet to meet Olivia's father." God, he hadn't even met his future father-in-law, the man whose blessing he would prefer to have for the union. This was moving almost as fast as the night he'd compromised Olivia and been caught by her stepmother.

It was better not to think about that too much—the fact that he was about to be leg-shackled, priest-linked, noosed . . . and every other slang term for a man entering the parson's mouse trap without considering the consequences.

In any case, he'd had enough of wedding plans. He still had to finish writing the final scene of the play, which he'd figured out this morning while waiting for Olivia to wake up. That would take him a few hours, no doubt. Then all he had to do was keep silent about his authorship of the plays until this last one was performed and published. After that, he could give it up. He could, couldn't he? Because if he told Olivia the truth about it . . .

No, that was unthinkable.

He rose. "Ladies, feel free to continue your discussion here or in the drawing room, whichever you find more comfortable. I have work to do before tomorrow's journey, so I must absent myself. I'm happy with whatever you decide, be it a church wedding, a ceremony here in our chapel, or a ceremony in the Norley home. Just let me know in the morning if I need to obtain a special license. Good night."

He left the dining room and headed for his study, but he'd barely entered the hallway when Olivia came hurrying out.

"Did you mean what you said about being happy with whatever we decide?" she asked.

"I generally mean what I say," he told her, hoping he was successful in hiding his irritation at the whole process.

Warily she came closer. "You seem annoyed."

She might have trouble understanding people, but she certainly had no trouble understanding him. He raked his hair with one hand. "I'm simply unaccustomed to being part of this sort of thing."

She smiled tightly. "Wedding plans? Or not always getting your way?"

"Very amusing, sweeting." He pulled her into his arms for a hard and thorough kiss that got him hot and bothered.

And her, too, judging from her quickened breathing after she drew back. "What am I to do with you?" she asked softly.

"A number of very wicked and wanton things you probably can't do until we are very properly and completely wed."

A light dawned in her face. "*That's* why you want to marry so quickly."

He smirked at her. "You certainly took your time about deducing that."

"You didn't explain it to me well enough." She walked back toward the dining room door, then paused to give him a come hither look. "But now that you have, I do believe we'll be marrying here by special license after all."

He chuckled as she reentered the dining room. This marriage might actually work. At least he could be certain she would match his eagerness for bed sport. And surely that would be enough for him.

Olivia said good night to her mother much later than she should have, but they'd had a great deal to discuss with Gwyn, who'd just gone down the hall herself to bed. Now Olivia felt at loose ends. She wasn't ready to retire, but neither did she feel like reading.

Perhaps she should ask Thorn what he wanted her to do with her laboratory. Would it remain here for her use? Would he prefer a building not so close to the house? If she had to pack it up tonight, that would be good to know.

You just want another fiery kiss, you wicked woman.

Yes. She did. When Thorn kissed her, he convinced her that she might not be making a mistake in marrying him. And she could use such reassurance right now. Because his continued insistence on seeing their future marriage as merely a physical and practical arrangement was starting to gnaw at her.

Looking both ways down the hall to make sure no one was around to see her, Olivia ran down the stairs and then found the door to Thorn's study. It was a little ajar so she tapped as loudly as she dared, not wanting to draw anyone's attention. And when he didn't answer, she slipped inside to determine for sure if he was there.

He certainly was, but sound asleep. She walked over to look at him, where he sat with his head resting on the back of the chair and his eyes closed. Hard to believe that this handsome fellow, with his rumpled hair and well-muscled body, would soon be hers.

And what were all these papers strewn across his desk? They didn't look like business letters or contracts or whatever other kind of work she'd assumed he was performing. With a furtive glance at Thorn to make sure he wasn't awake, she picked a page up and stared at it.

It was written in the form of a play. One of the characters was named Felix. How odd. She picked up other pages and read them. This was definitely one of the Juncker plays . . . but not one she recognized. She'd seen—and read—them all, and this one wasn't familiar to her.

Perhaps Thorn was reading Mr. Juncker's latest manuscript to give the man a critique of sorts. Writers did that sometimes, didn't they?

She carefully scanned through the pages on the desk, but she couldn't find a single one with markings in a different handwriting. And she knew Thorn too well to think he wouldn't have marked up Mr. Juncker's manuscript. He would have taken a fiendish delight in correcting his friend's mistakes.

Could Mr. Juncker have given Thorn the play as a gift, sort of like a poet offering a friend the first copy of his poem that hadn't yet been published? If he had, it would have only been to mock Thorn for being jealous of him. While that fit with what she'd observed of their relationship, she couldn't imagine Thorn reading Mr. Juncker's latest play and referring to it as work he had to do.

A thought crept into her mind that was too awful to comprehend. Thorn had grown up in Germany just as Felix had. Mr. Juncker's style of speech had been more poetic and flamboyant than the crisp wit of the dialogue in "his" plays.

Dear heaven, what if Konrad Juncker had merely given his name to Thorn's plays? It would explain why Thorn was so grouchy around him. It would explain Thorn's seeming jealousy. He wasn't jealous of Mr. Juncker's success—he was annoyed he couldn't acknowledge his part in that success.

But why wouldn't he at least tell *her*? It made no sense. If he was the true author of the plays, she would think he'd confess it if only to make her stop going on and on about Mr. Juncker's brilliance.

She leaned over the desk to note the quill still in Thorn's hand, and the words at the end of it on the paper in a sentence only half written. That *Thorn* had been writing when he fell asleep. He was the author. He had to be.

He'd created the wonderful characters that so delighted her. Felix was surely based on him. Lady Grasping—who might she be? Not to mention the amusing Lady Slyboots, with all her attempts to snag a husband . . .

Her gasp of horror awakened Thorn.

Her. Slyboots was supposed to be *her*. And Grasping was Mama. They were the basis of the characters all of London laughed at and mocked. *That's* why he hadn't told her he was the author.

"Olivia?" he asked, rubbing his eyes. Then he saw what she'd been looking at, and said, in a lower, guiltier voice, "Olivia . . . it's not what you think."

"You mean, you *aren't* writing plays under your friend Juncker's name?"

He blinked. "Well, that is . . . what I'm doing, but I never meant . . . it wasn't . . ."

Slyboots. He thought of her as some deceitful woman like Slyboots, always scheming for a husband. Oh, Lord!

That was how he saw her? With a broken cry, she turned on her heel and headed for the door.

"No, no, no, no . . ." he chanted as he jumped up and came around the desk. "Damn it, Olivia—"

"Call me *Slyboots*. That's who you think I am, isn't it?"

He caught up to her and grabbed her by the arm. "You're not Slyboots, I swear." When she shot him an arch look, he added, "Not anymore. You might have been at the beginning, but only because I was angry at what had happened, and I . . . I wanted to feel . . ."

"Powerful," she snapped. "In control. The almighty Duke of Thornstock surveying his domain as people curtsy and bow to him. Instead of the young man just landed in London whom people might mock for his odd sayings or awkward behaviors."

"Yes! You do understand."

She shook her head. "I understand you decided to take your anger out on the two women you thought had treated you ill: me and Mama. I understand you made us into . . . caricatures for people to laugh at. What I don't understand is what *I* did to deserve that."

He just stared at her, a flush rising in his cheeks.

"You had a right to be angry at Mama. She blackmailed you, humiliated you by forcing you to offer for me." Tears clogged her throat, and she swallowed them ruthlessly, determined not to let him see how badly he'd hurt her. "But all *I* did was turn down the marriage proposal you didn't even want to make! Why was that such an awful thing?"

"It's . . . hard to explain."

"No, it isn't." She choked down bile. "You've already admitted you weren't ready for marriage. Well, neither was I. It was the wrong time for us, that's all. Yet you made it into some vendetta I had against you. You made *me* into Slyboots. I—I did *nothing* to deserve that!"

"Olivia . . ." he murmured, and tugged on her shoulder as if intending to pull her into his arms.

"Oh, no, Your Grace," she said, wriggling free of his grip. "You will not try to kiss this away. It's unforgivable."

"Surely not," he said hoarsely. "I meant to tell you, but—"

"You had ample opportunity, yet you didn't say a word." Something occurred to her that made everything even worse. "I suppose this"—she flicked her hand toward the desk—"*this* is what you meant when you said you had secret hobbies! No wonder you didn't want me to know about it."

"I didn't want *anyone* to know about it. No one in my family does, not even my mother. Dukes aren't supposed to write plays, as you well know."

"Even so, I thought you and I . . . we were close enough that . . ." She shook her head. "I guess I was wrong." A weight descended on her chest, making it hard for her to breathe. "Either that or you simply didn't want me to catch on to your game."

He scowled. "What game?"

"How you must have *laughed* at me when I gushed about loving your plays. You must have found my . . . inability to see that Slyboots was based on me absolutely hilarious, especially when I said she and her mother were my favorite characters! Did you exult in the fact that as usual, I hadn't even understood I was being m-mocked?"

His face now bore a stricken expression. "I did none of that, I swear. And I am sorrier than you could ever know that I didn't tell you."

"Only because you got caught." She stared at him, her

heart breaking, just as she'd known it would eventually. Better to have it happen now while she still had her pride. "How can I believe anything you say? You pretended not to be who you are. You let me go on and on about your plays like some dim-witted fool—"

. "You are *not* a dim-witted fool. I never saw you as such, and I certainly don't see you as such now."

She ignored his claims. What else was he to say now that he'd been cornered? "If you can keep this secret, I have to wonder how many other secrets you're keeping. For all I know, you have mistresses strewn across London! Oh, Lord, was . . . was your behavior toward me, your determination to bed me, just part of some larger scheme for revenge?"

"Certainly not," he said brokenly. "How can you even think it?"

"I can think it because I don't know you anymore, if I ever did." She steadied her shoulders. "The wedding is off."

"Come now, Olivia, don't make a rash decision that will affect our whole lives. I ruined you!"

"For any other man, true. But not in the way you mean. You've ruined men for me. I don't know . . . if I could trust one again."

He winced. "At least take a day to consider the ramifications."

"I don't need a day," she said softly. "I have already considered the ramifications. It's clear I will never gain your respect, much less your love. And I find I require both of those for a marriage, after all."

As she walked away, feeling as if her chest was caving in, she realized she'd gone and fallen in love with him despite all her cautions. This mad urge to run back and say she forgave him, when she knew she shouldn't, matched the tales about unrequited love she'd read for years. Apparently pain was the other side to love.

She had once told him that science and hearts had nothing to do with each other. And now she knew how right she'd been. Because if they had, by now someone would surely have invented a cure for heartbreak.

Chapter Seventeen

With his stomach churning, Thorn watched Olivia walk away. She couldn't mean it, not after the way they'd made love, the dangers they'd endured together. Didn't any of that count?

Not if she thinks this has all been an elaborate ruse to humiliate her in revenge for how she humiliated you.

Surely she understood . . .

That you're an arse? A coward? You had all those chances to tell her, to explain, but you were too afraid about this very thing happening, to do what you should have. Because you didn't trust her to keep your secret. Because you didn't trust her to understand.

He ordered his conscience to shut up, and his legs to follow her. But when he went into the hall, he didn't see her anywhere.

Right, her room was upstairs. Taking the steps two at a time, he arrived on the next floor just in time to see her go into her mother's room. Damn, this was bad. Very bad.

Sure enough, when he walked up to the door and knocked, he got no answer. So he knocked again. On the third knock, the door swung open and Lady Norley stood there with her arm around Olivia.

"I already told you, Your Grace," Olivia said, her face a blank slate with no sign of caring for him etched upon it. "I cannot marry you."

Lady Norley looked grim. "We're leaving now, sir. Thank you for your hospitality, but I must ask you to have your servants bring my carriage around. We'll send for our things later."

"You can't leave now," he said, his throat raw. "Especially not in the dead of night, when thieves prowl the roads. We don't know for sure that the villain who hired Elias isn't prowling around himself, especially now that Elias hasn't reported to him. You could be in danger." He looked at Lady Norley. "You must convince her to wait until morning at least." And that would surely give him a chance to change her mind.

His reminder of what Elias had tried to do apparently affected Lady Norley, even if it looked as if it had done nothing to shake Olivia's resolve, for the baroness gazed at her daughter with earnest concern. "My dear, perhaps we should wait until dawn. The roads can be very dark at night."

"You brought two of our footmen as usual, didn't you, Mama?" Olivia said. "That should be sufficient."

"Are they armed?" Thorn asked. "Because they won't be much use if they're not."

Her gaze locked with his. "We're leaving, and that's final. It's a full moon, and the route to London is one taken by the mail coaches, so there will be plenty of traffic even at night."

He bit back a vile oath. "Very well. Then I will send two of my footmen with you, too, and they will be armed." When Olivia looked as if she might protest, he added, "That isn't open for discussion."

"As usual," she muttered.

Her mother was more gracious. "Thank you, Your Grace. That is very kind of you."

The next hour was spent in making the arrangements for travel, but though he tried to speak to Olivia again, her mother kept him at bay. Lady Norley even said once, "Give her time."

He wondered if Olivia had managed to tell her that she was Lady Grasping in the plays. Because somehow he didn't think she'd be looking on him quite so kindly if she knew.

Bloody hell, what a mess. He knew how to put an end to this madness. Tell Olivia he loved her. But he'd be damned if he buckled under to her demands. He wasn't in love, and he wasn't going to claim otherwise. Why should he? He'd already begged her forgiveness.

That gave him pause. He had, hadn't he?

Well, he knew for sure he'd said he was sorry. That was the same thing as begging her forgiveness.

It damned well is not.

"Shut up," he said to his conscience.

"Are you talking to yourself again?"

He turned to find Gwyn now awake. "Always."

Gwyn was draped in a wrapper that didn't hide her pregnancy as well as her gowns had been doing. She had a decided bump in her belly area.

Seeing it had an odd effect on him, reminding him that without Olivia, he might never have children himself. He might have ruined Olivia for men, but she had definitely spoiled him for women. No one but Olivia would do, it seemed.

The panic he felt now was decidedly different from the one he'd felt at dinner. What if he never was able to get her back? What if he died a hoary old bachelor like Olivia's uncle, the chemist? Another member of her family he hadn't yet met. He didn't even know the fellow's name! God, he should have asked her more questions.

He would do so once he got her back. Because he would get her back. He *must*. He would heed her mother's words to "give her time," and then approach her again. Although how *much* time he should give her was anyone's guess.

"What's going on?" Gwyn asked, as two footmen came past carrying a trunk.

He'd talked Lady Norley into going ahead and packing their things with the maids' help, in an effort to slow down the departing process. Obviously it hadn't slowed it down by much. "Lady Norley and Olivia are leaving."

"In the middle of the night?" She narrowed her eyes on him. "What did you do?"

He crossed his arms over his chest. "Why do you assume I did anything?"

"Because it's your particular talent—pushing away the people you care for."

Beyond his sister, Lady Norley approached. "We're leaving, Your Grace. Thank you again for your hospitality." She flashed Gwyn a smile, then added, "Both of you. Olivia is already in the carriage, and she would prefer that I . . . say her good-byes for her."

"Of course," he choked out.

Lady Norley patted his arm. "I don't know what happened between you, but I'll talk to her."

"I'd appreciate it," he said, though he suspected that once she did know, she would be as up in arms as her daughter.

With a nod, she started to walk away, then stopped to add, "Oh, and I'll send your footmen back as soon as we reach home."

"Home? You're going to Surrey and not London?" He

didn't even know where they lived when they weren't in London. The thought that he hadn't bothered to find out, either, made him cringe.

"Yes, home," she said. "But it's not too far from here. I'm sure your footmen will be back by tomorrow evening."

He let out a breath. His footmen would be able to tell him exactly where she lived.

Lady Norley headed down the stairs, and as if drawn by one of the magnets in Olivia's laboratory, Thorn walked over to the window to determine if he could see her in the coach. He was barely able to make out her profile. Even as they pulled away, she didn't look up.

"You really must have angered her," Gwyn said as she stared out over his shoulder. "That is one infuriated lady."

"You can go back to bed any time you like, sis," he said, turning from the window.

"Not until you tell me what happened. I won't let you push me away this time, Thorn. It's taken us a while to mend our broken relationship from before, and I refuse to go back to where we were barely speaking. I understand you better than you know."

"Then you don't need me to tell you what happened, do you?" He eyed her closely. "I'll make it easy for you. If you can guess what the issue is, I'll give you all the gory details."

"Fine," she said. "I would think it was something to do with her desire to continue as a chemist, except that I can't imagine you taking too much issue with that beyond the possible dangers."

He stared at her with his best deadpan face. He prided himself on having a good one, since it had served him well all these years of occasional gambling.

"So," she continued, "if it's not that, then it must be the plays."

"What plays?" Too late. He was fairly sure he'd let his deadpan face slip.

"The ones you write and have Mr. Juncker stand in as playwright for."

Shifting his gaze away, he said, "A lucky guess."

She snorted. "Please don't insult my intelligence. I've known for weeks."

"Weeks?" He gaped at her. "How?"

She began ticking things off on her fingers. "First, I saw one of them, which included so many references to our childhood in Berlin that it was impossible not to notice."

"Juncker is my friend. I could have told him those."

"He may be your friend, but if he had included in his writing that many personal details of your life you would have cut him off as a friend long before you were on play number six in the series. I know you—you're very private. You don't mind including such details in your plays yourself because everyone thinks those things happened to Juncker. Or were well-researched. It doesn't affect you or how people look at you. But you'd be terribly unhappy if *he* appropriated them."

God, sometimes his twin was too clever for her own good. "Fine. I'll concede the point."

"Could we sit down for the rest of this? I'm carrying far more weight on my hips than you are. No one tells a woman about that when they encourage her to have babies."

"Of course," he said hastily, and led her back to her sitting room.

Once he had them both comfortably situated on her sofa, she got right to it. "Second, after I saw one of your plays, I read them all to confirm my opinion. It was easy. You have copies of them in the lower right drawer of your desk."

"The *locked* drawer!"

"The key to which is in the upper drawer." Gwyn shrugged. "It's like you were begging to be caught."

He scowled. "I wasn't expecting to have my drawers rifled by my sister."

She clasped her hand to her heart in mock horror. "Never say that sentence again, if you please. I shudder to even think about rifling your drawers."

Belatedly, he heard what he'd just said. "So do I! And you *know* I meant desk drawers."

She grinned. "I rifled your *desk* drawers because, having seen the one play, I wanted to determine if you owned the others. It's really a compliment to your skill and talent as a playwright that I would be so enamored of the plays that I'd look for other copies."

"It's a compliment to your nosiness, you unrepentant hoyden," he said sullenly. "That's all it is."

"Third," she went on, "there's the way you behaved around Juncker. Fourth, there's your past with Olivia—"

"What do you know about my past with Olivia?" he asked as bile rose in his throat. It was one thing to have Olivia know the truth, but to learn that others had detected it, too . . .

"Everything, I think. I got it out of Grey when I noticed that you and she were behaving oddly around each other at my ball."

Damn Grey. "Our half brother is becoming as much of a gossip as a woman."

Gwyn lifted an eyebrow at him. "I'm going to pretend you didn't say that."

"Good idea," he said hastily. "I'm doing my best tonight to anger all the females in my life." He sighed. "Please tell me Grey hadn't also deduced that . . . that . . ."

"Miss Norley and her mother are Slyboots and Grasping? I daresay no one has deduced that."

"Except you."

She smiled crookedly. "I have the honor—and the curse—of being your twin. After I knew the history of your relationship with her, it wasn't hard to figure out how you would have taken what happened. Why *she* never deduced it is anyone's guess."

"For one thing, she doesn't see herself as Slyboots because she's never been Slyboots in reality. And . . . well . . ."

"She only found out tonight that you wrote the plays."

He shook his head. "This is becoming a bit spooky. How on earth—"

"Not that spooky. A simple deduction. She obviously didn't know the truth the night we dined with Juncker. *I* would have behaved the way she did just to torment you a bit for not revealing the truth, but she isn't me. She isn't good at pretending or lying, a fact which I think you discovered once you went to Grey's and spent time with her."

He nodded. "I could never have offered for her if I hadn't seen that. But once I did, I liked her at once. I felt a kinship with her. She and I both had trouble fitting in." He'd dealt with it by taking up his role as rakehell, and she'd dealt with it by hiding in her laboratory. "Neither of us was ever comfortable in polite society, she even less than I." It hit him how much he'd lost, and he buried his face in his hands. "Oh, God, Gwyn, how do I fix this?"

His sister reached over to rub his back. "Tell her the truth."

"She *knows* the truth. That's why she's angry. And I've already said I'm sorry."

"I don't mean that truth. And a hastily spoken 'I'm sorry' isn't going to wash away the enormity of what you've done to her. Because that's not the real reason she's angry. She's envisioning the whole world laughing behind her back. Until now, she thought you were on her side, both of you not fitting in. The fact that you were a duke and she a mere miss only reinforced how remarkable it was that the two of you felt that kinship. Now suddenly you've switched sides, and she's all alone save for her mother, the other victim of your mockery."

Shame swamped him. "Oh, God, you're right. All Olivia could speak of was the mockery. I hurt her very badly. I don't know how she can forgive me."

"You must do whatever it takes to reassure her you're still on her side."

"How?" he asked.

"I'm sorry, dear brother, but I've reached the end of my twin-sisterly ability to deduce the truths of your relationship. You alone can figure that out. You've already asked her to marry you, and I assume you've told her you love her—"

He groaned.

"You *haven't* told her you loved her, you dolt?" She dropped her hand from his back. "God, men are so stupid."

With a frown, he straightened in his seat. "She hasn't said she loves me, either."

"Then I take back the 'dolt' part." She tapped her chin with one finger. "On the other hand, she probably didn't want to tell you how she felt once she discovered you'd essentially been lying to her all this time about who you really are."

Olivia had said something to that effect: *If you can keep this secret, I have to wonder how many other secrets you're keeping. For all I know, you have mistresses strewn across London!*

"What if I don't know if I love her?" he asked. "I'm not going to lie to her about it."

"Good Lord, of course you love her. Would you be in this agony right now if you didn't?"

"This agony is why I pray I'm *not* in love. After spending the years since I met her sure that our father didn't truly love our mother, no matter what we'd been told, I—"

"Why?"

Damn. He'd forgotten Gwyn didn't know about the blackmail. And since it probably wasn't based on anything real, he wasn't about to tell her and prejudice her against Lady Norley for no good reason. "Something I heard through gossip. It doesn't matter. I've since heard evidence it might be false. My point is I've spent years hardening my heart against love, sure that those who feel it are either deluding themselves or asking for trouble by giving their hearts to someone who invariably doesn't appreciate it."

"My, my, you *are* cynical about love."

"But with Olivia . . . I don't know."

"Well, you have to decide that before you do anything. There's almost no point in mending fences if you can't say you love her. Women want that. Actually, men generally want that."

Olivia's final words to him rang in his memory: *It's clear I will never gain your respect, much less your love. And I find I require both of those for a marriage after all.*

"She wants my love," he said. "She told me that much." His love . . . and his respect. She already had the latter, whether she knew it or not.

"It seems to me if you're asking how to fix things, then you don't want to let her go."

"You deduced that, did you?" he said, now a bit embarrassed by his show of emotion. Except that if he couldn't show emotion to his twin, he had the feeling he would be truly lost. He'd be confirmed as an arrogant arse undeserving of any love.

"You'll know for yourself soon enough. But promise me that if you do feel love for her you won't fight it out of some determination to be a world-weary rakehell. Because that will only lead to more heartbreak."

"Speaking from experience, are we?" he asked.

"Well, not the part about the world-weary rakehell. But the fighting love? Perhaps a bit. Love is funny that way. Embrace it with someone who loves you, too, and it's the most beautiful, wonderful experience imaginable. But try to fight your feelings? It's like . . . like trying to push the needle of a compass away from magnetic north. You can push it all you like, but the moment you let go, it will swing back to magnetic north. Unless you break the compass entirely. And a broken compass isn't useful to anyone, is it?"

No. He should know. He'd been a broken compass for a long time. And protecting his heart had only been . . . numbing.

He didn't want to be numb anymore. He didn't want to be *alone* anymore.

So now he would have to decide what to do about that.

Chapter Eighteen

Olivia stared out the window blindly. She'd had her fit of temper, then had a cleansing cry, and now she felt the way an element must feel when it couldn't bond to any other element: alone and useless.

Deluded.

No, an element would never feel that. Just her.

Mama had remained quiet while Olivia cried, save to give her soothing pats and soft "there, there, now" comments, rather like what one would give a child. Olivia didn't feel like a child right now. She felt very much like a woman wronged. And she had the wet handkerchief to prove it.

"Do you feel better now, dearest?" Mama asked.

"I suppose."

"Do you mind telling me what you and His Grace quarreled about?"

"It will anger you," Olivia warned.

Mama shrugged. "But at least then I would know how to help."

Olivia didn't want to be all alone in her misery, but some sense of discretion kept her from revealing what

Thorn's family didn't even know. Instead, she decided to give Mama a slightly modified version of the truth.

"You know those Juncker plays we like so much? Well, Mr. Juncker is a friend of Thorn's. Years ago, the duke revealed to Mr. Juncker *his* version of what happened that night at the Devonshire ball. Then Mr. Juncker created Lady Grasping and Lady Slyboots out of that. Those two characters we laugh at so much? They're supposed to be us."

"You don't say!" her stepmother exclaimed. "But we're nothing like that!"

"*He* thinks we are."

"Mr. Juncker? Or the duke?"

"The duke. Well, both men, I suppose."

She could feel Mama's eyes on her. "I don't think the duke thinks we're like that," Mama said. "At least not anymore."

Dear heaven, Mama was practically saying what Thorn had said. It was eerie.

Olivia twisted her handkerchief into a soggy ball. "For a woman who was irate over me marrying him, you've certainly changed your tune."

"I'll admit, I didn't approve of him when I first came rushing to Berkshire. But then I saw how he was with you and how he looked at you."

"You mean, with calculation and disrespect?"

"With affection, perhaps even love."

She stiffened. "Mama, I don't know what you think you saw, but that wasn't it."

Mama laid a hand on her arm. "Weren't you the least bit softened when he insisted on sending his own footmen to protect you? And arming them, too?"

"He was just . . . trying to impress you."

"Why would he do that? You'd refused him—again—

and he had every right to throw you out of his house. Instead, he didn't want you to go."

That was true, though she hated to admit it. "Thorn doesn't know what he wants. It's part of his mercurial nature."

"Last night, he told you to plan whatever you wished for the wedding, and he would go along with it." She snorted. "I daresay there isn't another man alive who would do so." When Olivia had no answer for that, Mama asked, "Why does it bother you so much that he told his friend about that night at the ball, and his friend created characters out of what he said?"

"Thorn knew we were being mocked—by his friend, I mean—and he did nothing to stop it. He just let his friend keep putting those characters in situations where people could laugh at them."

Mama shrugged. "They were meant to be funny. Perhaps they started out as us, but I daresay his friend made them into something wholly different. I'm told that writers do those things. Especially playwrights. They need amusing bits for the audience, so people don't get bored. Besides, the duke had a right to be a little angry back then. I did blackmail him, after all."

"You were looking out for me," Olivia said. But her stepmother had a point. "The thing is, he had no reason to be angry at *me*. I did nothing to him, except remove a stain from his waistcoat and engage in a kiss with him."

"True. But you have no idea how much mothers are encouraged, by everyone around them, to snag a duke for their daughters. There are few enough eligible dukes around, and three are in Thornstock's family alone, so he's probably been warned many times that young women and their mothers are lying in wait to trap him into marriage, just for his title and wealth."

"I'm not," Olivia said stoutly.

"How could he know that? Admit it, until you learned that Grasping and Slyboots were based on us, you thought them enormously amusing. That's because you've met many a lady like those two. It's why they're funny—we all know someone they resemble. And Thornstock probably knows more people they resemble than most. I'm rather surprised he didn't do more than tell his playwright friend about us. Thank goodness Mr. Juncker never put in his plays the real tale of what happened that night. Thornstock must have put the fear of God into him."

Olivia stayed silent. If she opened her mouth at that moment she would spill the truth about everything, and that still seemed wrong. For all she knew, Thorn had some other, more important reason for keeping his writing secret from even his family.

All of a sudden, she remembered how she'd teased him about being jealous of Mr. Juncker. Embarrassment heated her cheeks. It was odd how he'd behaved at those times. He'd been grumpy, annoyed. Not because he was jealous, but because he was having to hide something he was surely proud of. He didn't need whatever money he got from his writing—that much was clear. He did it for pleasure. And because he obviously had a passion for the theater.

"But Mr. Juncker's shenanigans aren't the only reason you're angry at Thornstock, are they?" Mama went on. "Surely something more is upsetting you."

She sighed. Mama might not understand her step-daughter's chemistry work or how Olivia thought or even what she wanted out of life, but Mama could always tell when Olivia was upset.

"I'm just . . . worried about his reputation," Olivia said. "What if he means to keep on bedding married women?"

And then lying to her about it as he'd lied all this time about being her favorite playwright. "Or going to his club every night after spending all day in Parliament? Or—"

"Being like your father."

Reluctantly she nodded. "I . . . I love Thorn so much, Mama, that I don't think I could bear knowing he was doing such things. This betrayal already hurts almost too much to endure."

Her stepmother kissed her cheek. "Dear girl, marriage is no guarantee of a happy life. It's rather like . . . like playing billiards. You strike a ball with your cue, intending for the ball to go one place, and instead it careens in another direction entirely. But that doesn't mean you stop playing billiards. We have to try. Heartache is what we risk."

Mama clasped her hand. "So don't let your father's behavior convince you to give up on your dreams, whether they be to succeed as a chemist or to succeed at love or both. Your father made his choice, and I made mine. You must make your own based on your hopes for your life. Sometimes, we get lucky." She kissed Olivia's hand. "I certainly did."

Tears stung Olivia's eyes as she squeezed Mama's hand. She didn't believe in luck. So she had to figure out how to make her own, whether by burying herself in her work for all time or taking a chance on marriage to Thorn.

Or, as Mama had said, "both." She wanted both. And she began to believe that Thorn was the only man in England who could and would give her that.

The next day, Thorn accompanied Gwyn to her Mayfair town house. While there, he told Wolfe he'd spoken with the coachman injured in his father's accident. It was a difficult endeavor given the state of the man's mind, and

Thorn had only gleaned one bit of useful information. The coachman had said he'd seen a stranger walking away from the coach on the day Thorn's father had left, but given the number of guests in the house and the hooded cloak the person was wearing, he couldn't say for sure if the person was a man or a woman, or even if the person had fooled with the carriage. Since it had been raining that day, he hadn't thought the hooded cloak odd at the time.

Then Wolfe and Thorn discussed how to convince Elias to reveal who'd paid him, but the truth was it might be easier to check those guest lists from the two house parties and see who was at both. That meant talking to Mother. Thorn wasn't sure how much to tell her, but he had to tell her something.

Unfortunately, out of concern that Mother might hear of his engagement before he could share the news in person, he'd sent a hasty note to her as soon as Olivia had accepted his offer. Now he ought to tell her the wedding was off. But if he asked for the guest lists without giving her a good reason for wanting them, she would try to get the truth out of him, and he wanted to consult with his siblings before he told her about their investigation. So he was just going to pretend he was still engaged, ask for the guest lists, and pray that Mother believed his explanation for why he needed them.

When he reached Armitage House, he paused only to doff his hat and greatcoat. Wolfe had already told him Mother was here and not in Lincolnshire. She had elected to stay in London because Sheridan was in town, and they were attempting to unravel the tangled business affairs of Thorn's stepfather, Sheridan's father. Not that Mother had much to do with it, but apparently she wanted to be around in case Sheridan had questions.

As Thorn passed through the foyer, he glanced at the

salver with its pile of calling cards. That stopped him short. William Bonham's card was on top. Perhaps Mother had another reason to be in town. He released a long breath. Gwyn approved of the friendship between Mother and their stepfather's man of affairs, but Thorn wasn't sure it was a good idea. After three marriages, surely Mother was ready to be done with the wedded state.

Not if she's in love.

He grimaced. It was such an unequal match she'd *have* to be in love to pursue it. Her friends would cut her off if she married so far beneath her. Then again, she didn't seem to care that much about her society friends. Rather like Olivia, actually.

Ignoring the pain that thinking of her provoked, Thorn joined his mother in the breakfast room, her favorite spot in the afternoon, since that's when it—perversely—got the best light. Gwyn had always said that whatever architect had deemed it a breakfast room needed to find a new profession.

"Thorn!" Mother exclaimed. She leaped out of her chair and hurried over to kiss his cheeks. "How was Berkshire?"

"Fine," he said.

"And how is your new bride-to-be? I'm so happy for you, though I had no idea you were looking for a wife, let alone one like Miss Norley."

The blow to his gut was swift and painful, made all the more so because he had to hide it. "What's wrong with Miss Norley?"

"Nothing, as far as I know." She lifted an eyebrow. "I barely exchanged two words with her at the ball. You never even said you were courting her, so it didn't occur to me to ask her any questions. She seemed very quiet, that's all."

"She is. But you'll like her once you get to know her." *If I can ever get her back.* "She loves the theater."

"Wonderful! Someone who can accompany me to see my favorite plays." She cast him a sly smile. "And where is she just now?"

"In Surrey with her mother."

"Oh, of course." Mother tucked her hand in the crook of his arm and led him over to a cozy arrangement of chairs near the windows. "When she's back in town, you must bring her by so she and I can discuss wedding plans."

"You and Olivia and Lady Norley with all your wedding plans," he grumbled as he settled Mother into her favorite chair. "Between the three of you, you act as if a wedding requires the same strategic planning as a concerted attack on the French."

"Speaking as a woman who's had three weddings, it does. You can trust me on this, son."

"I suppose I can." Taking the chair opposite her, he flashed her a wan smile. "And regarding weddings and such, I was wondering if you happened to have kept the guest list for the house party you threw for Grey's christening."

"What? Why?"

This was the part where he had to lie to his mother. Damn. "Well, Olivia and I would like to have a very intimate wedding at Rosethorn, with only those people who are closest to you and the family."

"The list from Grey's christening wouldn't help you," she said. "Many of those people were your father's friends, not mine."

"That's why we also want the one for the house party from when you were about to give birth to me and Gwyn. We figure if we compare the two lists, we can weed out those people who were just friends to Grey's father or mine and Gwyn's. Anyone who attended both affairs would be family friends. *Your* friends and ours."

"Why not just ask me for a list of my current friends?"

"It's more complicated than that, Mother," he said irritably.

"Isn't it always with you?"

He narrowed his gaze on her. "What's that supposed to mean?"

"Of all my sons, you have most been the one to keep secrets."

"Nonsense. Grey is—"

"He's secretive, too, I suppose, but he thought he was protecting me by not telling me what his uncle was putting him through years ago. You're just secretive in general. About everything." She eyed him askance. "And now there's this sudden engagement. Why do I feel there's more to it than what you're saying? I know the five of you are up to something, but no one will tell me what it is."

"We're not up to—" He fought for calm. "Can you give me the lists or not, Mother?"

She smoothed her skirts with a primness that belied her backbone of steel. "I'm sure I have them somewhere. I packed up everything from Grey's christening and stowed it in the Carymont attic after his father died. Lord knows I didn't want to keep anything from my wedding to that man." Her voice softened. "Of course, I kept everything from my wedding to your father and the birth of you two. That's in the Rosethorn attic."

"Then I'll look for that one there, and Grey can look for the other at Carymont."

She got a faraway look in her eye. "I loved your father so much. I want for you and Miss Norley what he and I had. If I've learned anything through my three marriages, it's the importance of trust and affection and real love. Your father meant everything to me. I swear, if I hadn't had you and Gwyn to cuddle and care for, I don't know how I would have survived the loss of him."

In the past few years, whenever she started talking like this, he would make an excuse to leave. It had been so hard to hear her gush about the man Thorn had thought was betraying her with another woman. But now he wanted his questions answered. And this time he wouldn't avoid the truth.

"Mother," he said, "I heard a rumor some years ago that Father had been hurrying to London when he had his accident, because he was going to see his mistress. Do you think it's true? And if not, do you know who started the rumor and why?"

Astonishment lit her face. "Lord help me," she then said with a snort, "that bit of nonsense has been going around since before I married your stepfather. Of course it's not true. Your father was hurrying to fetch a London accoucheur for me."

"But he never made it there."

"No. The last time I saw him, he kissed me and said he would return as soon as he could. But he never did." With tears welling in her eyes, she cupped Thorn's cheek. "By morning I had you and Gwyn in my arms. The constable told me about his accident later that day."

The fact that there were conflicting stories about his father's reasons for racing to London nagged at him. "And you're certain our father wasn't going to London for . . . some personal reason."

"Like a female friend?" she said archly. "I'm certain. The woman people were touting as his mistress was my good friend Eliza. The whole thing was ludicrous—your father never even liked her, always thought her a shameless flirt. It was one of the reasons he didn't court her for long. Besides, she was *here* at my bedside when your father died. Obviously, he wasn't going to London to meet *her*."

"Apparently not." But as far as he was concerned, Lady Hornsby still wasn't eliminated as someone who might have arranged his father's murder. She could have damaged his father's carriage at any point while she was at Rosethorn, perhaps to get back at him for not offering for her.

Hell, his father could have taken her as a mistress and then broken that off with her *before* marrying Mother. Lady Hornsby could have been simmering with anger over it all that time.

His mother sniffed. "Why on earth are you dredging up this stuff from my past? What brought this on? Between you asking for guest lists and Sheridan wanting to know what *his* father had been up to when he died, you both have me scratching my head."

"I promise, Mother, we will tell you all eventually, when we've pieced everything together. But in the meantime, you may want to be careful about whom you allow into your inner circle. We think there are people around you and the family who aren't to be trusted."

She tilted up her chin. "Who in particular?"

"Lady Hornsby. Grey's Aunt Cora. Other women you came out with."

"You're not making any sense." She made a dismissive gesture. "And you're being overly suspicious. Will you throw your new fiancée's mother in with those 'other women'?"

"I would." Although he honestly didn't think she was one of the ladies to be concerned about.

"You'd best not tell *Olivia* that."

"I wasn't planning on—"

"Forgive me, Your Graces," said Mother's butler from the doorway. "But Major Wolfe is here."

With that, Wolfe came into the room, wearing an expression of dark intent as he approached Thorn. "I've been looking for you everywhere."

"Major!" Mother exclaimed. "Can you not even give your mother-in-law a kiss before you launch into a discussion with my son?"

"Good afternoon, Duchess," he murmured as he bent to kiss her cheek. "I'm afraid I must tear Thorn away from you."

He straightened and fixed his gaze on Thorn. "I must speak with you privately. It's about our friend Elias."

Thorn's heart began to pound. That couldn't be good news. Not with the look the major wore.

"Of course," Thorn said. "Pardon me, Mother, but I'll have to take my leave of you." It was a convenient time to do so, anyway, since it got him out of maneuvering Mother's pointed questions. "I'll see you again soon, I promise."

Thorn and Wolfe had barely cleared the door when Wolfe murmured, "Elias is dead."

"What? How?"

"From a large dose of arsenic," Wolfe said grimly.

"Good God." Thorn lowered his voice as they neared the footmen. "How do you know it was arsenic?"

"The poison was in his food *and* his drink. He didn't eat it all, but the rats finished it for him. They too were dead by the time he was found this morning. The coroner has him at present, but I spoke to the man, and he said he was fairly certain it was arsenic."

"Does anyone know who administered it?"

"It was in his food, and it passed through a number of

hands, so it could have been added anywhere." After Thorn paused to get his hat and greatcoat, he and Wolfe went out the door. "Especially since Newgate is practically run by the criminals themselves. Lots of nasty sorts in there, trust me."

Thorn shuddered. "I'll take your word for it. But is it possible the poison was meant for someone else?"

"Not likely. Although he hadn't had any visitors since I had him put in a cell after leaving Rosethorn yesterday, the food was definitely meant for him."

"Bloody hell. Someone is going to great pains to make sure we never find out who was behind the poisoning of Grey's father."

Wolfe nodded.

"So what next?" Thorn asked.

"I suggest you hurry off to wherever Miss Norley has gone and warn her of the danger."

Damn it all, Thorn hadn't thought of that. If this villain could get to Elias in Newgate, he could obviously get to Olivia in Surrey. And given that Olivia could prove Grey's father had been poisoned, she could very well be in danger.

If something happened to her, Thorn would never forgive himself. He should have ordered his armed footmen to stay with her, at least until he could get there.

Wolfe went on. "Gwyn said Miss Norley went home to Surrey, but she didn't know where."

"My footmen will have arrived from Surrey by now. I told them to come back here rather than go to Berkshire." Thorn quickened his steps toward his abode a short distance away. "They can tell me where she is."

He would go to Surrey, and he would tell her what had happened to Elias. Then he would do what he'd never done with any other woman: beg her to forgive him and take him back.

Gwyn was right about one thing: trying to fight his feelings *was* like trying to stop a compass needle from pointing north. He wanted Olivia, needed Olivia.

And yes, he loved Olivia. She was the ink in his well, the quill in his hand. Every word he'd written last night of the final scene of his latest play had been laced with Olivia, with her humor and eccentric observations, her logic and her warmth.

He had to make her see they belonged together, that he could be the kind of husband she said she wanted. That he would never again hide himself from her. Because if he couldn't be himself around Olivia, he couldn't be himself around anyone.

Chapter Nineteen

Olivia paced the house like one of the deer Papa was presently out stalking. Mama wouldn't be back from her visit to the rector for at least two hours, and then she and Olivia would go to London. Olivia had a number of reasons she must see Thorn again, mostly related to the items she'd left in her laboratory at her estate. It had nothing to do with wanting to work things out between them. No, indeed.

What a liar she was. She *did* want to work things out.

Yet every time she thought about apologizing to him for what Mama called her "overreaction" to his characters, her blood heated and she couldn't think straight. Mama was right about one thing. Olivia had an involuntary reaction when it came to Thorn and his plays. She just kept imagining herself and Mama on the stage being mocked by the audience.

She plopped down into her favorite window box, which overlooked the garden Mama so diligently nursed along. She had to get past this. Why couldn't she?

Their butler came into the room, appearing decidedly flustered. "Miss, there's a man here to see you who claims to be the Duke of Thornstock." He skimmed his gaze over her wrapper and nightdress, then said blandly, "Do you wish to . . . see him?"

Her heart began to race. Thorn was *here*? Dear Lord. "Yes." When their butler raised an eyebrow, she added hastily, "I'll see him in the garden. That will give me time to dress."

Their butler was right—she couldn't see Thorn like *this*, for heaven's sake.

The minute their butler left the room, she flew up the stairs, calling for her maid. Thankfully, her maid was able to get her dressed and her hair put up in under an hour.

When next she was on the stairs, she walked as primly as Mama always wanted her to. But her blood was pounding, and her hands were clammy, no matter how much she told herself that *he* was the one who should be nervous.

She found him near the rosebushes, looking pale and lost and still handsome, even in profile. Why must he always look so delicious, even when she wanted to stay angry at him?

"Your Grace?" she said.

He turned to her, relief on his face. Now she could see his impossibly blue eyes filling with remorse. "You're here," he said, as if he couldn't believe it.

"And so are you. Why have you come?"

"To tell you that Elias is dead."

That caught her entirely off guard. "Dead? How?"

"Poisoned. By arsenic, we think."

Her heart sank. "And you're here to ask me if I'll test his remains to be sure."

Judging from his startled expression, she'd managed to catch *him* off guard. "What? No. We don't need you . . . I mean, there's no reason. The dead rats around his food pretty much confirm he was poisoned by arsenic. I merely thought you should know so you wouldn't worry anymore about him escaping and coming after you. Or sending the man who hired him after you."

"I—I wasn't worried about that." She gazed at him. "At least not until now."

"But you needn't fret. He had no visitors, which means he couldn't have told the man who hired him that you were doing your experiments elsewhere. So you're safe."

She stared down at the pebbled garden path. "Then . . . was that the only reason you came?"

"Certainly not."

The vehemence in his tone gave her hope. She lifted her gaze to him expectantly.

"I came to say how very sorry I am," he said. "I have no excuse for not telling you right away about Grasping and Slyboots. Or at least telling you once I knew you liked the plays."

She swallowed. "Why didn't you?"

"By the time we started talking about the plays . . . I was already beginning to like you. To remember why I liked you when we first met." He threaded his fingers through his beautiful hair. "I knew you'd be hurt to realize I'd based Lady Slyboots and Lady Grasping on you and your mother, so I kept quiet rather than risk hurting you. I was a coward, pure and simple. I should have told you long before."

She was still taking that in when he added, "But I come bearing a gift that I think, I hope, will make it up to you."

So help her, if he gave her a piece of jewelry like Papa always gave Mama when he'd done something beyond the pale, she would throw it at him.

Fortunately, it wasn't jewelry or even a traditional gift. Instead, he held out a sheaf of papers.

As she took it, he said, "I've made some alterations to

the beginning of the Felix play I just finished. Please read them before you decide to give up on us."

Curious now, she started reading what looked to be one long scene, marked up with a pencil. She frowned when she realized she couldn't easily make out the marked-up parts.

"You'll have to forgive my handwriting," he said. "I made the changes in the carriage on the way here."

"That explains why it's in pencil," she said dryly.

He shrugged. "It's hard to manage an ink pot and quill in a moving carriage, even with a portable writing desk."

"I can well imagine." She continued reading until she got to a mention of Grasping and Slyboots. Taking a deep, bracing breath, she read the passage. Then her gaze shot to him. "You killed them off!"

He nodded, then gestured to the pages she held in her hand. "I did it in a comic way, as you can see."

She said nothing, too absorbed in rereading the sentences where Felix talks about them dying in an avalanche in the Alps while pursuing an Austrian count.

At her continued silence, Thorn added, "But if you want it to be more of a tragic event, I can do that, too."

She lifted an astonished gaze to him. "You . . . you killed off Grasping and Slyboots for *me*? To please *me*?"

"I'll do whatever I must to get you back," he said earnestly.

She waved the pages at him. "You shouldn't have done *this*."

His face fell. "Because you can't forgive me. Still."

"No!" she said quickly. "That's not what I meant. I meant . . . they're two of your greatest creations. You can't kill them off." She flashed him a tentative smile. "Assuming you intend to keep writing about Felix and his friends, that is. Because I heard a rumor you might not."

He stepped toward her, his eyes bright. "To tell the truth, I haven't decided. I figured I would see how this latest play fares in the theater. If it does well, I might consider another."

"It won't do well at all if you kill off Grasping and Slyboots. They're your funniest characters! You simply cannot kill them off."

"I thought you hated them," he said softly.

She thought so, too. But seeing him kill them off also felt wrong. When she could separate them from her and Mama, she adored them. "I did. But the more I think about it, the more I realize no one knows it's Mama and I. So unless you use your own name for your plays—"

"Which I will never do. As I told you, dukes aren't supposed to write plays."

"Then no one will ever guess whom they're based on." She toyed with the gold chain about her neck. "It will be our secret."

His breath seemed to falter a bit as he took her hand in his. "Does this mean you forgive me?"

"For which part? Basing your comic characters on me and Mama? Or not telling me you're actually my favorite playwright."

"I'm your favorite playwright?" he said. "Really?"

She laughed. "Of course that's the part you choose to focus on. You're as vain as Juncker."

"Better and better—you think Juncker is vain."

"I shall need another dinner with him to determine that," she said with a coy smile.

"The hell you will. I barely made it through the last one." He paused a moment. "Oh, and by the way, I told you that no one in my family knew of my writing. It turns out that Gwyn knew. I just didn't know she knew."

"Why does that not surprise me?" she said lightly. "Your sister is a very clever woman."

When he sobered, she knew they were still dancing around the main issue.

"So you do forgive me," he said.

"Only if you promise never to lie to me again. Because unlike your sister, I can't bear it if you tell me anything less than the whole truth, warts and all." She blinked back tears. "If I found out you had a mistress or spent your evenings in the stews when you told me you were at your club, it would destroy me."

"I wouldn't want to do that, ever," he said earnestly. "So yes, I promise never to lie to you."

"I promise never to lie to you, either." She cupped his cheek. "And I forgive you."

"Good," he said. "Because I don't think I could bear to live unforgiven by you."

Oh, but the man had a way with words sometimes. She flashed him a teasing smile. "You need to explain that better."

"I beg your pardon?"

She lowered her voice to what she hoped was a temptress's thrum. "The way you explained why you wanted the wedding done at Rosethorn by special license. Remember?"

He gazed at her a long moment before a smile crept over his lips. "I *do* remember."

When he tried to pull her into his arms, she danced back toward Mama's clematis and ivy bower, tugging him along. "I believe we'll need privacy for this, Your Grace. Unless you want to be forced into marrying me when we're caught in an embrace."

"That would be dreadful," he said, his eyes darkening

as they entered the cold arbor. "But I warn you, if we're to stay in here, in the chill of autumn, we'll need to keep each other warm, and that will mean a more . . . intimate encounter."

"You'll have to explain what you mean by that," she whispered.

He dragged her into his arms, kissing her so thoroughly she could hardly keep her wits about her. He pulled back only long enough to glance around. As he spotted the stone bench there, he pulled her over to it and took a seat.

She tried to sit beside him, but he wouldn't have it. Instead, he tugged her between his legs. "You wore this front-opening gown for me, didn't you, sweeting?"

"And what if I did?" she said lightly as she dropped the scene from his play onto the bench beside him.

"Then I shall take full advantage." He had her gown open within moments and her short stays pulled down in even less time. But he took his time with her shift, unfastening each tiny button with care. "Ah, yes," he murmured as he bared her bosom. "Just what I was looking for."

By the time he had his mouth on her breast, she thought she would die of waiting. As he sucked at one and fondled the other, she let out a fractured breath. "You are shockingly . . . good at that. It's a bit . . . worrisome."

"I'll admit to"—he tugged at her nipple with his teeth—"gaining experience in an . . . unsavory manner. You would probably disapprove." He licked her quite deliciously. "But those days are over."

She gazed down at him. "Are you sure?"

"Oh, yes." He tongued each nipple until she gasped. "You like that, my wanton wife-to-be?"

"Yes," she choked out, and clasped his head. "Though I don't remember . . . agreeing to marry you after my . . . most recent refusal."

He paused to stare up into her face. "Don't tease me about that. I thought I'd lost you forever. And I had no one to blame for it but myself. So take pity on me. I won't survive the loss of you again, my love."

"You . . . you love me?" she stammered.

"More than you can imagine." He worked loose the buttons of his fall and then his drawers and pulled them down and open in front to expose his very aroused flesh. "Shall I explain it some more?"

"Definitely." She smiled. "I fear your wife-to-be is a slow learner."

Lifting her skirts, he urged her to straddle him. She noticed he was careful to spread his coat on the bench on either side so she didn't have to kneel on the cold stone as he guided her onto his member. That small gentlemanly bit of concern warmed her heart.

As she slid down atop him, he groaned. "You feel like heaven, sweeting."

"So do you," she whispered, surprised to find that the discomfort from their first time was gone, replaced by the pleasing feeling of his thickness inside her. "*My* heaven. *My* love."

"Mine," he growled possessively as he teased and sucked her breast. "Forever."

Using his hands to urge her to move up, he finally made her realize what she was supposed to do. "Oh!" she said. "How interesting."

"An experiment, if you will," he rasped. "In driving me to distraction."

She gave a choked laugh. "I could get used . . . to such experiments. As long as they don't lead to . . . sudden fires."

"Oh, trust me, this will lead to sudden fires." With his

eyes gleaming, he licked her nipple. "Just not the chemical kind."

Then he thrust up against her, and she took his instruction and began to move. Between his thrusts and her urge for more, they fell into a rhythm that made her feel like a queen mastering her subject. Except he was far too big and masterful to be a mere subject.

"I love you," she murmured as her blood began to heat. "I love you even more than chemistry."

His face lit up at those words. "I love you . . . even more than the theater." He was driving up into her now with a glorious excess that made her ache and moan and shimmy atop him. "I love you," he said hoarsely, "as the ocean loves the shore."

"As phosphorus loves the air." She came down on him faster now in response to his frenzied motions. He was rousing her own need, drawing her ever closer to the edge . . . to where she would find . . . her match . . . and light them both.

"For all time." He pounded into her. "In all places. Mine. *My love.*"

And just as her body erupted and she clutched him to her with a cry, he thrust up into her with a cry of his own, her cascade of echoing eruptions milking him. Then she collapsed on top of him, spent and satisfied.

Some time passed while they held each other close and basked in the warmth of their joined bodies.

Then Thorn stirred beneath her. "I take it that your parents are not home?"

That brought her back to herself rather abruptly. "Oh, Lord, Mama will be here any minute. She'll come looking for us once she hears from the butler that you're here in the garden. With me." Feeling a bit panicked, she slid off him and began setting her clothing to rights.

"What can she do?" he said, a hint of laughter in his voice. "Force us to marry?"

Casting her gaze heavenward, she grabbed the pages of his play and swatted him with them. "You won't find it humorous when she demands that we hurry to London and marry right away. Especially after all the travel you've been doing."

"Ah, but after that we can be together in the master suite at Rosethorn by tonight. Sounds perfect to me."

"Doesn't it, though?" She paused to imagine that and smiled. Then she imagined Papa chasing Thorn around with his hunting gun, and she went over to pull on Thorn. "You have to get up and button up your clothes!"

With a laugh, he rose and buttoned his few buttons, then pulled her into his arms. "Calm down, will you? While I was waiting for you, I told your butler I was your fiancé and paid him to leave us be. I also paid him to warn us if he saw either of your parents arriving."

"You were rather sure of yourself," she said, fighting a smile.

"I was sure I would say or do whatever I must to make you mine."

"Allow me to continue as a chemist?"

"Done," he said.

"Even if it means not always having me readily available?"

"Even if it means I have to wait on you hand and foot."

"Don't be ridiculous. You have servants for that."

"There are certain things I'd rather do myself," he said, eyes gleaming. Then he turned serious. "I do have one caveat. That when you're enceinte, you don't perform any experiments with dangerous chemicals."

"Done," she said, smiling broadly. "You see how easy it is to negotiate with me?"

"You're content as long as I 'explain' things, right?"

She laughed at his smug smile. "Oh, yes. I am a blank slate when it comes to those sorts of explanations, my love."

"Well, then," he said. "I can see a great deal of explaining in my future."

And as he bent to kiss her, she decided there was something to be said for marrying a writer.

Epilogue

It had taken some wrangling to get his siblings and their spouses, not to mention Mother, in one place, but Thorn had them all together at last. Now if only he could stop grinning, a highly inappropriate behavior given the subject of the meeting.

But he couldn't help it. Yesterday, he and Olivia had finally been married, although it had taken three weeks instead of the three days he'd wanted, thanks to the women clamoring that they needed time to plan the wedding, special license or not.

Now Olivia sat with the others around the large table at Rosethorn, smiling coyly as if remembering last night's wild lovemaking. He would have to keep from looking at her. Or remembering how it felt to be inside her last night, knowing that she was his forever. Or remembering waking to the sight of her in his bed, his *wife*.

That, rather than the actual wedding, had been the crowning moment for him.

"What's this about, Thorn?" Sheridan demanded.

He wiped the grin from his face. "Mother and the deaths of her husbands. A subject that has weighed heavily on our minds of late."

"I *knew* you children were up to something!" Mother exclaimed. When everyone turned to look at her, she added, rather petulantly, "Well, I did. A mother knows these things." She paused to regard them all with a quizzical gaze. "So, what *are* you up to, exactly?"

"Are you going to explain, Grey, or shall I?" Thorn asked.

"It's your house," Grey drawled. "You should do it. Besides, you and Wolfe are the only ones who know the whole story."

"All right," Thorn said, and turned to his mother. "As you may remember, last year we came to the conclusion that Maurice and his predecessor were both murdered." When her eyes widened, he added hastily, "That was what got us all thinking about the fathers of Grey and us twins. We think perhaps they were both murdered, too."

"That's absurd." Mother shook her head. "Thorn, your father was killed in a carriage accident!"

"Yes, but we now think Father's was caused when the perch screws were loosened enough to send the coachman flying off and to startle the driverless horses. And if not for Wolfe's swift intervention earlier this year, you, Gwyn, Wolfe, and I might also have been killed on our way to London for the debuts. Since both accidents involved the perch screws being loosened, both were probably also deliberate."

"What?" Mother said. "I—I don't understand."

Gwyn covered her hand. "We didn't want to bother you with what we uncovered, Mama, until we were certain we weren't imagining things. But it does seem as if someone has been systematically murdering the gentlemen close to you. And if not for Joshua and I seeing the fellow fooling with the carriage, you too would have been in an accident. We four might have been killed or maimed!"

"So we decided to start by investigating the death of my father," Grey said. "We suspected he might not have died of an ague because I, who supposedly infected him, did not perish, but Father did. That's why I asked Thorn's wife to use her extensive knowledge of chemistry to test my father's remains. That's the real reason Thorn and Olivia traveled to Carymont with me and Beatrice."

"That was all a sham?" Mother sat back with a huff. "You four ought to be ashamed of yourselves."

"We didn't want to worry you," Beatrice said hastily.

"Hmph," Mother said.

"Anyway, Mother," Thorn said with a smile for Olivia, "my brilliant wife found arsenic in the remains. But before she did, someone attempted to put an end to her tests by destroying her laboratory." His voice turned steely. "She could have been killed. Thankfully, she wasn't there. And although the lad named Elias, who did it, fled, Joshua tracked him down and arrested him. But Elias was murdered in Newgate before he could reveal who hired him."

Everyone else gasped.

"Do we know how?" Sheridan asked.

"We know he was poisoned by arsenic," Thorn said. "We don't know how it ended up in his food in the prison."

Sheridan leaned over the table. "Is it possible he was also responsible for the deaths of Uncle Armie and Father?"

"At this point, anything is possible," Thorn said. "Well, except that Elias couldn't have done the two earlier murders. He was too young. Still, we have a number of suspects."

"A *number* of suspects?" Mother exclaimed. "Good Lord. Who would do such a thing?"

"We're getting to that, Mother," Grey said.

Thorn laid down two sheets of aging paper. "As you know, Mother has a tendency to store her entire past in boxes in the attic." Everyone laughed. "So we have a list of who was present at Carymont for Grey's christening, which is when Grey's father died. We also have a list of who was present at Rosethorn for the birth of me and Gwyn, which is when *our* father died. Excluding Mother, three names appear on both lists, all female. Grey and I figured that if we're correct and both men were murdered, someone had to have had access, which means they attended both events."

Mother stood. "I can't believe this . . . this conspiracy you suspect. It seems outlandish. Those people were our friends. Why would any of them kill your fathers?"

Sheridan sat back in his chair. "I don't know, Mother, but you heard the evidence from last year about Father and Uncle Armie. So that's three of your husbands and one of your husband's brothers. It definitely seems to be a pattern."

The color drained from her face. "Then why should I be excluded from the list of possible guilty parties?"

"Because you couldn't have managed all four murders," Thorn said gently. "In our father's case, you would have been in labor. It's highly unlikely you were sneaking about, unscrewing carriage perches. In Uncle Armie's case, you were abroad. In fact, we think that's why this villainess waited so long to kill our stepfather. Her reach didn't extend to Prussia. We think she grew frustrated when you and Maurice stayed so long in Prussia, and so she murdered Uncle Armie to get you and Maurice, Uncle Armie's heir, back here so she could murder Maurice, too."

"And possibly me," Mother said.

Grey nodded. "The truth is, we have no idea why

someone would have committed so many murders. And until we understand that, we can't unravel this conspiracy, if that's what this is."

Mother sank back into her chair. "So who are the three women on both lists?"

"First is Grey's Aunt Cora, a vicious and most ambitious woman, as you well know," Thorn said. "Then there's Lady Norley, whom my wife assures me could not be the culprit. And there's your friend, Lady Hornsby."

"Surely not her," Beatrice said. "She was so kind to me during my presentation at court."

"As far as I'm concerned," Thorn said, "we must treat all three as possibilities, even if my wife does claim she can vouch for her stepmother's character."

Grey took up the tale. "But although we've proved to our own satisfaction that my father was murdered by poison, it would be difficult to investigate the other components of a crime that happened thirty-four years ago. So Thorn, Gwyn, and I have agreed that our best hope of catching this fiend lies in trying to unravel the most recent murders—that of the two Armitage dukes."

Thorn nodded to Sheridan and Heywood. "So we'll be relying on you two for that investigation. Although I realize Heywood has only been in that area a year, and Sheridan a year more, you know the town and its residents better than the rest of us. The local populace trusts you, and you've shown your measure by now. Besides, the questions of a local duke and his brother will carry more weight than those lodged by any of us. And I don't want to put any of that burden on Mother."

"I beg your pardon." Mother sniffed. "I am as much a member of that area as the boys, so I certainly mean to do my part. And I refuse to give the townspeople any hint that my sons are investigating a murder I might be involved in."

Sheridan put his arm around her. "I promise Heywood and I will make it clear that we don't suspect *you.*"

"Not good enough," Mother said. "Put me to work."

"We'll talk about that later, Mother," Heywood said.

"One last thing," Thorn said. "Our other reason for this meeting is to advise caution. Thus far, our villainess hasn't tried to kill any of us, except for Elias's bungled attempt to damage the carriage, but that may change. After engineering the murders of so many, she may not stop at those. So every one of us must be on our guard. At the same time, we think it prudent *not* to share these suspicions with anyone unless it's necessary. We don't want to paint targets on our backs."

"So don't tell Vanessa that we suspect her mother, Grey," Sheridan said. "Because that woman will drive us all mad trying to find out why."

Heywood laughed. "You're the only one she drives mad, brother. Especially her infatuation with that Juncker poet friend of Thorn's."

"*That's* the poet my cousin has been talking about all this time?" Grey scowled at Thorn. "Did you know?"

"I . . . er . . . only found out a short time ago. And I wasn't about to mention it to *you.* I knew you wouldn't be happy about it."

"Vanessa and Juncker," Grey muttered. "God help us all."

"Before the conversation degenerates further into gossip irrelevant to the subject at hand," Thorn said dryly, "I have one more piece of business to mention. Wolfe has agreed to be in charge of gathering and documenting our efforts. He has powerful friends in London, including Bow

Street runners and others who investigate crimes. So if you need a bit of information you can't uncover, turn to him."

"We should enlist Mr. Bonham," Mother said. "He was a solicitor before he became Maurice's man of affairs, so he knows something about the law."

Thorn had to stifle a curse. "We're not bringing in people outside the family except to gain bits of information from them, Mother. I doubt that anyone would put together those isolated bits, but if we involve Bonham, he'll see them altogether and know what we're up to. We can't be sure that your suitor won't gossip to the wrong person."

Mother was blushing. "He's not my suitor," she said.

Gwyn and Beatrice exchanged a knowing smile.

"No matter what he is, he can't be part of this, Mother. Do you understand?"

She thrust out her chin. "Whatever you say, Thorn. God forbid I should have a male friend. Or female friends, for that matter, without having my children suspect them as criminals." She rose. "I'll see about ordering us some tea."

"I'll help you," Olivia said, jumping up to follow Mother, with a chiding glance for Thorn.

Then he caught Gwyn and Beatrice glaring at him. "What?" he asked.

"Couldn't you have put it more delicately?" Gwyn said. "Mother just heard the news that practically all of her friends are suspects. She's still taking it all in. You could have been more tactful in telling her not to reveal what we know to her friend Bonham."

"Thorn?" Grey said. "Tact isn't his forte. I mean, he was right about Bonham, but he doesn't have a tactful bone in his body."

"Do you remember the time when the king came to visit our stepfather—" Sheridan began.

"Meeting adjourned!" Thorn said and marched out the door. He was done dealing with his family for the moment. He wanted his wife.

His *wife*. And duchess and bed partner and the woman who knew him better than anyone. He smiled in spite of himself. She made everything better. He must have been daft not to fight harder for her nine years ago.

He found her talking to his mother in the drawing room and stood back to listen.

"You have to understand," Olivia said. "Thorn is a typical bullheaded man when it comes to ordering his mother around. He thinks he has every right to tell you what to do."

Mother said something he couldn't hear.

Olivia laughed. "Exactly."

Mother said something else, and not being able to hear it frustrated him, so there was no point in eavesdropping. Besides, Olivia would tell him later.

He entered the room. "Mother, I'm sorry. I didn't mean to upset you."

His mother rose and came over to give him a kiss on the cheek. "It's all right. Olivia explained how you were just being a man."

"And you agree with her?"

"I do, actually." She smiled faintly, then leaned up to whisper, "I like your wife a great deal. And she seems to love you quite a bit, too."

Even as he was grinning to himself about that, Mother went out into the hall to oversee the delivery of the refreshments to the crowd in the dining room.

Meanwhile, he went to join his wife. "Mother likes you," he said as he offered her a hand to get up off the sofa. "I'm not surprised. She'd have to be out of her wits to dislike you."

"Why?" Olivia said with a wry smile. "Because *you* like me?"

"Precisely," he said. "And I have excellent taste in women."

She lifted an eyebrow. "I'll have to take your word for it since you have yet to give me the name of even one of your former paramours."

"And I don't intend to do so ever," he warned. "You'll just have to trust me when I say that none of them could hold a candle—or a bit of phosphorus—to you."

She laughed. "You are incorrigible."

He pulled her into his arms. "Precisely why you like me, sweeting. Women are always drawn to us wicked fellows."

"That may be true," she said, smiling up at him. "But what drew me to you wasn't your wickedness."

"Oh?" he said as he kissed a path from her temple to her ear.

"It was your acceptance of me and my quirks. Before we got caught that first time, you clearly liked me, despite my obsession with chemistry and my refusal to take anything in society at face value."

"I liked you *because* of all that, my darling wife," he murmured. "It just took me a long time to realize it. Apparently, you're not the only slow learner in this marriage."

"Then let me do the explaining this time," she whispered. "Though perhaps we should close the door before we scandalize your family."

"Or retire to our bedchamber?" he suggested.

"Thorn!" she cried. "It's still morning! If we return to our bedchamber *now,* everyone will know what we're doing."

"I should hope so. You married into a family of wicked fellows like me, sweeting, and we're all rather unrepentant about such things." He released her, only to go over and shut and lock the drawing room door before returning to her side. "On the other hand, enjoying another consummation of our marriage in the drawing room might actually scandalize them, my love. Shall we experiment?"

"Oh, yes," she said with a laugh. "You do know how I like experiments."

All in all, the experiment was a resounding success.

Read on for a preview of the next book
in Sabrina Jeffries's Duke Dynasty series...

UNDERCOVER DUKE

*Coming in Summer 2021
from Kensington Publishing Corp.*

London Society Times

THE LAST DUKE STANDING

Dear readers, I, your esteemed correspondent, cannot believe it. Not only has that randy devil, the Duke of Thornstock, actually married, but he chose Miss Olivia Norley as his bride! And this, after she refused him most soundly. He must have reformed because Yours Truly knows full well Miss Norley would never have married him otherwise.

This means that his half brother, Sheridan Wolfe, the Duke of Armitage, is the only one of the Dowager Duchess's offspring not yet married. What a coup it will be for the young lady who snags him! Although the usual wagging tongues claim he must needs marry a fortune to shore up his estate, that will not matter to anyone with an eligible daughter. He's a duke, after all, and a young, handsome one at that, which is particularly rare. I daresay he will not be left unwed for long.

How delicious it will be to watch him hunt for his bride. Armitage is discreet where Thornstock was not, and he's more reclusive even than his other half brother, the Duke of Greycourt. So it will have to be a most intriguing lady to pierce his armor and seize the rare heart that surely beats beneath. We await the result with bated breath.

Chapter One

Armitage House, London
November 1809

"The Duke of Greycourt is here to see you, Your Grace."

Sheridan Wolfe, the Duke of Armitage, looked up from the account ledgers for his family seat, Armitage Hall. "Show him in."

Grey, his half brother, was supposed to be in Suffolk, but Sheridan was glad that wasn't the case. Grey would be a welcome distraction from the thing Sheridan detested most. Numbers. Arithmetic. Double-entry accounting. Which, try as hard as he might, he could not fathom.

Unfortunately, running a ducal estate required dealing with endless permutations of the method, so he *must* master it.

But not just now. Sheridan would rather have a brandy and a pleasant chat with Grey than continue slogging through the books. To that end, he poured himself a glass and was about to pour one for his half brother when the butler showed Grey in, and Sheridan's idea of a pleasant chat evaporated.

His brother looked as if he'd drunk one too many brandies already and was now about to cast up his accounts. Pale and agitated, Grey scanned the study of Sheridan's London manor as if expecting a footpad to leap out from behind a bookcase at any moment.

"Do you want anything?" Sheridan asked his brother, motioning to the butler to wait a moment. "Tea? Coffee?" He lifted the glass in his hand. "Brandy?"

"I've no time for that, I'm afraid."

Sheridan waved the butler off. As soon as the door closed, he asked, "What has happened? Is it Beatrice? Surely you're not in town for the play, not under the circumstances."

In a few hours the whole family would be attending a charitable production of Konrad Juncker's *The Wild Adventures of a Foreign Gentleman Loose in London* at the Parthenon Theater. Although Sheridan barely knew the playwright, Thorn had asked him to go because the charity was a cause near and dear to his wife's heart: Half Moon House, which helped women of all situations and stations get back on their feet.

Grey shook his head. "Actually, I came to fetch an accoucheur to attend Beatrice. Our local midwife says my wife may have our baby sooner rather than later, and the woman is worried there will be complications. So I rushed to London to find a physician to examine Beatrice, in case the midwife is right. The man awaits me in my carriage even as we speak."

Lifting an eyebrow, Sheridan said, "I would suspect you of having taken Beatrice to bed 'sooner rather than later,' but you've been married ten months, so this is hardly an early babe."

"No, indeed. And the midwife might be wrong, but I

can't count on that. That's why I stopped here on my way out. Because I need a favor."

Sheridan cocked his head. "Sadly I have no skills in the area of birthing babies. So I don't see what sort of favor you could possibly—"

"Do you remember how we said I should be the one to question my Aunt Cora about what she remembers of those two house parties we suspected were attended by my father's killer?"

"I do indeed."

Their mother's five children had finally come to the conclusion that her thrice-widowed status had not been just a tragic confluence of events. Someone had murdered her husbands, including the father of Sheridan and his brother. They suspected it was one of three women, all of whom had been at the house parties going on when the first two husbands had died. So Sheridan and his siblings were engaged in a covert investigation, trying to learn who it had been. To that end, they'd each taken assignments, Grey's being that he question his Aunt Cora, otherwise known as Lady Eustace, who was no relation to any of the rest of them.

Belatedly, Sheridan realized what the "favor" must be. Damn. "No. God, no. I am not doing that."

"You don't know what I'm going to ask," Grey said.

"I can guess. You want me to question Lady Eustace."

Grey sighed. "I find it necessary, given the situation."

"You'll be back in town soon enough. It can wait until then, can't it?"

"I don't know. I honestly have no idea how long I shall have to be in the country."

Sheridan dragged in a heavy breath. "Yes, but why ask *me* to do it? I barely know her."

"The others don't know her at all," Grey snapped.

"But you're friendly with Vanessa, and that gives you an excuse."

Which was precisely why Sheridan didn't want to do it. Because it meant being around Lady Eustace's daughter, Miss Vanessa Pryde, who was too attractive for his sanity, with her raven curls and lush figure and vivacious smile.

"I've chatted with Vanessa a handful of times," Sheridan pointed out, although he knew Grey was right. "That hardly makes me ideal for this."

"Ah, but my aunt and I hate each other. That hardly makes *me* ideal, since it seems unlikely she'd share her secrets with me."

"And why should your aunt share them with *me*?" Sheridan sipped some of his brandy.

"Because you're an eligible duke. And her daughter is an eligible young lady. Not that I'm suggesting you should even pretend to court Vanessa, but her mother would certainly offer you more confidences if she thought it would snag you."

"I would never court Vanessa, pretend or otherwise," Sheridan said. "For one thing, she's spoiled and impudent, a dangerous combination for a man who won't ever be able to afford expensive gowns and furs and jewelry for his wife. I'm already barely treading water. A wife like Vanessa would drown me."

Grey narrowed his gaze. "Vanessa isn't so much spoiled as determined to get her own way."

"That's even worse since it means having constant strife in my marriage."

"Beatrice and Gwyn are both of that ilk, and so far their husbands are quite content. Indeed, I rather like being married to a woman with spirit who knows what she wants."

"Good for you," Sheridan clipped out. "But you have

money, and I don't. Nor does *your* wife have an absurd fixation on that damned poet Juncker."

"Ah, yes, Juncker." Grey stroked his chin. "I doubt that's anything more than a girlish infatuation."

"Trust me, I've heard her babble on about Juncker's 'brilliant' plays plenty of times. She once told me some nonsense about how Juncker wrote with the ferocity of a 'dark angel,' whatever that means. Frivolous chit has no idea about what sort of man she should marry."

"But *you* know, I take it," Grey said with an odd glint in his eye.

"I do, indeed. She needs a fellow who will curb her worst excesses, who will help her channel her youthful enthusiasm into more practical activities. Sadly, she has romantic notions that will only serve her ill, and those are leading her into wanting a fellow she thinks she can keep under her thumb, so she can spend her fortune as she pleases."

"Juncker," Grey said.

"Who else? You know perfectly well she's been mooning after him for a couple of years at least."

"And that bothers you?"

The query caught Sheridan off guard. "Certainly not." When Grey smirked at him, Sheridan added, "Juncker is welcome to her. She could do better perhaps, but she could also do a hell of a lot worse."

"You've certainly convinced me," Grey said blandly. "Unless . . ."

"Unless what?"

"You're merely chafing at the fact that she thinks dukes are arrogant and unfeeling, or some such rot. So she would never agree to marry you anyway."

"Yes, you told me," Sheridan said. More than once. Often enough to irritate him. "And I'm not looking for her to marry me, anyway."

"I suppose it's possible you could coax her into *liking* you, but beyond that . . ."

When Grey left the thought dangling, Sheridan gritted his teeth. "You've made your point." Not that Sheridan had any intention of making Vanessa "like" him. She was not the right woman for him. He'd decided that long ago.

"Didn't you agree to fund Vanessa's dowry?" Sheridan said as he took another swallow of brandy. "You could just bully Lady Eustace into revealing her secrets by threatening to withhold the dowry, you know, unless your aunt comes clean."

"First of all, that only hurts Vanessa. Second, if my aunt is cornered, she'll just lie. Besides, all of this depends upon the women thinking they got away with it while we pursue our investigation. That's why I haven't told her *or* Vanessa that we've already determined my father died of arsenic. Which is another reason you should question Lady Eustace. She won't suspect you."

"What about Sanforth?" Sheridan asked. "Originally we decided that I was to ask questions in the town. What happened to *that* part of our plan to find the killer—or killers—of our fathers?"

"Heywood can manage Sanforth perfectly well."

That was probably true. Sheridan's younger brother, a retired Army colonel, had already made significant improvements to his own estate. Compared to that, asking questions of Sanforth's tiny populace would be an afternoon's entertainment.

"So you see," Grey went on, "there's no reason for you to even return to the country. As long as you're in town for the play you might as well pop into the box my aunt has at the theater and see what you can find out. You can pretend you're there to chat with Vanessa."

"That's assuming they even attend the play," Sheridan

said. "Charitable productions don't sound like things Lady Eustace would enjoy."

"Oh, they'll be there," Grey said. "Vanessa will make sure of it. It's Juncker's play, remember?"

"Right." He stared down into the shimmering liquor and bit back an oath. "Very well. I will endure Lady Eustace's suspicions to learn what I can." Which meant he'd also be enduring Vanessa's foolish gushing over Juncker.

His throat tightened. He didn't care. He *wouldn't* care.

"Thank you," Grey said. "Now if you don't mind . . ."

"I know. Beatrice is waiting for you at the estate, and you've got quite a long journey." He met his brother's anxious gaze. "It will be fine, you know. The Wolfes come from hardy stock. Not to mention our mother. If she can bear five children to three husbands before the age of twenty-five, I'm sure my cousin can give you an heir without too much trouble."

"Or give me a girl. I don't care which. As long as Beatrice survives it, and the child is healthy . . ."

"Go." Sheridan could tell from Grey's distracted expression that the man's mind was already leaping forward to the moment he would reach his wife. "Go be with her. I won't disappoint you."

Sheridan knew firsthand the anguish love could cause, how deep it ran, how painful the knot it tied around one's throat.

That was precisely why he never intended to be in such a situation. Just seeing Grey's agitation was more than enough to caution him. Love could chew a man up and spit him out faster than a horse could run. Sheridan already had plenty of things to worry about. He didn't intend to add a woman to that number.

* * *

"Wait, girl," Vanessa's mother said as she stopped her daughter from entering the Pryde family box. "Your headpiece is crooked." She shoved a hat pin into Vanessa's fancy turban, skimming her scalp.

"Mama! That hurt!"

"It's not *my* fault it won't stay put. You must have put on the trim unevenly. Serves you right for not buying a brand new turban in the first place."

Her mother always wanted her to buy new instead of remaking something. Unfortunately, the small estate of Vanessa's late father didn't produce enough income and the widow's portion for her mother never stretched far enough for Vanessa to buy anything she liked. So she was always practicing small economies to make sure they lived within their means.

Mama didn't approve of living within one's means. For one thing, she was incessantly trying to impress someone with how lofty they were. For another, she was pinning her hopes on Vanessa marrying well and being able to support the two of them quite handily.

"It's not the trim, Mama," Vanessa grumbled. "The whole thing is lopsided from all your fooling with it."

"I'm merely trying to fix it. You want to look nice for the gentlemen, don't you?"

"Of course." Vanessa really only wanted to look nice for *one* gentleman, but he would probably ignore her as usual. If he did, she would give up hope of ever gaining his attention. So far nothing seemed to have worked in that regard.

Uncle Theo, her favorite relation, patted Vanessa's arm reassuringly. "You know your mother—always thinking about your suitors."

"And with good reason," her mother said. "The girl doesn't have the sense God gave her when it comes to suitors. She *should* be married to Greycourt, but instead she dragged her feet, and now he's married to that low chit Miss Wolfe."

"That 'low' chit," Vanessa put in, "is the granddaughter of a duke just like me. So if she's low, then so am I. Besides, I like her."

"Of course you do." Mama sniffed as she fussed a bit more over the turban. "You always prefer the wrong sort of people."

"I find they're generally more interesting than the right sort," Vanessa said.

"Like that playwright you're enamored of." Her mother shook her head. "Sometimes I think you want to marry the poorest fellow you can find just to vex me."

"Mr. Juncker is very talented," Vanessa pointed out, precisely for the reason her mother had given—just to vex her. He was handsome, too, with a winning smile, teasing eyes, and good teeth, but Vanessa didn't care about any of that.

Her uncle huffed out a breath. "Are we going to enter the box sometime before the end of the century, sister?"

"Oh, stubble it, Theo. The orchestra is still tuning its instruments."

"That sounds like an overture to me," he said. "That's why the corridor is empty except for us."

"Almost done." Her mother *finally* left off adjusting her turban. Instead, she gave Vanessa's bodice a tug downward.

Vanessa groaned. "It will just creep back up. Honestly, Mama, do you *want* me looking like a strumpet?"

"If it will catch you a good husband? Absolutely. You're not getting any younger, you know." Her mother pinched Vanessa's cheeks.

"I fail to see how pinching rolls back the years."

"You must trust your mother in this," Mama said. "I swear, someday I hope you have a child as recalcitrant as you. 'Twould serve you right." When Uncle Theo cleared his throat, Mama scowled at him and opened the door. "Very well, *now* we can go in."

"Are you expecting someone in particular tonight?" Vanessa asked as they entered the box. Her mother usually primped her, but this went beyond the pale.

Mama lowered her voice. "I heard that most of Lydia's family will be here. And if His Grace, the Duke of Armitage, happens to come . . ."

"He will magically decide to marry me because my cheeks are rosy and my bosom is half-bare?"

"Men do that, you know. Anything that will make him notice you is good."

Someone nearby shushed them, and they took their seats.

Vanessa sighed. Saint Sheridan was unlikely to notice her. He clearly had relegated her to the position of little sister, even though she was twenty-five years old to his twenty-nine. She didn't want to be his little sister. She wanted to be his *wife*. Unfortunately, she'd tried a number of the time-honored tactics of young ladies, and none seemed to have changed his image of her.

Including her attempts to make him jealous. She'd stared after Mr. Juncker with seeming longing, and she'd gushed about the man's talent to Sheridan. She'd even hinted to her cousin Grey of her adoration and had gone so far as to say she would never marry a duke, hoping that her remarks would get back to Sheridan. Having grown up with a consummate liar for a mother, that was going about as far as Vanessa was comfortable in dissembling to her cousin.

But as far as she could tell, all her efforts had merely annoyed her mother and irritated Grey, not to mention made her feel ridiculous. The three times Sheridan had danced with her—only because he couldn't avoid it—he'd been as distant and aloof as usual. Granted, he was a duke and they were supposed to be like that, but she *was* related to his half brother. Surely that should have coaxed a smile or two out of Sheridan.

If anything, he'd pulled away from her even more, curse his hide. And that made no sense, if his financial situation was as bad as the gossips said. Despite her family's own strained finances, Vanessa had a sizable dowry, which he ought to know, since Grey was the one who'd funded it. Still, she didn't really want him interested in her for her fortune. She wanted him to see the real her, to desire the real her.

She feared that would never happen.

Was he even here? Her mother would surely have told her if he was. If, that is, she'd spotted him. But leaning forward enough to see if he sat in the Armitage family's box would give Vanessa away.

Then a thought occurred to her. "Mama," she whispered, "do you have your polemoscope with you?"

With a nod, her mother drew it from her reticule. But before Vanessa could seize it, her mother asked, "Who are you using it to observe?"

"The duke, of course." Vanessa would have lied—the only time she ever stooped to do so was when she was dealing with her mother—but in this case there was no need.

"Don't toy with me, girl." Funny how Mama always assumed other people lied as much as she did. "I know you have your heart set on that playwright, and he is far beneath you."

"Yes, Mama."

She took the polemoscope from her mother and put it to her eye as she leaned forward. Her mother had bought it after Papa's death, but Vanessa had never used it.

Until now. Other people would assume she was trying to view the actors and actresses more closely, because the polemoscope looked exactly like an opera glass or spyglass, which was ironic since it literally allowed one to spy on the people in the boxes to one's right.

It took her a moment to adjust to seeing things to the side of her rather than on the stage. Once she did, however, she could observe everyone in the Armitage box. Sheridan sat between his half sister, Lady Gwyn, and his mother. The two ladies were clearly chatting, but he wore his usual stoic manner. Like a saint. Or a sphinx.

A sphinx fit him better, given how hard he was to understand. Suddenly, he looked over at her, and she started, unnerved by his attention, even though she knew he couldn't tell she was watching him.

She dropped the polemoscope into her lap.

"Is he there?" Mama asked.

"Who?"

"Your Mr. Juncker."

Good Lord, she hadn't even checked. "Yes," she said, praying he was. She lifted the polemoscope and scanned the boxes she could see. And there he was, Mr. Konrad Juncker, the supposed object of her affections. He was flirting with some lady whom Vanessa didn't even know. That was why she would never actually be enamored of him. He was a rakehell, and she wanted nothing to do with such a man. He was too much like her late father.

Still, she wished she'd never started her foolish plan to seemingly pine after Mr. Juncker to make Sheridan jealous. The playwright didn't interest her in the least. And now she was stuck. If she switched her affections to Sheridan at this late juncture, he would think her fickle. Curse it all to blazes.

She handed the polemoscope to her mother, but Mama seemed fully engrossed in the play. Vanessa was not. She and her mother had seen this one when it was first performed, but Mama had either forgotten or was enjoying the repeat performance. Her mother had only attended tonight in hopes of having Vanessa be able to speak to Sheridan. She despaired of that ever happening. Especially as the play reached the end of the first act, and a quick glance at the Armitage box showed he'd disappeared. No doubt he was flirting with some other—

"Good evening," said a smooth-as-brandy voice. "I trust that you're all enjoying the performance?"

Vanessa's pulse jumped. Sheridan had come to her. He felt the same pull as she did. At last.

"We're liking it as much as one can, given that it's not new," Uncle Theo said from his seat next to Mama. "Still, I'll take an old play by Juncker to a new one by just about any other author. He knows how to entertain, I'll give you that."

"Do join us, Your Grace," Mama said and gestured to Vanessa to move over so Sheridan could sit between them. "Vanessa was just saying she would love your opinion on it."

When Sheridan focused his gorgeous green eyes on her, Vanessa pasted a flirtatious smile to her face. "Nonsense, Mama. I already know his opinion."

His expression didn't change one whit. It exhibited a

perfect blend of boredom and nonchalance as he took the seat between her and her mother. "Oh? And what might that be?"

"That the shenanigans of Felix and his friends are ridiculous. That you don't find such frivolity entertaining in the least."

"If you say so." He shrugged. "Honestly, I have no opinion whatsoever."

"That's absurd," Vanessa persisted. "You always have an opinion. And generally, it's contrary to everyone else's. Why, I once heard you tell the Secretary of War that Napoleon was a masterful strategist who would win against us if we didn't recognize it and act accordingly."

"That wasn't an opinion; it was the truth." Turning to stare her down, he said, "Just because the man is our enemy doesn't mean we should assume he's stupid. Greater men than our Secretary of War have made that mistake, to their detriment."

"And what would you know about military strategy?"

"More than you, I would imagine. You may not realize it, but Father trained me from an early age to follow in his footsteps in Britain's diplomatic service."

Mama snorted. "I'm sure he was relieved when you became his heir to the dukedom instead. What a fortuitous event that was."

Sheridan shifted his attention to Vanessa's mother. "I'm not sure he would call the death of his brother fortuitous." As if realizing that Mama might take offense at that, he softened his words. "Personally, I'd have preferred a post abroad over inheriting the dukedom, but that wasn't meant to be."

Mama lifted an eyebrow. "You would have been happy

to live outside of England all of your life as some low envoy?"

"I wasn't born in England, Lady Eustace. So if I'd had the chance to live the remainder of my days in Prussia, for example, I would have been perfectly content."

"But surely you would have missed entertainments like this or hunting house parties or our glittering balls," Mama said.

Uncle Theo snorted. "I'm sure they have those in Prussia, too, eh, Duke?"

"But not peopled by Englishmen," her mother persisted. "And those Prussians are not to be trusted."

Vanessa stifled a groan. "Do forgive my mother, Sheridan. She finds all foreigners suspect."

Sheridan ignored her. "I will say, Lady Eustace, that the house parties in Berlin paled beside those my mother always describes. Prussian house parties were orderly events, with every activity scheduled. Whereas my mother says that her first husband's affairs were madcap and not the least scheduled. Everyone had differing plans for activities, and no one consulted with anyone else concerning those plans."

"Exactly," Mama said, brightening. "That's how they were indeed. We did as we pleased in those days. None of this 'Oh, the young gentlemen must be appeased' nonsense. We enjoyed ourselves however we could."

"I suppose that left plenty of time for guests to roam the estate and explore a bit," Sheridan said.

"And have assignations," her uncle added, slyly.

Mama swatted her brother with her reticule. "No one was having assignations, Theo. I was newly married and not about to jeopardize my marriage for any fellow. And my husband wasn't there." She glanced at Vanessa and colored. "Not that he would have done such a thing either."

It was all Vanessa could do not to roll her eyes. How could Mama think that Vanessa hadn't noticed Papa's many payments to ladies through the years? Vanessa had done the books for him from the time she was old enough to know what an account book was. Papa had been woefully bad at managing money. "Wasn't that the house party where—"

"Grey's father died at that house party," Sheridan drawled, without even glancing at her. "How did the guests feel about that, Lady Eustace? It must have lowered their spirits dramatically."

"Well, it did indeed. Although Lydia kept his illness quiet until she couldn't anymore. Besides—"

A boy came out onto the stage and began a comic introduction to the second act. It should have ended all conversation but her mother continued whispering to Sheridan and Sheridan to her, at least until the action of the play began.

Then Sheridan leaned back in his chair and stretched his legs, unwittingly drawing Vanessa's attention to his fine physique. The man had the best-crafted calves she'd ever seen, not to mention a chest as broad as a pugilist's and clearly capable of any test of strength. As if that weren't enough to tempt a young lady, his hair . . . oh, she must not even think of those glorious ash-brown curls. It made her want to run her fingers through it, a possibility that clearly escaped him, since he continued to whisper only to her mother and ignore Vanessa completely.

Like a balloon deflating, she felt the air go out of her joy. He was here to see—to talk with—Mama. Vanessa couldn't understand why, but the point was he wasn't here to be with *her*. She must get him to converse with her, do *anything* that might prove he noticed her.

Using Mama's polemoscope, Vanessa surveyed the boxes nearby, racking her brain for something to say to Sheridan that might get his attention. Then she spotted Mr. Juncker, who was clearly getting up to leave his box.

And that gave her an idea.

Books by Bestselling Author
Fern Michaels

___The Jury	0-8217-7878-1	$6.99US/$9.99CAN
___Sweet Revenge	0-8217-7879-X	$6.99US/$9.99CAN
___Lethal Justice	0-8217-7880-3	$6.99US/$9.99CAN
___Free Fall	0-8217-7881-1	$6.99US/$9.99CAN
___Fool Me Once	0-8217-8071-9	$7.99US/$10.99CAN
___Vegas Rich	0-8217-8112-X	$7.99US/$10.99CAN
___Hide and Seek	1-4201-0184-6	$6.99US/$9.99CAN
___Hokus Pokus	1-4201-0185-4	$6.99US/$9.99CAN
___Fast Track	1-4201-0186-2	$6.99US/$9.99CAN
___Collateral Damage	1-4201-0187-0	$6.99US/$9.99CAN
___Final Justice	1-4201-0188-9	$6.99US/$9.99CAN
___Up Close and Personal	0-8217-7956-7	$7.99US/$9.99CAN
___Under the Radar	1-4201-0683-X	$6.99US/$9.99CAN
___Razor Sharp	1-4201-0684-8	$7.99US/$10.99CAN
___Yesterday	1-4201-1494-8	$5.99US/$6.99CAN
___Vanishing Act	1-4201-0685-6	$7.99US/$10.99CAN
___Sara's Song	1-4201-1493-X	$5.99US/$6.99CAN
___Deadly Deals	1-4201-0686-4	$7.99US/$10.99CAN
___Game Over	1-4201-0687-2	$7.99US/$10.99CAN
___Sins of Omission	1-4201-1153-1	$7.99US/$10.99CAN
___Sins of the Flesh	1-4201-1154-X	$7.99US/$10.99CAN
___Cross Roads	1-4201-1192-2	$7.99US/$10.99CAN

More by Bestselling Author
Hannah Howell

__Highland Angel	978-1-4201-0864-4	$6.99US/$8.99CAN
__If He's Sinful	978-1-4201-0461-5	$6.99US/$8.99CAN
__Wild Conquest	978-1-4201-0464-6	$6.99US/$8.99CAN
__If He's Wicked	978-1-4201-0460-8	$6.99US/$8.49CAN
__My Lady Captor	978-0-8217-7430-4	$6.99US/$8.49CAN
__Highland Sinner	978-0-8217-8001-5	$6.99US/$8.49CAN
__Highland Captive	978-0-8217-8003-9	$6.99US/$8.49CAN
__Nature of the Beast	978-1-4201-0435-6	$6.99US/$8.49CAN
__Highland Fire	978-0-8217-7429-8	$6.99US/$8.49CAN
__Silver Flame	978-1-4201-0107-2	$6.99US/$8.49CAN
__Highland Wolf	978-0-8217-8000-8	$6.99US/$9.99CAN
__Highland Wedding	978-0-8217-8002-2	$4.99US/$6.99CAN
__Highland Destiny	978-1-4201-0259-8	$4.99US/$6.99CAN
__Only for You	978-0-8217-8151-7	$6.99US/$8.99CAN
__Highland Promise	978-1-4201-0261-1	$4.99US/$6.99CAN
__Highland Vow	978-1-4201-0260-4	$4.99US/$6.99CAN
__Highland Savage	978-0-8217-7999-6	$6.99US/$9.99CAN
__Beauty and the Beast	978-0-8217-8004-6	$4.99US/$6.99CAN
__Unconquered	978-0-8217-8088-6	$4.99US/$6.99CAN
__Highland Barbarian	978-0-8217-7998-9	$6.99US/$9.99CAN
__Highland Conqueror	978-0-8217-8148-7	$6.99US/$9.99CAN
__Conqueror's Kiss	978-0-8217-8005-3	$4.99US/$6.99CAN
__A Stockingful of Joy	978-1-4201-0018-1	$4.99US/$6.99CAN
__Highland Bride	978-0-8217-7995-8	$4.99US/$6.99CAN
__Highland Lover	978-0-8217-7759-6	$6.99US/$9.99CAN

Available Wherever Books Are Sold!

Check out our website at
http://www.kensingtonbooks.com

More by Bestselling Author

Lori Foster

Romantic Suspense from
Lisa Jackson

Absolute Fear	0-8217-7936-2	$7.99US/$9.99CAN
Afraid to Die	1-4201-1850-1	$7.99US/$9.99CAN
Almost Dead	0-8217-7579-0	$7.99US/$10.99CAN
Born to Die	1-4201-0278-8	$7.99US/$9.99CAN
Chosen to Die	1-4201-0277-X	$7.99US/$10.99CAN
Cold Blooded	1-4201-2581-8	$7.99US/$8.99CAN
Deep Freeze	0-8217-7296-1	$7.99US/$10.99CAN
Devious	1-4201-0275-3	$7.99US/$9.99CAN
Fatal Burn	0-8217-7577-4	$7.99US/$10.99CAN
Final Scream	0-8217-7712-2	$7.99US/$10.99CAN
Hot Blooded	1-4201-0678-3	$7.99US/$9.49CAN
If She Only Knew	1-4201-3241-5	$7.99US/$9.99CAN
Left to Die	1-4201-0276-1	$7.99US/$10.99CAN
Lost Souls	0-8217-7938-9	$7.99US/$10.99CAN
Malice	0-8217-7940-0	$7.99US/$10.99CAN
The Morning After	1-4201-3370-5	$7.99US/$9.99CAN
The Night Before	1-4201-3371-3	$7.99US/$9.99CAN
Ready to Die	1-4201-1851-X	$7.99US/$9.99CAN
Running Scared	1-4201-0182-X	$7.99US/$10.99CAN
See How She Dies	1-4201-2584-2	$7.99US/$8.99CAN
Shiver	0-8217-7578-2	$7.99US/$10.99CAN
Tell Me	1-4201-1854-4	$7.99US/$9.99CAN
Twice Kissed	0-8217-7944-3	$7.99US/$9.99CAN
Unspoken	1-4201-0093-9	$7.99US/$9.99CAN
Whispers	1-4201-5158-4	$7.99US/$9.99CAN
Wicked Game	1-4201-0338-5	$7.99US/$9.99CAN
Wicked Lies	1-4201-0339-3	$7.99US/$9.99CAN
Without Mercy	1-4201-0274-5	$7.99US/$10.99CAN
You Don't Want to Know	1-4201-1853-6	$7.99US/$9.99CAN

Available Wherever Books Are Sold!
Visit our website at **www.kensingtonbooks.com**